Dark Village

AN ANTHOLOGY OF TWISTED FICTION

curated by

Mallory Cywinski & Karly R. Latham

Copyright © 2023 Mallory Cywinski and Karly R. Latham
DBA Dark Village Publications

ISBN: 9798394376467

Each contributing Author retains the rights to their individual contributed stories. Unless by the original Author, this book or any portion thereof may not be reproduced or used in any manner whatsoever without the express written permission of the publisher except for the use of brief quotations in a book review. All rights reserved.

Cover Design by Mallory Cywinski

Follow Karly R. Latham @karly.latham
Follow Mallory Cywinski @coffeebooksandghosts

To my crotch goblins, everything I do is for you. You're my motivation and my reason to keep growing. And to my friends for keeping me going when I needed it the most, I wouldn't have found my footing as a writer or the confidence to pursue it without y'all.

- Karly

To my spooky community of weirdos, for all your support: you know who you are. To Cade & Maya, because every book is for you. And a special thank you to my publishing partner and one of my BFFs, Karly, for always being my cheerleader and joining me outside my comfort zone—with enthusiasm and inappropriate jokes along the way.

- Mallory

CONTENTS

	ACKNOWLEDGMENTS	*i*
1	GOOD GIRL Mallory Cywinski	1
2	PREY ANIMALS Noelle W. Ihli	19
3	THE DOORWAY BETWEEN Amelia Cotter	25
4	DOWN TO THE RIVER TO PRAY Morgan McKay	39
5	HEATHER HAS THREE DADDIES Katharine Hanifen	43
6	WITH A NOD TO THE SPACE BETWEEN STARS Harlow Dayne	51
7	DON'T EAT THE YELLOW SNOW Cassie Marozsan	63
8	SHE WAITS FOR ME Jason A. Jones	69
9	THE WENDIGO Heather Moser	79
10	CARNIVAL GAMES Loki DeWitt	83
11	SURVIVING THE CHANGE Amanda Woomer	99
12	THE BENSON Karina Halle	111

13	BODY BOX Shawn Proctor	153
14	THE CUTTING OF THE OUROBOROS E.E.W. Christman	159
15	THE MIDDLE OF NOWHERE Stacey Ryall	169
16	GOOSEBUMPS Joy Johns	175
17	BUILD-A-TWIN Torrence Bryan	187
18	SCYTHE AND SICKLE Mae Dexter	195
19	DAISY, DAISY Bethany Drillser	205
20	A SHELTER Jordan Heath	209
21	OBSCENE Phil Rossi	215
22	BROTHER Lauren Hellekson	229
23	THE RAIN Lorien Jones	237
24	UNTIL THE NEXT TEN YEARS Allison Kurzynski	243
25	KANSAS FOREVER Amy Bennett	253
26	THE WRITER Bizzy Blank	263
27	TO BE WITH HER Karly R. Latham	269

DARK VILLAGE

ACKNOWLEDGMENTS

We would like to thank the authors who contributed their time and efforts to the stories that make up this book, and for trusting us with your work. It's truly an honor to have read each and every submission, and to share them with our readers. We cannot express how grateful we are for such incredible authors' contributions; this project would not be possible without you all.

We would also like to add an extra special thank you to Karina Halle for inspiring us with her writing, and for lending us Dex and Perry. (We are huge fans and shamelessly fangirled behind the scenes.) Thank you for being a part of this journey.

To our family and friends: we are so grateful for your help and support.

GOOD GIRL

By Mallory Cywinski

Trevor was handsome, not her usual kind of guy—he was tall, but on the slim side, with short spiky hair perched above a too-big forehead. He had an easy smile though, and kind eyes. They were a little feminine—something about the lash length, but she chose to ignore that thought, tucking it away in the back of her mind. He was objectively attractive, and he'd piqued her curiosity at a glance as she sat down in her usual spot at the polished wood bar. She'd come here to play, after all, so she wanted to see if he'd take the bait. She moved the cherry around the bottom of her glass, holding the little straw delicately with two manicured fingers.

    Sure enough, she'd seen him watching her while she sat sipping her drink, doing a well-practiced job of pretending not to notice anyone around her, though really, she took in every detail. It was the writer in her; she couldn't help it. He watched her, half paying attention to his friends' conversation. A little while later, she noticed him working up the nerve to come speak to her by way of a quick tequila shot. Liquid courage. When he finally came over—it had taken a full forty minutes, during which she had kindly but curtly given the cold shoulder to two other men, wanting to see how Shy Guy would proceed—she made it easy on him and gave him a warm smile. This red lipstick never failed to dazzle, and it seemed he was ensnared.

He was a little awkward asking her about herself, but she answered without guile ("Yes, I'm here for a few weeks visiting from Philadelphia.") and if she wanted another Cosmopolitan. ("Yes, thank you very much.") She could tell he wasn't feeling as confident as some of the other men who approached her on nights like these, all swagger and alpha energy, but she wondered if a change from her usual kind of man might be fun. He ordered another rum and soda for himself and seemed to relax slightly after some long sips. A little dimple peeked out when he smirked down at her, though he kept his distance.

Usually after awhile, the man would drape his arm over the back of her chair in a territorial way. In her first few weeks up here in this small lakeside town, that had thrilled her, made her feel wanted and a little nostalgic, but lately she'd grown tired of the overconfidence and quick assumptions they made about their success in claiming her. They hadn't really earned it, but her expectations were probably too high. This one had a different, quieter energy, and he was pleasant, but was he boring? She was just starting to question whether he'd be too dull to be any fun at all, when she asked him about his line of work and his features lit up. His passion was suddenly obvious, and she wondered if she could redirect it. His enthusiasm for his photography business was attractive. She reached the bottom of her cocktail while he talked editing programs, she thought to herself, "Ok let's try this one," even though she knew he wouldn't be as rough with her as she liked.

Mara had started to make a habit of visiting the rowdy bars in town to find occasional male companionship shortly after arriving in the Adirondacks. She wasn't interested in more than one night with any of them, and she always insisted on going back to her rental cabin, never ever his house or apartment or whatever ramshackle hovel he was renting for the summer. The cabin wasn't hers, but she knew it well by now and if things went south, she knew every exit. Not that they would, just if they did.

Trevor was still discussing his latest shoot when she abruptly hopped up from her chair and, interrupting him mid-sentence, invited him back to the cabin. He hesitated slightly, his shyness suddenly creeping back up and threatening to end their night right there, but after a moment and a deep inhale he didn't think she noticed, he agreed. When they stepped out of their rideshare (where he hadn't even moved a pinky finger toward her) fifteen minutes later in the driveway, she saw his expression change to awe when he saw the cabin. She could tell he was instantly fascinated. They moved inside, and he was like a little kid on Christmas, his original carnal motives for coming back with her seemingly forgotten in his inspiration at seeing the beautiful architecture and interesting décor within. They crossed the foyer to the Great Room with its wall of windows, and it was as if he couldn't help talking to himself, mumbling about wishing he had his equipment.

She let him peruse the photographs and oddities along the walls while she stepped just inside the butler's pantry to pour some drinks. As she mixed, he called out questions to her about the names of those in the photos, but of course she couldn't relay much of the information he sought. This wasn't her cabin, after all, she was just here temporarily on a self-prescribed sabbatical. She said as much but it didn't seem to bother him in the slightest, if he even heard her, as he moved around the room. Drinks made, she slipped off her light jacket and draped herself invitingly on the leather sofa, trying to refocus his attention. He was, however, distracted by the large built-in bookcase and the dusty tomes within. Some quiet minutes passed, and she sat up, huffing a bit, and gulped her drink, less ladylike than before. His drink sat untouched on the coaster in front of her, sweating condensation down the sides of the icy glass. When he pulled out a book and sat on one of the tufted chairs to flip through it, she rolled her eyes, hoisted herself up and went to pour another glass for herself.

When she came back into the room, feeling a little less sultry and leaning increasingly more toward annoyed, she walked right up to him and held out the drink she'd made for him at eye level. The ice had partially melted and a clear layer of water floated at the top. He closed the book and accepted the drink as he stood, though he still seemed preoccupied. He opened his mouth, and with a lukewarm flutter in her stomach she hoped he would return to his flirtations and they could have some fun after all, but instead, he asked with a crinkle between his brows, "Can I get a tour of the upstairs as well?"

There was a fraction of a second in which she thought maybe he was being coy and finally getting down to business, but seeing the earnest look on his face, she realized he really did just want a tour of the rooms.

Her shoulders slumped a bit as she understood her night was shaping up to be more of an historical tour than anything steamy. She regretted ignoring those other two men, and wondered if she could get this guy out and get back to town before the bar closed for the night. She sighed, knowing it was too late in the evening for that, and agreed to give *Junior* here the tour he requested. They circled back to the foyer and went up the grand staircase, reaching the central hallway upstairs. A small greenhouse room was directly off the hall, and he entered it excitedly, grazing the pots and tools on the table, musing at the potential for great light in the room. She nodded absently. He wasn't even phased by the alluring, cozy-looking bed when he poked his head into one of the rooms, such as his attention was commanded by his artistic eye at the moment. She trailed behind him, and having grabbed the bottle of vodka on their way up, was now taking small sips as they went.

As he reached the end of the hallway, having seen all the main bedrooms, he started down the servant's hallway. Mara's heart suddenly froze up.

"No! Nothing down there," she quickly called out. "I think it's best if our little tour wraps up here." She took a moment to calm the trembling in her voice. "You know, I'm pretty tired and I have a long day tomorrow." She didn't really–a writer makes their own hours, more or less–but she sure as hell didn't want to visit the servant's hallway, especially this late in the evening. He giggled–*giggled*–and she was suddenly struck with the honest truth of how unattractive she found this man, dimple be damned. She was disgusted that she had considered sleeping with him, and felt a pang of guilt as a familiar whisper of dismay breezed by. When Trevor took off down the hallway despite her protest, she had no choice but to follow him.

She turned the corner and the hallway loomed out into the dark of the late hour in front of her. It was oddly quiet. Sentient. She couldn't see Trevor anywhere. Her heart rate started climbing as she crept along the wooden floor and called out to him quietly but urgently.

"Hey! Have you seen enough yet?" She raised the bottle with quivering hands, taking another sip to dilute her rising fear, when a creak from the small bathroom to her right startled her. She almost dropped the vodka as she spun around and came face to face with The Painting. She hadn't realized how far down the hallway she'd walked.

At the tail end of Spring, she'd come across the cabin on a website for just a few hundred dollars a week. In the height of summer? What a steal. She'd decided to escape to the Adirondack mountains for a breather when the rush of the city and its memories became too much for her, and progress on her book stalled. When she'd arrived at the cabin weeks before, the owner had simply left the keys in a lockbox outside and texted her the combination to retrieve it. So, she was alone when she'd heaved open the heavy wooden front door and saw the interior for the first time.

The private cabin-mansion stood amidst towering pine trees with a view of the lake beyond, but inside it had many ornate, expensive-looking flourishes, and little oddities arranged throughout. (In truth, Trevor was probably apt to gawk at its beauty and intricate curiosities; she certainly did when she first arrived, but it was still unattractive under the circumstances.) Gold-and-crystal chandeliers dotting the rooms and ornate sconces hanging along the walls hinted at old money. Strange shadow box displays with taxidermied rodents were unexpected and fascinating. Drippy candles were arranged across the bulky fireplace mantle. Big raw wood beams careened across the high ceiling of the great room. Again, she idly wondered how she'd been so lucky to get this place for such a bargain, before setting her bags down and dashing up the broad stairwell to give herself a tour.

She felt the load of stress and grief she usually carried momentarily lift from her shoulders as she explored what was to be her new home for the next few weeks, or months, depending on how well the writing went while she was here. Her publishers had been kind enough to extend her deadline a bit, but she still needed to buckle down and get her project finished. She smiled as she peeked into each of the big bedrooms off the main hallway, deciding to run and flop onto the comforter in the brightest room, all white curtains and walls and plush rugs. Sighing contentedly, she stood from the glorious pile of blankets, already looking forward to bedtime, and walked more calmly back into the hallway. She was about to return downstairs when a slight chill licked at her shoulder blade, bare in her tank top. Turning her head, another hallway snagged in her periphery.

This one was much narrower, and as she gingerly made her way down it, the air felt more compressed, somehow, with a nagging sense that she wasn't supposed to be there. The smile unconsciously fell from her face as she realized this was probably the old servants' hallway. Yes—there was the stairwell that led right down into the kitchen so the guests in the old days would never have to see the maids and butler moving about. There were two small bedrooms at the end of the hall; the curtains were yellowed and everything felt very, very still. She was immediately uncomfortable here. She moved to go back toward the airiness of the rest of the house, keeping her eyes on the rooms as she went, like backing away from a predator. "Don't be ridiculous," she thought to herself with venom. She turned and suddenly a pair of large, dark eyes were directly in front of her face.

Stifling a surprised scream, she whipped back, eyes still on the face that a moment ago was much too close for comfort. She cursed at her own jumpiness, suddenly irritated, when she fully took in the painting hanging on the wall beside the bathroom door. She'd moved right past it earlier, her attention having been so fully absorbed on the seeing the rooms at the end. The painting showed an odd-looking little girl with sloping shoulders, wearing a poofy pink dress. The girl stared blankly out of the picture with big round eyes that were darker than the rest of the painting, with subtle greyish streaks painted around them. One of her hands pointed toward the bottom of the canvas, where an ugly cat lay. The cat's face was as creepy and knowing as the girl's; the artist had given it slightly humanoid features that made Mara feel unsettled. Looking back up at the girls' face as the light outside shifted, the grey streaks seemed darker than they did a minute ago. She instantly disliked the painting and wondered why on Earth the owner would hang this piece anywhere in a vacation home. Or really, why anyone would hang it *anywhere*.

The longer Mara stared, the more her uneasiness grew. No, she thought, she didn't just dislike it, it repulsed her. All at once, her unease transformed into something sharp and the painting made her unreasonably angry. Her emotions were a visceral thing; she had to stop herself from punching the stucco wall beside it. She frightened herself with her sudden violent urge. Her belly roiled, the burger she'd eaten in the car on her way to the cabin twisting in her stomach uncomfortably. Gone was the glow of exploring her new temporary lakeside retreat; she turned and shuffled back down the main stairwell, forcing herself not to walk backward nor even look back at the painting. It was too pathetically cliché to admit, even to herself, that it felt like the painted girl watched her leave, with equal disgust in her gaze.

Over the next few weeks, she'd settled in and avoided entering the servant's hallway. She had plenty of room throughout the rest of the cabin anyway. She'd come up to the lake to finally finish her novel and move on; it didn't need to be perfect and homey here, but it was imperative she felt reasonably comfortable and that her creativity be untethered.

She had briefly considered finding somewhere else to stay, but decided against it. She was paying next to nothing for this place, and she felt foolish for feeling afraid of an inanimate object. Though really, who wouldn't be at least mildly uncomfortable around an old painting of a creepy kid? Not to mention a human-cat thing. Maybe she'd just watched *The Shining* one too many times– a writer living alone in the mountains was probably never a great idea. She would forget about the painting, do what she needed to do, and leave.

However, now and then while she sat working on the other side of the house, or sprawled on the floor in front of the big windows in the Great Room, typing as the light off the lake danced across her fingers, the image of the girl in the painting swelled to the forefront of her mind. She'd feel cold down to her bones, shuddering as the girl's inky blank stare filled her brain without warning. Each time, she told herself to use it, this fear– her storyline was dark anyway, but even as she attempted to shrug off her discomfort, her fingers stilled on the keyboard and she knew she'd lost the moment. *Damnit!* she thought. Her publishers' deadline loomed closer and closer. These little failures ate at her confidence, feeding her pervasive guilt, and days like this often led to evenings down at the bars, finding a man to use her body and clear her head with heat.

Early one morning when she'd groggily entered the kitchen to make coffee, she heard light footsteps patter down the hallway above. And a swish of fabric? She whipped her head toward the stairwell, keenly listening, and so distracted was she by the unexpected sounds that she poured the scalding hot coffee on her hand instead of in the mug before her. She couldn't type properly for two weeks afterward without pain.

She told herself she'd been overtired and overdoing it on drinking. She was still healing from Philadelphia. She was stressing over the kind but eager emails from her publishers. All of it was coloring her thoughts. But no matter how many times she tried to convince herself all was as it should be in the cabin, she'd started to build in her heart a growing stone of resentment toward the painting and its meddling. It was a black spot of rot in this beautiful place. She focused on the fact that she would be gone soon, and she honestly couldn't wait to put miles of road between herself and that awful little girl in the frame.

Now, tonight, forced back into this hallway because of Trevor, increasingly irritable and fuzzy from the buzz of the alcohol soaking her senses, she stared at the painting. She still hated the sight of it, and the streaks around the girl's eyes looked even worse at night. She felt infuriated to unreasonable levels, and that in itself angered her even more; she didn't like that it affected her so much. The liquor warmed her, simultaneously comforting and disorienting, and she swayed on her legs a little.

For the first time, she whispered aloud to the painting, "I hate you." And she stared hard at the girl's face. "What is the matter with you, you little bitch?" she said, surprising herself with her own vehemence. Taking another sip, the sides of her vision rippled in waves. All she could properly see were the girl's dark eyes.

Bottle hanging in one hand at her side, she lifted her other hand. Slowly she reached out toward the little girl's hand, finger to finger, only an inch or so of space between them. Just then the painted girl's finger twitched in a "come hither" movement. Mara jumped back, a small shriek escaping as she slammed her body into the other side of the narrow hallway, cracking the back of her head against the wall.

Trevor appeared suddenly in front of her. He looked so condescendingly concerned; she couldn't stand the sight of him, the sight of this hallway a second longer. The commotion had finally brought him out of his childish excitement over the house.

"Hey, are you OK?" he asked, the sweet soda-and-vodka smell of his breath washing over her, as he finally started to lean in as if to kiss her. He was too close; she didn't want this. She shoved him away aggressively.

"Get out!" she screamed explosively. He instantly lifted his hands, shock replacing the concern on his face.

"I'm sorry, *sorry!*" he said, "I get so caught up in these old houses, I wasn't paying attention—"

"Get the fuck out!" she cried, interrupting his pathetic apologies, storming down the hallway and back stairwell, ricocheting a little side to side, holding the back of her throbbing head, and bursting into the kitchen.

He followed her, and he opened his mouth to speak before deciding the better of it. He hurried down the butler's pantry hall, grabbed his coat, crossed the foyer, and with a dull slam of the large wooden front door, was gone. Mara took a deep breath and placed the bottle on the kitchen island in front of her with shaking hands.

"What a Goddamn mess," she mumbled. She pivoted to the sink behind her and flicked on the tap, bending to slurp from the running faucet. She turned it off and stood, sloppily wiping her mouth on her arm and dribbling water between her breasts and onto the red material of her low-cut top. Her eyes moved to the stairwell, and her entire body sensed something was listening to her, anticipating what she would do.

She froze in mute terror as a muffled laugh rang down the stairwell through the stillness of the kitchen.

A mile or so down the road, Trevor walked along the side, kicking gravel as he went.

"Idiot," he mumbled to himself, his coat slung over his arm. "She wanted to fool around and you went off on some dumbass rant about the damn cabin." He paused to kick a larger stone into the middle of the road. It was late and quiet; he decided his stupid ass deserved a long miserable walk home. He strolled, the fresh air sobering him up a bit as he recounted the lame things he'd said. He stopped and stared up at the stars for a moment.

"Damn," he said. "Beautiful place though, seriously." He turned to check if he could still see the cabin from how far he'd walked. The sudden glare of headlights was blinding, seconds before the car slammed into him, propelling him ten feet off the side of the road. The driver didn't even pause before peeling away, and Trevor lay there, breathing wetly, his body suddenly broken in many, many places. Too many. Moments later, he lay in the dirt and roadside litter, as dead as the fallen tree beside him.

And back at the house, the dark streaks on the painted girl's face receded, just a little.

All the while, Mara stood rooted to her place in the kitchen, holding her breath and keenly listening for more laughter. She knew the laugh had to have been from a neighbor kid, probably that one with the yappy dog she despised. That had to be it. She may write dark fiction, occasionally throwing a spooky twist in her storylines, but she didn't *actually* believe in any of it. Not really. She sighed irritably. She came here to write in the fresh mountain air and enjoy sexy local men whenever it suited her mood. She did not come here to fuck around with creepy paintings and freak herself out because it was dark outside and she'd had too much to drink. With that thought, she slammed two aspirin, chugged the rest of the OJ left in her fridge, and went to bed. On the other side of the house.

After that night, the energy in the cabin seemed calmer, and normal days passed by. She woke, ate, wrote, sipped coffee with her feet propped up on the picnic table outside, staring out across the lake. Many nights she wrote until her eyes burned at the edges and she was forced to succumb to sleep. Other nights she let herself have a break from working and brought someone back to the cabin.

She enjoyed the feel of a hot body slamming hers into the soft cotton sheets of her rented bed. She loved when they came, and she loved to watch them leave; she didn't want commitment, she simply wanted the physicality, the chance to close her eyes and remember. No one else insisted on a tour of the house beyond her bedroom. Trevor never came back to the bar, at least not when she had been there. Embarrassed, probably.

To her relief, all the nonsense with the painting had obviously been a figment of her imagination. There had been no giggles, no footsteps, nothing. Part of her mused that it was as though the awful painted girl had been sated somehow. Whatever the change was, there were even some days when her fear of that part of the cabin didn't come to mind even once. It appeared it had forgotten her, too.

As summer was coming to a close, Mara had nearly completed her book. Her heroine had solved the mystery, survived the villain's vicious attempts on her life, and had enjoyed some sexy men along the way—what writer didn't add a bit of themselves into their characters? She smiled, knowing she'd set herself up to finish the entire manuscript by tomorrow; she'd even purchased a bottle of champagne for the moment when she'd tidy up some minor aesthetic issues, email the file to her publishers, and close her laptop. It was always her favorite part of the process—closing her computer feeling she'd poured her heart into something her readers would love. It was the moment when she could fantasize she'd written a New York Times Best Seller. She never had, of course, but the dream filled a space in her heart, and she really needed it this year.

She was proud of herself for nailing her goal, despite everything that had happened recently, both here and at home. The day after tomorrow, she could be done. She'd pack her stuff, email the owner to say thanks for the creepy fucking "Overlook Hotel" accommodations, and be on the road to wherever she wanted to go next. She hadn't decided that part yet, and that was fine—a little freedom sounded wonderful. She stretched her arms above her head, feeling pleasantly sleepy, and after changing into an oversized tee shirt and brushing her teeth, she crawled into the cozy bed in her favorite room and was asleep in minutes.

The girl in the painting wasn't feeling drowsy in the slightest. Nor was she satisfied any longer.

Sunlight was just filtering in the window the next morning when Mara woke up screaming, though no sound passed her lips. Her throat was parched dry, though her sheets and her shirt were soaked with cold sweat.

She flung forward into a seated position, putting a palm on her forehead. She took some deep breaths, staring down at her legs, her wild sleep-addled hair making a curtain around her face. She blinked and let her heart rate return to its normal pace in her chest, breathing deeply through her nose. The terror of her dream was still fresh.

She hadn't dreamed so vividly in so long. Now, she could still feel his fingers ripping into the flesh of her stomach, trying to drag her back through the front door and back to the living room where they'd been talking. She'd been done with him; it was over and she'd finally told him so, as much as it broke her heart.

In South Philadelphia, the front doors of the houses are practically on the street; a few paces across a narrow cement sidewalk and you're in the road. And while she'd been lucky and run the twenty steps safely to the other side in the early morning hours, he hadn't fared so well. When he gave chase, eyes only on her, he had been immediately hit by a pickup truck on its way to delivering baked goods from the Italian market a few blocks away.

She stopped and screamed, and the truck skidded to a halt, the driver flinging the door open and at his side in seconds. Sandwich rolls and small colorful cookies littered the road, thrown on impact from their secured bins in the bed of the truck. The driver was on his cell phone dialing 911 before she had the capacity to take in the scene before her, even while she numbly moved toward his body. The cheerfully decorated cookies on the pavement beside the spatters of blood looked obscene.

She'd known she had to leave him; his increasingly firm and dominant behavior had started to frighten her.

"It's a game," he'd say, forcing her to comply. In truth, at first she'd loved it, it had gotten her riled up and ready for him to throw her onto their bed, but over time it became a prison. He dictated what she could wear, where she could go. Even five dollars spent on a cup of coffee was questioned when he checked their joint bank account.

That morning, with an aching heart, she'd told him it was enough, and whether he thought her words were more roleplay fun or not, he'd bruised her and denied the immediate release their safe word was supposed to promise. She'd run and now he lay in the street, blood trickling from his ears and his skull, pooling around his head.

At first the dream was as clear as her waking memory; that really *was* how he'd died in front of her eyes that morning. But as she stared at him, this dream version, his blood started moving strangely, pulsing rhythmically. It gathered in globs and moved sloppily toward his face, leaving a vivid red trail across his forehead as it inched further up into his hairline. It coagulated into two horn shapes on top of his head. He was dead and he had blood horns and suddenly his skull turned toward her and with vacant eyes blindly staring in her direction, he spoke.

"I died for you, Baby. Do you understand?"

"Yes, Daddy," she said automatically, nodding. It was an instant, easy response for her, given so many times she didn't even consciously think about it anymore.

"That's my good little girl."

His body convulsed then, twisting around itself into a grotesque form; his elbows popped backward in their joints. He rose to broken feet, blood falling freely from the crack in his head, pouring from his mouth and eye sockets. The awful, horned thing stumbled toward her and she was frozen in shock, the air gathering close, smelling stagnant. Her legs were lead, glued to the floor as he lunged forward in jerky movements, and he grabbed the back of her head. He forced his bloody mouth to hers, his rotten tongue exploring her mouth, running along her teeth.

She screamed into his bleeding maw as his dead blood filled her mouth, spilling out the corners. It would drown her. She gagged. Her tearing eyes frantically searched the space behind him for someone, anyone, to help. Suddenly the girl from the painting shifted into her view, staring calmly like she always did. He still assaulted her face, and she felt the bile rising in her throat as she watched the girl raise her arm, pointing. Right at her.

That was when she abruptly awoke, the bile still in the back of her throat. She sat shaking, neck bent, still trying to find calm and leave the dream behind. Taking another deep breath, she reached for the glass of water on her bedside table without looking up, and her hand was met with air. She blinked, sat up a little further, and was puzzled to see small yellow flowers on the blanket pooled around her lap. The air smelled off—old and musty and *wrong*.

Looking around in abject horror, she realized she was in one of the servant's rooms at the end of the awful hallway. The night before she'd fallen asleep peacefully in her favorite room; how had she gotten here? She scrambled from the bed, landing hard on her knee on the wooden floor as blankets tangled around her legs. She clambered down the hallway, half crawling, half running, not looking at the painting as she scrambled past it. Perhaps she should have looked.

She moved clumsily toward the main hallway, groaning, knee twinging, and limbs still stiff with sleep and adrenaline from her nightmare. She was going to slam the door behind her in the other bedroom, catch her breath, and get the fuck out of this place. She'd had enough—she'd finish the damn book sitting in her fucking car. Her chaotic brain barely noticed the scene blocking her way before she skidded to a halt at the last second.

As she reached the split in the hallway at the top of the kitchen stairwell, a huge, writhing pile of dead things sat before her. At least three feet of dead mice, bleeding bodies of shrews, still twitching, squirrels, eyes bulging, their fluffy tails smeared with gore. Some of the taxidermied animals wrenched from the displays downstairs stuck out of the pile. She whimpered, completely disoriented, and stared in revulsion at the hundreds of small furry dead bodies.

She heard something approaching from the other side of the heap, and she could not fathom what she was seeing when suddenly the cat from the painting leapt gracefully up to the top of the pile, a dead rat in his teeth. He dropped it atop the pile and stared placidly at her, calm and knowing. Mara's mouth stretched wide in a silent scream, too stunned to make a sound.

Maintaining eye contact, the cat-thing made his way down and stalked toward her. She backed away, tears streaming down her face. He tracked her every step, before his eyes subtly moved to something just over her shoulder and he appeared to smile, somehow. She turned to follow his gaze and spun to see the painted girl there, corporeal and standing in the hallway.

Her expression was no longer serene. Her dark pit eyes were larger than before and full of malice, dark streaks like ink under her skin leaching down into her pale cheeks and around her mouth. She still looked painted; Mara could see the brushstroke texture across her terrible blackened skin. Mara's mind couldn't keep up with what she was seeing; this reality would not form properly. Surely this was another nightmare.

The girl and the cat moved forward in eerie, terrible unison, closing in on Mara from either side, and she crept backward. She couldn't let them touch her, nothing would be worse, nothing more foul than these painted figures touching her. But they wouldn't relent, walking slowly toward her as she continued to back away. The girl's expression was livid, ravenous for something Mara couldn't comprehend. She was so transfixed by shock and terror at this impossible sight that she didn't realize she'd reached the top of the kitchen stairwell. She took another step backward and found her foot had no purchase on solid ground. The painted girl smiled.

Mara completely lost her balance, and as she began to fall, a split-second of time stretched into minutes as thoughts flashed through her mind: Her book, a mere sentence or two from completion. The deep pink color of a Cosmopolitan as the candle on the bar glowed behind it. The glitter of sunlight on the lake. But mostly, the arousing intensity of Daddy's gaze when he towered above her, and whether he was mad at her for how she'd acted that morning and all the weeks since. *I'm sorry, Daddy*, she thought toward the fleeting vision. His eyes softened.

A beat later, time sped back up, and she was falling head over feet, down and down, around the landing, cracking her head over and over, against the wooden treads and the walls as she fell. Her sweat-soaked nightshirt tumbled askew, now stained with blood. She fell to the kitchen floor in a heap, legs splayed at wrong angles.

The last thing she ever saw was the girl and the cat standing quietly on the landing, looking down at her. The girl's face had returned to its pale porcelain hue, no streaks to be seen, a portrait of calm. Somewhere in her dying brain, Mara had a last fading thought that she was grateful to finally leave this cabin, even if this was the way.

When Mara had taken her final breath, her chest falling still, the girl and the cat turned as one and walked up the stairs with unnatural grace.

They disappeared around the corner, toward their empty canvas in the hallway.

PREY ANIMALS

By Noelle W. Ihli

Lulu pinned her ears and planted her hooves.

Fuck no, in horse.

She stopped at the edge of a barbed wire fence, which was nearly obscured by waist-high weeds. The trail narrowed here, threading past a craggy butte. I nudged her forward with a gentle squeeze, but the muscles in her withers tensed under the saddle.

No.

I nearly listened. We'd already ridden farther than usual, and it was getting late. But after the fight I'd had with Joel, I wasn't ready to turn around. Besides, this happened all the time.

Horses are prey animals, my old riding instructor explained. *Your horse is always on the lookout for predators, but she'll take her cues from you. The way you react is the difference between a minor hiccup and a runaway horse.*

I stood in the stirrups, scanning for the "predator." The rustle of quail set to burst from the sagebrush? A candy wrapper flapping in the weeds? An approaching dog? Impatient with my analysis, Lulu took a step backward, shifting her weight and tossing her head. I nudged her flanks, studying the cheatgrass beyond the barbed wire. I would have assumed it was rangeland if not for the three dusty trailers tucked into the slope. There were no vehicles in sight. No signs. Not even a real road. Idaho claimed its share of prepper hideouts, but most of them screamed, *don't tread on me.*

Suddenly, I saw the source of Lulu's distress: a line of dingy, pit-stained t-shirts hanging from a cord strung between two skeletal trees. Her ears pricked forward as one of the shirts billowed in the breeze. I settled back into the saddle. "Just a fashion emergency," I soothed.

You've got a serious death wish, Joel had muttered before I walked out the door. He hated it when I rode alone, convinced I'd break my neck in the hills. He had a point. If something happened out here—miles from the nearest cell signal—I was screwed. I rode anyway. I needed it too much.

Lulu wouldn't let anything happen to me, I'd replied with less conviction than I felt. Lulu was a good horse, but she was still a horse. A prey animal.

As if reading my mind, Lulu took another step backward. I tugged the left rein, and she eagerly swung her body around. I kept up the pressure on the bit, squeezing her flank with my boot until we'd made a full circle. Then I gave her a firm kick. "Come on, Lulu." It did the trick, like it usually did. "Let's go," I encouraged with another kick, eager to avoid a second standoff with the undershirts. She moved into a lope, kicking up her back hooves in one last gesture of protest. As we flew along the barbed wire fence, one of the shabby undershirts caught in the breeze again. It was stained a slightly different shade than the others: mottled brown.

We rode for an hour, until the tawny ocean of weeds and yarrow yielded to steeper trails and scrawny pines. Lulu's ears pricked again as the trail crested a slope. This time, I saw what attracted her attention immediately: bones.

"Probably a stray calf," I murmured. The nearest stockyard was miles away, but it wasn't unusual to see the remains of some unfortunate animal that had separated from the herd. This kill looked fresh though—and strangely neat. The color was wrong for a carcass picked this clean. Bright, crimson strips of gore and sinew still tied the ribs together like a pulpy bow. Nostrils flaring, Lulu kept one eye on the gore but obediently plodded on.

"Good girl," I murmured.

Lulu could abide bones. Just not undershirts. Even so, I was ready to turn around. The sun was dangerously low in the sky, and I wasn't eager to meet whatever had so quickly dispatched that carcass—especially not after dark. Once the stripped bones were out of sight, I dismounted and let Lulu drink from a small stream while I stretched my legs. When my foot hit the ground, something crunched beneath my shoe. Another bone, a vertebra, this one old and dusty. Next to it were several others. My eyes followed the grayish-white breadcrumbs into the brush.

Sun-bleached ribs peeked through a stand of bitterbrush—along with something pale and round. My pulse pounded as I took a step closer to see.

It was a skull, unmistakably human.

I yanked the reins harder than I intended as I stumbled backward, my eyes locked on the dark sockets. Lulu whipped her head back hard, and I heard a faint *snap*. The reins clutched tightly in my hand suddenly went slack. In a daze, I tore my eyes from the skull just in time to watch Lulu's bridle slide over her ears and into the dirt. The chin strap had snapped. She spit out the bit—the tiny piece of metal that made it possible to control a thousand-pound animal—with nervous whinny. Thinking quickly, I looped the reins around her neck like a lasso.

You can ride without a saddle, not without a bridle, my riding instructor told me. *Not unless you've got a death wish.*

We'd both have to walk—back the way we'd come. And we'd both have to stay calm. If I panicked, Lulu panicked. And if Lulu panicked, I'd never see her again. Not alive, anyway. Beyond the trail, the hills were riddled with badger holes: "Leg-breakers" to a runaway horse. I didn't look at the skull again, but I couldn't stop the words running through my mind.

Prey animal.

Our pace was agonizingly slow. By the time we made it back to the barbed wire fence, the sun had disappeared behind the butte, tucking the ribbon of trail into darkness.

"Almost home," I repeated like a broken record.

When we reached the fence line, she stopped short and tossed her head hard, nearly pulling the reins from my hands. "It's just undershirts—"

The words died on my lips.

A dark shape blocked the narrow trail. From the way it suddenly shifted, I knew it was human. I froze, torn between the urge to scream and the pressing need to stay calm. Lulu pulled harder at the pathetic bridle, desperate to run. She knew as well as I did that the only way home was through. I blinked hard, forcing the figure into focus: A wiry man wearing one of the stained undershirts. Most of his face was obscured by a dark beard.

Jump on her back. Hang on like hell, my gut demanded.

I reached for her mane with one hand, then hesitated.

She'll break a leg. You'll break your neck.

The breeze shifted, carrying a whiff of something acrid and metallic. Lulu snorted and whipped her head up. The leather cut into my palm as I struggled to hold on. The man didn't react, but his eyes traveled to the wrecked bridle.

Get on the fucking horse, my gut screamed.

Finally, I obeyed. I hadn't even managed to get my foot in the stirrup before he darted forward—not at me, but at Lulu. He let out a wordless whoop, clapping his hands in a clatter that echoed off the butte. Lulu bolted past him in a dark blur. The leather burned through my hands as my heel caught on the stirrup, sending me hurtling toward the rocks.

Everything went black.

When I woke up, I couldn't move—even though my vision shifted like a seesaw. My head throbbed, but what hurt most was my throat. When I tried to turn my head, the pressure intensified. Either something was choking me, or I'd actually broken my neck. I couldn't move my arms or legs. I stopped struggling and blinked, gasping for breath and trying to make sense of my surroundings. The cold, dry air smelled like meat. And blood.

Through blurry eyes, I suddenly saw my riding helmet hanging from a hook on the wall to my right. A smear of something shiny and dark glazed one side. I was sitting, slumped in a round metal trough. Dangling chains and hooks layered the far wall of the trailer. Dark, lumpy objects of different sizes hung from the ends.

The trailer door creaked open, letting in a warm breeze from outside. My throat constricted again, threatening to cut off my airway completely as I turned to see. That was when I understood: I hadn't broken my neck. There was no unseen hand on my throat. It was the strap from my helmet, still on my head, pushed back so far the nylon dug cut into my throat. I wasn't paralyzed: My arms and legs were zip-tied to a metal chair.

My eyes swiveled back to the helmet hanging on the hook.
It wasn't mine. Neither was the hiking backpack beside it.
Or the bike chain.
Or the dog collar.
Or the yellow apron, stained a mottled brown.
Or the circular saw, glinting in the moonlight as the door flung open wide.

THE DOORWAY BETWEEN

By Amelia Cotter

Deep in the northern wilderness, where for months it is night, firelight glowed from the windows of a small cabin in a small settlement at the edge of a forest. There were two adjacent cabins in the settlement, together occupied by one family, along with an outhouse and a storage shed. In the cabin with the glowing light were a mother, father, their teenaged son, and their old dog Fritz. The other cabin stood, for the time being, empty.

It was the dead of winter, and the snow was deep. Parents and son alike were sick, each ailing and weak in their beds. The grown daughter, Zina, was nearing the end of a three-day journey to bring her family medicine and supplies.

Zina marched steadily toward the settlement. Her face and feet were frozen, but she was sweating underneath her clothes and furs and the large pack she was carrying. The moon was low in the sky and she could see the firelight from the distant cabin's windows growing bigger on the horizon. She walked to the rhythm of her footfalls crunching in the snow. She longed for the warmth of the cabin and some hot soup, and hoped that everyone had been okay in what felt like her eternal absence.

As she neared the settlement, which the family had been occupying since the last long winter, she heard an odd noise rising over the sound of her footsteps. It was shouting. She quickened her pace, drawing the pistol she carried, just in case.

The shouting sounded shrill and desperate, and soon turned to screams. Zina dropped her pack on the ground and ran as fast as she could. The door to the cabin stood wide open. She ran inside, gun pointed, and found her mother and father already dead in their beds. She turned and found a man bent over her brother, holding him close, drinking deeply from his neck in long gulps.

Zina stood staring in shock, until the man looked up at her. His face was flush and smeared pink with her brother's blood. He dropped the young man, who was clearly dead, and stood up, taking a single step toward her. She backed away, assuming he could move extremely fast if he wanted to. Her pistol was of no use to her now. She turned and made a run for the adjacent cabin, hoping he couldn't enter without an invitation.

Her skin crawled with the anticipation that he would be on her any moment. She made it in a dozen long strides, threw the door open, and stepped inside. She turned around, panting, clutching the doorway. He came pacing, in no hurry, across the snow in her direction. He cocked his head to one side and looked at her with curiosity.

"Come out," he taunted her.

"No," she said, gritting her teeth.

"Then let me in," he smiled.

"No, I'm not stupid."

"No. No, you're not. I can see that."

She could see by the moonlight that he was young, around her age. He was tall and dressed plainly in a black sweater and black pants. He was also handsome, with a broad, boyish face and what may once have been warm, dark, human eyes. Shaking off the thought, she realized that her pack was still out there, just beyond the yard. She looked around the mostly vacant cabin for a lamp and firewood. She found both, but supplies were meager. Enough to wait out a hungry vampire?

He stood before her in the doorway, but as she had hoped, could come no further. She set to work making a fire.

"I don't know what you'll do," she said, "standing there and waiting like that. You'll be here a while because I'm not coming out and I'm not letting you in." She looked up suddenly and remembered the dog.

"Where's Fritz?" she demanded.

"Fritz? I'm Fil," the vampire answered casually and pointed to himself.

"Did you hurt Fritz?" she asked, quivering, and then—"Your name is *Fil?*"

The vampire smiled again. Zina shook her head and approached the doorway as closely as possible without coming within his reach. She tried looking over his shoulders and calling out to Fritz.

"Fritz!" she cried. Nothing was out there but the silhouettes of trees over the blue-tinted snowy ground. She called his name a few more times, and soon a small white shape appeared at the tree line. It was Fritz, and first he bounded toward her, but then locked eyes with Fil and slowed to a stalk.

"Please don't hurt him," Zina begged. "Don't you hurt him."

Fil took a few steps out into the snow and called to the dog. "Fritz," he said, and then whistled. Incredibly, the dog went to him. Zina realized she had made a great mistake calling to the dog, and almost ran out after them. Fritz crouched in front of Fil with his ears slightly back and tail down. Fil looked back at Zina and then bent down and pet Fritz gently on the head. The dog looked from him to Zina and back, and then ran to her. She bent down to meet him and hugged him tightly. Fil took his place in the doorway again.

"I don't eat *dog*," he told her.

Zina comforted the old dog, his fur damp with snow, and led him over to where the fire would soon be blazing. Keeping an eye on Fil, she started making a fire again, found some blankets, and settled down near the fireplace, her beloved dog and her useless pistol resting by her sides. Fil settled down into the doorway across from her and Fritz, resting his feet against the doorframe, and watched her.

"I need my pack," she told him. "It's still out there."

"What's your name?" he asked, unfazed.

"Zina," she told him.

"Zinaida?" he asked. She nodded.

"I'm Filipp. Yes, I saw the pack." That was all he said for a while, still watching her. She watched him back, his robust black form filling the doorframe and her view to the outside world. After a while, she was overcome with exhaustion and began to cry.

"*Why?* Why us?" she asked.

"I was hungry," he answered, gazing off into the distance, in the direction from which Zina had come. "Are there still others?" he asked, looking back at her. She shook her head no, thinking of the thirty or so people who lived at the outpost she had just been to.

"But why did they let you in? How? You're wearing only a sweater. They must have known something was *off*."

"Because I asked them to," he answered. "They didn't know. They were humble, polite people. And sick out of their minds."

He paused, then continued, "Their blood will sustain me for some time. You're in no danger now."

Incredulous, Zina reached for a piece of firewood and flung it at him as hard as she could. He flinched and put his arm up to block it. It hit him in the elbow with a thud and fell limply to the floor.

"Get out of here!" she screamed. Even Fritz jumped to attention, but then settled down again.

He sighed deeply. "Zinaida," he said slowly. Only her father called her by her full name. "I didn't know you would come. I didn't know you existed."

"I want you to *leave*," she begged.

"But I'd rather stay," he replied calmly.

She didn't know what to say and just kept shaking her head.

He reassured her, "It's night. You can sleep."

Zina opened her eyes. Fil was no longer in the doorway, but her pack was. The ever-present hint of twilight made it difficult for her to tell sometimes if it was morning or not, but she sensed that it was, and sat up, one side of her face hot from the fire and the other bitterly cold from the door being open all night. She rubbed her eyes. Fritz was with her. Where was the vampire?

Getting her bearings, she could hear muffled sounds coming from the other cabin. She crept to the open door and looked out. The bodies of her family members were lined up next to each other in the yard, each wrapped in a blanket. Fil was coming and going from the cabin, bringing out blood-soaked sheets and other items and dropping them next to the bodies. He gazed across the yard to Zina.

"I'm cleaning up," he called to her. "You're welcome."

Zina felt the blood drain from her head and leaned into the doorway. She searched for her words. "What will you do with them?" she called back.

"Do you prefer I burn them or bury them in the snow?"

She thought for a moment. "Bury them?" she asked.

He nodded.

Fritz bounded out of the cabin past Zina and ran to the bodies, examining them carefully, running around them and sniffing them with his tail between his legs. Finally, he sat down by her father's head. But when Fil called to him, he stood at attention.

Zina cried.

She felt sick and realized she might also be hungry. She had enough food in her pack to sustain her for another day or so, and then she would be out of luck in this mostly empty cabin. She gathered a snack and her thermos for some hot coffee, and spent the morning watching helplessly as Fil and Fritz walked back and forth from the cabin to the woods, Fil carrying the bodies away until there was nothing left but a stain in the snow.

When Fil returned, he acknowledged Zina with a nod and then retreated into the cabin, where he stayed for the rest of the day. Zina wondered if he would leave on his own eventually, or if he was settling here for the remainder of winter, or just waiting her out so he could make a meal of her, too. She had to think of a way to get to the other cabin or to the storage shed. The cabin had everything she needed. The storage shed had food, too, but no warmth. If she just ran for the shed, she would still have to run back.

The vampire was probably too fast, and she knew she couldn't defend herself. He had brought her the pack like she had asked, and he seemed to either like or pity her, or both, so maybe she could leverage that to get him to bring her more supplies.

But that didn't sit right with Zina.

Maybe she could somehow reach the other cabin when he wasn't inside, and then "uninvite" him in. Did that even work, and would he actually go away? She was going to have to leave the settlement again someday. *If he does leave*, she told herself, *I'll be alone. Completely alone in this world, save for Fritz. And the outpost.*

The thought made Zina weary. She was tough. She was also dangerously isolated. Of course, she had always felt alone, even in the presence of others. This was too much. She sat down in her mother's broken sewing chair. She would have to do what her parents had taught her about survival and resilience: she had to focus on what she could do in this moment–which didn't appear to be much.

Zina slept for the rest of the day. Sometime in the late evening, she woke to the sound of footsteps approaching. She had let the door stand open in a small show of self-empowerment, and there was the vampire, filling the doorway again. It was snowing heavily behind him. He crouched down and resumed his position from the night before, resting across from her with his back against the doorframe.

"Zinaida," he said, shaking the snow from his black sweater. "I cleaned everything. The cabin is ready for you to return. I buried the bodies in a mound of snow near the tree line, and I found some stones to mark the graves. Maybe tomorrow you will let me show you."

Zina took a moment to process what he was saying, and just blinked.

"We'll worry about it tomorrow," he said.

Zina was certain this was some kind of test, a trick. The vampire's demeanor was strange. Maybe in the morning she would pretend to need something from the shed, and then when he went to get it, she would *run*...run to the cabin, and get this over with.

"Thank you," were the words she chose.

They stayed up half the night, taking turns watching each other while the other pretended to sleep. At some point, Fil began to tell a story, an old folktale Zina had heard many times. Her mother used to read her that story from an old book, and the way he told it now was as if he was reading from those same time-worn pages. She listened to his voice and let it soothe her, overcome her, until she fell into another exhausted sleep.

In the morning, the doorway lay empty. The snow was still falling. She wanted to go out and bathe in it, take her clothes off and let it shroud her, pick it up from the ground in big fistfuls and run it over her bare skin. Fritz was snoring quietly at her side. She checked her pack for the last scraps of food: not enough to ration for another day. She would eat everything left and take her chances with Fil. Now, where was he?

When she turned around again, Fil's shape was growing bigger in the doorway.

"Good morning," he said, appearing through the falling snow. "Are you ready?"

"I'm ready," she replied. "But first," she added, her voice shaking a little, "will you bring me some…some potatoes from the shed?"

"Potatoes?" he asked, furrowing his brow. He glanced around the cabin. "Are you out of food here then?"

"Yes."

"Are you hungry?"

"Yes," she answered, feeling a little lightheaded.

"I'll bring you something."

Zina watched him curiously until he disappeared into the snow again. Now was her chance to run, somewhere. But she decided not to. Fil returned a few minutes later with a sandwich. He handed it to her through the doorway. *It could still be a trick*, she thought, but what did she have to lose? When she reached for it, the bread was warm and soft in her hand, as if freshly baked. Her fingertips grazed the backs of his fingers, which were icy cold.

"You're so cold," she told him.

"I'm dead," he said with a shrug. "Now, come on. Eat. There's more where that came from."

She ate the sandwich ravenously. It was delicious, and she felt much better afterward. She went to her thermos for some of yesterday's cold coffee and gathered herself. Fritz was still curled up and sleeping next to the fire, which was burning on its last bits of firewood.

"If something happens to me, will you look after Fritz? Will you surrender him to somebody you don't kill?"

"Nothing is going to happen to you or Fritz," Fil replied.

Zina picked up her pistol from the floor and the lamp from the table, and looked into Fil's dark eyes. She kept eye contact with him as she approached the doorway. "Let's go then."

She felt the meager warmth of the slowly dying fire at her back and looked down at Fritz for what she guessed could be the last time, and then at Fil, and then out into the dreary world. Fil stepped aside to let her pass.

She placed one foot outside. He looked down at it.

She stepped halfway out. He didn't move.

She stepped all the way out. He still didn't move.

She walked in short, careful steps toward the cabin, and could hear Fil's footsteps behind her, keeping pace with her. She didn't look back. She saw the form of the cabin materializing in front of her and felt her way to the front door, opened it, and stepped inside.

It was like another world.

The interior of the cabin was cleaner than she had ever seen it, and it was warm and softly lit with fire- and lamplight, just as she had hoped to find two nights before, except now there were no parents and no brother, and no one was sick, and no one needed her. The aroma of fresh bread and hot soup filled the cabin. She could hear Fil's heavy footsteps pass over the threshold behind her. She turned around. Here was another chance. She could ask him to go.

But she didn't.

He stood just inside the doorway and looked as if he knew she was mulling it over. "I did everything I could, Zinaida," he said, showing her his hands. "Everything to make it right."

Zina felt a wave of heat and vertigo. "What do you want here?" she asked.

"I want to stay."

"*Why?*"

He didn't answer, but smiled a nearly human smile.

Zina took a deep breath and pushed past him, back into the yard and into the steadily falling snow. She tore off her furs and her coat and pulled down her pants and her long underwear. She removed her shirt, pulled off her boots, and in a matter of seconds was all but completely naked, up to her knees in the snow.

She closed her eyes and fell forward into it. It took her breath away. She rolled in it, let it freeze on her sticky, warm skin. She rubbed it on her body, washing away the sweat, the static, the dread.

She stood up, shaking, and went to Filipp, who stood still in the doorway of the cabin. He opened his arms, and when she came into them, he pulled her inside and pressed his mouth into hers.

The kiss was as cold as the snow. Fil pulled her further and further into the warmth of the cabin, kissing her on her face and shoulders. She held him tightly and felt his teeth on her neck.

"Please," she said quietly.

"It will be quick," Fil promised.

Zina took him by the hand and led him to the small room around the corner, which had been her room. She pushed him down gently onto her small bed and surrendered.

She felt the unearthly sensation of being carried, transported thousands of miles from the burden of her ailing parents and the biting cold, thoughts of impending starvation, the fear of him and his darkness, her darkness, and her ever-present—even in this moment with him—solitude.

After they had both finished, and Zina lay in the warmth of Fil's arms—warmth he had gathered from her body and a bite's worth of blood—he stroked and smelled her hair, and told her, "Come late winter, before the sun rises, we can leave this place. Then, before winter comes again, I can make you like me, if you still want to be my companion."

Zina felt dreamy, languid, and fragile next to him. She reached up and ran her fingers over his face and through his hair. "I do want to be your companion. I don't want to be alone."

"Me neither," he said, and she buried her head in his chest.

The days passed, and the snow continued to fall. The two passed the time in the cabin preparing food and telling stories, reading, writing, playing her brother's mandolin, and sometimes idling in silence, just listening to the wind. They spent time outside walking Fritz in the deep snowdrifts of the woods, tending to the graves of her family, and playing in the snow.

Zina still couldn't regain the strength she had before her journey to the outpost. She felt hot, tired, and weak constantly. She asked Fil if it might have something to do with him feeding off her, which she allowed when they were in bed together, or if she might have what her family had. Fil promised that he was not the culprit and stopped biting her just in case.

It soon became apparent that Zina was very sick. Fil fed her the medicine that she had brought back for her parents and brother. She lay in bed for several days with a high fever. Fil and Fritz stayed at her side until it became apparent that the medicine was not taking effect. Her illness was serious.

"Zinaida, now may be the time," Fil told her, taking her hand.

Zina, who had grown up on fairy tales and ghost stories and romantic notions of *forever*, sighed heavily and said, "I know, Filipp. I'm ready."

She asked him to help her stand, and he walked her to the window. She looked out toward the forest where her family was buried, frozen solid beneath the snow.

"If you had never come, would we all have died anyway?" she asked.

"I don't know," he answered quietly.

"Will it hurt a lot?" she asked. "The transformation?"

"Yes," he told her.

Struggling for a deep breath, Zina clutched her chest and turned to Fil, her eyes filled with tears. "I'm scared."

"It will be quick," he promised, and nodded reassuringly. "You will live off my blood at first. Not for long, but for a little while, and everything will be alright after that."

She nodded back and cupped his face in her hands. They kissed and Fil gripped her tightly, told her to breathe in slowly, as deep as she could, and hold it. When she did, he plunged his teeth into her neck and drank her within a drop of her life.

Soon it was time to leave the settlement. The snow had stopped falling and the wind had stopped blowing it in all directions. The outside world was still dark but had at last gone quiet again.

Zina stepped outside, free of her heavy furs and old coat, and the weight of her pack—save for a few books and notebooks, and some keepsakes to pass the time and remember her family by. Fil carried her brother's mandolin, along with food and an old blanket bundled up in a bag for Fritz.

They stood hand in hand looking back at the cabins. Fritz stood between them looking up at them, his tail wagging in anticipation of this new adventure.

"Goodbye," Zina said to the settlement. She turned toward the woods and called out, her voice breaking, "I love you all."

Fil squeezed her hand, and they turned and headed for the outpost, where Fil would report a family missing out along the remote trail, at the settlement by the woods. They would both be long gone before anyone would have a chance to ask questions.

They marched steadily, away from the settlement. The moon was low in the sky and Zina turned back occasionally to see the darkness of the distant cabin's windows growing smaller on the horizon. They walked to the rhythm of their footfalls crunching in the snow. Fritz bounded back and forth around them, and Fil remarked that he was a good old dog, with so much life left in him. Zina took Fil's hand and kissed it, and he smiled at her with the warmest and most beautiful human eyes she had ever seen.

DOWN TO THE RIVER TO PRAY

By Morgan McKay

A s I went down to the river to pray
Studying about that good ole way
And who shall wear the starry crown,
Good Lord show me the way."

Summer fell upon Natchez, stifling and damp. Thunder rolled in the distance as the sky turned a sickly greyish-green. All was quiet, aside from the angry grumbles overhead. No squirrels skittered through the trees; no cicadas screamed from the pines. Silence fell on ears that knew the silence was neither pleasant nor kind. You see, down here the trees scream.

Incessant humming and wailing and crying *usually* rings through these trees at all hours of the day and night. The crunching of dead grass and snapping twigs can be heard echoing for miles. But not tonight.

"As I went down to the river to pray
Studying about that good ole way
And who shall wear the starry crown,
Good Lord show me the way."

Tonight, the world is silent, save for the eerie voices that seem to draw you in, ever further. A white wooden chapel stands on a hill, looking over the small town as the air churns and clouds bubble. No lights adorn her windows; no children roam her halls. But if you listen closely, the ever-present stillness that resides in her pews will occasionally be disrupted by the random plink of a piano. Out of tune notes fill her foyer, almost as if new students were learning to play. But if you push open the doors and press your way inside, you'll see naught but dust and cobwebs.

Life has not had a home in this holy place for quite some time. Blood stains blend in with the old wooden floors, leaving the barest trace of the travesties that occurred here. Somewhere in the distance, a clock chimes midnight. And suddenly, the church comes alive.

Candles in the windows light as if by themselves. A ghostly breeze fills the foyer and dusty cobwebs are replaced by gleaming hard woods, recently shined and polished. Empty pews no longer empty, but filled with lively families chattering and talking amongst themselves. And if you turn at just the right time, you'll see him. Brother Grady O'Neil approaches the pulpit, worn leather bible in hand. His face is obscured by a wide-brimmed black hat that matches the perfectly black satin of his Sunday best.

The piano comes to life, tunes beginning to play beautifully as otherworldly voices lift up to the heavens. Skeletal hands clutch charred crosses to crushed chests as the congregation lifts their praises to the King. The walls of the church begin to drip and leak, blood covering the once beautiful stained glass. Hymns echoed through the building, hauntingly beautiful melodies a stark contrast to the gruesome sight before you.

As the song comes to an end, light from the candles slowly flickers out, leaving you in an unsettling darkness. A hand claps onto your shoulder. Before you can turn and meet the eyes of the apparition, your vision goes hazy and you feel yourself collapse into the worn wooden floor.

Warmth, comforting and welcome, surrounds you. The soft scents of clean laundry and fresh baked cookies fill your senses. Your eyes flutter open, ever so slowly, and you're bathed in warm sunlight that filters through your bedroom window. The horror of the previous night slowly slinks into the depths of your memories, a terrible nightmare. Nothing more. But as you leave your bed and prepare for your day, faint voices echo from somewhere over your shoulder, sending a chill down your spine:

"As I went down to the river to pray

DARK VILLAGE

Studying about that good old way
And who shall wear the starry crown,
Good Lord show me the way."

HEATHER HAS THREE DADDIES

By Katharine Hanifen

Heather kicked her feet, carefully selecting which crayon to use for her masterpiece: a portrait of her family. Daddy was in blue, while Papa was in red. She stood in between them, dressed in pink. Heather had used her special sparkle crayons to make an extra pretty picture for Father's Day. She knew it wasn't for another month, but the rest of the class had all been making gifts for Mother's Day, and she didn't have a Mommy. Just three daddies.

Invisible Daddy was the hardest to draw. White crayon doesn't show up on white paper, so she settled on the grey and drew him in short, sketchy strokes instead of the long strokes she used for the rest of her family. He floated on the other side of the paper, apart from the family, but still happy and smiling.

No one else could see Invisible Daddy, so he sometimes followed her to school. Her other daddies thought he was an imaginary friend, but he was real. She could see him, hear him, and touch him, though she didn't do the last one very often. His skin felt … weird. It was cold and clammy, making her stomach flip like she'd just touched a slug every time she touched him. But she still loved Invisible Daddy as much as she loved Daddy and Papa.

"What are you doing?" Stupid Dylan Jacobs asked. His first name wasn't stupid, but it might as well have been. He'd been a real jerk to her ever since he and his mom saw her two dads pick her up from school.

"Drawing," she replied, selecting a bright yellow for the sun in the corner.

"Why?" he sneered. "You can't make a Mother's Day card. You don't have a mom. Or a real dad either."

She smiled, finally able to use the response that Invisible Daddy gave her whenever bullies wanted to bother her about her family. "I'm adopted. That means that my dads chose me. Your parents just got stuck with you."

"Well, at least mine aren't going to Hell," he snapped, snatching the picture from her desk and forcing her to ruin it by running a streak of sky-blue crayon right through Papa's head.

"Hey!"

"What's that?" he asked, pointing to Invisible Daddy.

"Give it back!"

He stepped out of reach, glancing over at the desk where the teacher was busy making paper flowers with another student. Old Mrs. Watkins was practically deaf, which meant that misbehaving students had to be especially loud to get her attention. Otherwise, she was utterly oblivious, not that she would have been all that much help anyway. Mrs. Watkins didn't approve of her dads' "lifestyles" and tended to ignore the jerks who hated her because of her parents. "Not until you tell me what that grey thing is," he said.

"He's my Invisible Dad," Heather replied.

Dylan stared at her like she'd grown two heads. "What's an Invisible Dad?"

"He's my dad, but I'm the only one who can see him." She reached for the paper again. "Now, give it back!"

Dylan laughed in a way that made her skin crawl. "You're so weird. There's no such thing as an Invisible Dad."

"There is!" She managed to grab onto the corner of the paper, holding it tightly as he tried to yank it away. The paper split down the middle with a terrible ripping sound. Her half was the one with her and her dads while Stupid Dylan had the side with Invisible Dad.

"No, there isn't," he said, making eye contact as he tore his half of the paper into tiny confetti pieces.

With a primal scream of rage, Heather punched him in the stomach, knocking him into the cabinet with the force of her blow. He grinned at her a moment to tell her he'd won before turning on the waterworks. "Mrs. Watkins," Dylan sobbed. "Heather hit me!"

Her head snapped up. "What was that?"

Tears burned in Heather's eyes as she cried, "He started it! Dylan said my parents were going to Hell and ripped my picture!"

"I didn't," he sniffled. "I swear!"

"Come with me to the principal's office."

"But he—"

Mrs. Watkins cut her off. "Now!"

Tears flowing freely, she ran out of the classroom and through the halls before Stupid Mrs. Watkins could drag her to the principal's office. It just wasn't fair! Dylan could do whatever he wanted with her, but the moment she fought back, she was the one in trouble.

She ran into the bathroom and locked the door of the largest stall before pushing herself into the far corner. Invisible Daddy appeared in front of her, his one good eye looking at her sadly. The other eye was completely gone from his head, leaving only a bloody red hole. His whole body was covered in cuts and bruises like he'd lost a fight with an army. When she first saw him, she was very afraid, but fear turned to confusion when he introduced himself to her as her first Dad. She knew what it meant to be adopted—her dads had explained that to her—but whenever she asked about her first parents, her dads got very sad, so she stopped asking.

After all these years with him, though, she wasn't scared because she knew Invisible Daddy was nice and funny. He always knew how to cheer her up. "Hey Heather," he said, kneeling beside her, "I saw what happened, and it wasn't okay."

"Why do I have three daddies?" she asked, sniffling. "Why don't I have a Mommy?"

"I guess you're old enough to understand." He sighed, clearly trying to collect his thoughts. "I'm kind of both. When I was born, the doctors thought I was a girl, and for a time, my parents and I thought so too. But then I realized that I was a boy, and became one—"

"Like Pinocchio?" she asked, making Invisible Daddy laugh.

"Yeah, like kind of like Pinocchio. But then, I decided that even though I was a boy, I wanted to have a baby, so I had you. But someone didn't like the fact that I was a boy, and he hurt me. Luckily, though, I got your daddies to promise to look after you in case anything happened to me, and they love you just as much as I do."

"Why don't they talk about you?" she asked, her pain forgotten in favor of learning more about her mysterious Invisible Daddy.

He gazed her, his eyes sadder than any other grownup's she'd ever seen. "What happened to me was … bad. They didn't want to scare you or give you nightmares, so they decided to wait until you were older. They have no idea you can see me." He shook his head as though he was trying to dispel these sad thoughts. His lips quirked up in a smile. "But it's okay because I'm a lot scarier now than the person who hurt me, and I won't let anyone do to you or your daddies what they did to me."

"Promise?" she asked.

He offered his pinkie, and she hooked hers around his. "Pinkie promise."

Heather decided to face the music and head to the principal's office. As always, Dane followed close behind, ever proud of his daughter's courage. The parents had already been called in, and all four looked furious, but Dane couldn't bring himself to pay attention to the back-and-forth. No, he was focused on Dylan's father, Winston Jacobs, currently purple-faced with rage. If he had a beating heart, it would have stuttered in his chest. He knew that face. It was the face of the man who killed him.

And now his son was torturing Dane's daughter.

When they went to school together, Winston had always been proudly bigoted. He'd protested the funerals of queer people and attended pro-confederate statue marches. He'd killed a man just for being different, and after his wife saw Heather's dads in the pickup line, had their kid treat his daughter like trash. The Jacobs were rotten to the core, every one of them.

Heather was given detention and ordered to write an apology letter, something she'd begrudgingly agreed to because it was better than getting expelled.

But Dane wasn't done with them. He'd been more focused on caring for Heather than on revenge for what happened, but now, everything had changed. His fury blazed within him like Hellfire, and they were going to burn. He was going to make them pay for killing him and continuing to hurt his family. So, that night, after Heather and her dads went to sleep, he slipped out of the house. As a ghost, he could come and go as he pleased, but he preferred to stay close to his daughter.

Now, he made his way into the Jacobs' house, a well-appointed home in a nice area of the suburbs. The lawn was immaculate to the point of being lifeless, and the inside looked like that of a catalogue. He took the sharpest knife from their block and ascended the stairs. Mr. and Mrs. Winston Jacobs both slept peacefully in their beds, oblivious to the angry spirit standing over them.

Mrs. Jacobs went first—and swiftly—with a quick slice through the throat. A mercy she did not deserve. The sound of her death gurgles and the sudden warm wetness on the bed woke Wilson, whose eyes widened uncomprehendingly at the scene.

Dane focused on his form, making it visible to someone other than Heather for the first time since his death.

Winston went pale. "No, no, this isn't possible."

"You fucked with the wrong family," Dane said and buried the knife in his guts just like Winston did to him all those years ago. He stabbed him again and again, turning his chest into bleeding mincemeat, keeping him alive long enough to cut out his eye.

"If thy right eye offends you, pluck it out," he hissed as he tossed it aside like garbage. Those were the last words anyone had ever said to him while he was alive, and he felt a certain degree of satisfaction throwing them back into Winston's face as he lay dying.

Dropping the knife, he headed to Dylan's room, just to get a good look at the brat asleep in his bed, oblivious to the fact that he'd just become an orphan. Dane considered killing him too—in his view, the kid deserved it—but he was still a kid. He had time to change. So, instead, he left him a note to find when he woke, painted on the walls in his parents' blood:

NOW YOU DON'T HAVE A MOMMY OR A DADDY!

WITH A NOD TO THE SPACE BETWEEN STARS

By Harlow Dayne

Dani's grandfather stared at each of us in the circle; the last flames of our campfire were mirrored in his eyes. The quiet power of the mountains encompassed us. No light pollution from the city dulled the panoramic beauty of endless stars overhead. Gazing upward, I could feel my heart swell, my soul getting lost in it, integrally connected.

The rich tone of his voice filled the silence.

"Even now, there are secret, ancient places of Mother Earth as yet undiscovered by man."

I could feel Ridley squirming on the log beside me as he fought the urge to pipe up with some asinine remark, likely something to do with goblins. Dani's grandfather felt it too. His white, dangling, spider leg eyebrows furrowed as he shot Ridley a scolding glance. Ridley slumped a bit lower in silence.

"I speak of elementals, and the nameless who took refuge here from the cosmos before humans walked. Most lie dormant in caverns, (Ridley's foot twitched), the depths of lightless ocean, or in primordial forest where magical creatures remain vigilant. Such beings should never be disturbed."

The old man allowed a question from his Granddaughter.

"*Have* they been disturbed?"

"Of course," he nodded with a sigh. "Humans blunder in, chopping down trees, excavating land to build. No offering is made to Spirit or the Earth. No reverence to what came before. Entities awaken and are not pleased. This is why people go missing."

"Goblins take them," Ridley mouthed. Dani's grandfather ignored it.

"This is when otherwise unexplainable activity begins to manifest. Shadows dart. Curses activate. An omnipresence seeps into foundation stones. Crimson eyes blink open in the depth of an old well. A stand of trees begins to vibrate with song from a distant nebula. Planes and ships go lost at sea."

"The great mysteries of the world," I thought, suddenly realizing I had spoken aloud.

As his head swiveled toward me the old man's face softened.

"That they are, Ghost. For many people, at least. There are few who understand."

The nickname didn't reference my pale skin and blue eyes. Comanche blood intermingled with my English, Irish and German ancestral lines. It had just taken a backseat countenance-wise, preferring to manifest when I walked in nature or sat beneath the moon. Dani had been the first to call me Ghost when we were kids. She had watched through a window, absorbing my secrets as I donned stealth mode to sneak past my drunken father. It was either that, or because I seemed invisible to most folks, including our teachers at school.

We said our goodnights as the last ember winked out. Faces that had absorbed the heat of our campfire for hours were now instantly numbed by the cold. As the two girls of the group, Dani and I were always thrown together, but we got along fine. The truth of the matter was that I felt so different from her that I often considered myself a separate species. She was pretty, outgoing, and confident–things I felt sure I could never be. And thankfully, she was a quiet sleeper. Red-headed Jetson rarely spoke, but his snores could levitate large animals. How Ridley slept through it was a mystery.

I longed for the loving reassurance of the moon as darkness pressed against my closed eyes. Ambient noise from the other tents stirred the quiet now and then. I curled up like a ball in my sleeping bag, slowly drifting away as the old man's words whispered through my head.

True to form, I rose early. Without waking Dani, I slipped out, partly to relieve my bladder, partly to chat with her grandfather. He always greeted me by the fire with hot chocolate and hotcakes from his trusty black skillet. But no fire burned this morning.

Even before the possible significance of the unmanned fire ring reached my brain, panicky ache fluttered in my chest. A rush of adrenaline like paint fumes surged up my throat. My eyes darted across camp; nothing had been disturbed, but there was no sign of him. Despite my heart's refusal to believe that this beloved mentor could still be asleep, I reluctantly approached his tent.

"Sir Elwyn?"

When no answer came, I lifted the canvas flap. Just inside, an empty sleeping bag lay crookedly folded open, as if its occupant had merely gone for a stroll. An involuntary sigh of relief eased the tension in my chest.

Dani brushed past me and kneeled down, laying a hand on the bag. The concern in her dark eyes reignited my fear.

"It's cold."

With every fiber of my being, I believe her connection to the universe kicked in. She sensed the severity of the moment, internally receiving that unknowable knowing. I caught hold of her arm before she could rush off alone just as Jetson and Ridley emerged from their tent. We set off in pairs to search in different directions.

The boys headed east toward the river. Trusting Dani's lead, I followed her into a densely wooded area, holding up a hand to shield my face from pine needles. She hadn't said another word, but I had watched her scour the camp for tracks. Something on the ground had perked her interest. She knew what she was doing.

Holding onto hope, I offered words of encouragement. Dani didn't respond or even once lift her eyes from the trail, until she stopped suddenly. In pure reflex, I put a hand on her shoulder for support, stepping beside her to view her discovery. Before us was not her grandfather gathering sticks for the fire, lost in time with the beauty of nature, or any other possible scenarios running through my brain. Elwyn Bale was dead.

I've never been so utterly heartbroken. Neither of us said a word as the profound gravity of the moment imprinted itself into our corneas and hearts. Devastated, we held each other. A few feet away lay Sir Elwyn. He had surely known his time was near. Rather than pass in his tent he had chosen to seek refuge in the woods, lying beneath a great oak tree and covering himself with a blanket of leaves. The last blanket he would ever need.

Ten years later

The Devore mansion was haunted. Whispers stirred among a stand of oaks surrounding the immense property as I walked up. Layers of time, people, and their emotions resonated as I scaled the steps to its once grand porch. A subtle chill like a small spider crawling up the back of my neck made me shudder and quickly glance over my shoulder. It might only have been an odd trick of the light, or my imagination, but shadows beneath the old trees had taken crude form. One of the monstrous shapes gestured toward me. Shaking it off, I took a seat on the porch.

A house can radiate emotions. No murders or death need take place in a location for it to pulse with energy. Fear and anguish can lodge in walls. Floorboards repetitively creak as if still bearing the weight of a sleepwalker. Doors swing open soundlessly. A room can radiate malice absorbed over time from a wretchedly bitter soul a hundred years earlier.

An omnipresence seeps into foundation stones, Elwyn's words from ten years ago echoed in my brain. He had been speaking of more magical, ancient entities, rather than the common, residual energy of humans. Yet as I sat quietly alone on the porch, the memory was triggered.

When the first adult had entered the scene of Elwyn Bale's death, Dani and the boys were led away. I was unnoticed (as was so often the case). In truth I had eased deeper into shadows of the trees. Silent, I waited for the ruckus of their movement through the forest to dwindle. Alone with the body, time stopped. The very air pulsed with the profound consequence of the moment.

I spoke to him quietly, sitting cross-legged on a bed of leaves. It would not have shocked me had he answered. He did not, but I sensed slight movement overhead. Lifting my gaze, I felt his presence near the crown of the tree where he lay. I felt him call wordlessly to me, felt the essence of his soul as it acknowledged our connection and then danced into the sky with joy. I believe my eyes detected an odd anomaly–eight or ten small sparks of light hovering among the branches, but as I blinked, they were gone.

Tears had streamed down my young face. The moment had been incredibly bittersweet. My racing mind and heart soared and ached simultaneously. With a deep breath, I had pondered the future. Yet before I could dive too deep, a swallowtail butterfly fluttered against my cheek and landed on my nose. I have no idea where it came from. The gorgeous wings opened and closed slowly with the rhythm of a beating heart. Its tiny feet adjusted and then launched into the air, vanishing through sun-kissed branches.

The front door of the Devore house creaked open, dragging me back into reality.

"They're ready for you."

I was to perform a psychic sweep of the place.

Members of Southlake Paranormal stepped aside as I entered. The living room was set up as their command center. Shadows lay heavy in corners, but elegant antiques and heavy floor-to-ceiling draperies were bathed in pale illumination from a row of monitors. Cameras were set in place, but no investigation had yet occurred. My job was to scout out hot spots and identify any spiritual energy or entities.

An unfamiliar fellow in a black Lacuna Coil sweatshirt pointed his camcorder at me and nodded. High cheekbones and a well-trimmed, dark beard framed his face.

I'd learned to tread carefully. Not only is darkness in an unfamiliar, often deteriorating house a danger, but cables and other equipment can pose a threat as well. It hasn't happened to me, but I have heard of cases where living human beings interfered with investigations. Whether it's blundering upon vagrants in a massive sanitorium, or locals getting wind of an investigation and deciding to slip inside to wreak havoc for kicks, staying alert is essential. Even stray pets, bats, rodents, and snakes can pose complications.

"Stay a few steps behind me," I instructed.

Pulling a flashlight from my coat pocket, I switched it on and played it slowly around the room. There were arched, wooden doorways to both right and left. Ornately carved dragon pediments sat atop them both. Straight ahead lay a winding staircase. Light from my beam played over the first few steps like a diver's lamp driving back the extreme darkness of deep ocean. Beyond that the blackness was impenetrable. An image from the film *Nosferatu* flashed in my mind. Anticipation of inhumanly long, white fingers curling slowly around the corner distracted my focus.

Sometimes being a horror fan can float to the surface at inopportune times. I shook my head to dislodge the image and headed for the stairs.

"Pick up on something?"

Turning toward the cameraman as IR light hit my eyes, I explained for the record.

"There's a lot here, but most is residual and natural energy. Not much more than what you'd find in average homes. Layers of emotion from those who have lived here in various incarnations of houses or land. Of more interest is what's in the bedroom to the right. Had me fooled for a minute, but it's a thoughtform created by years of focused, repeated reading of the same children's book. There's a sweet five-foot-tall mouse in there."

"No way…"

Fighting the urge to defend my impression, I pushed on, laying a hand atop the banister. Many Sensitives receive actual images. I do on occasion, but generally information comes in an unspoken sense of *knowing*. Some people refer to it as a download. Already it's becoming an annoying new age term, but it is actually an accurate explanation. The information or knowledge is suddenly received as if invisibly transferred from one place to another, or wordlessly spoken within my brain by some solemn omnipresence. And despite the dramatic jolt portrayed in television shows of Sensitives while picking up images, the truth is that intuitive information comes with incredible subtly. Interpreting it correctly is an art form in itself.

Slight vibrations from the wood banister pulsed through my hand. Glancing up into the sheer darkness of the landing above me, I felt a surge of hesitation mixed with anxiety. Something eluding my focus was hiding there.

"Keep your guard up," I said sternly, catching the cameraman's eye. Likely in his early thirties with shoulder length hair and deep-set eyes, he had the look of a solid, unflappable soul. "What's your name, by the way?"

"Zane."

"Ok, Zane. We've got something upstairs I haven't identified yet, but it doesn't feel friendly. It may or may not interact, but stay centered."

"Got it."

The air was dense and considerably colder on the landing. I was drawn to a doorway at the end of the hall. Call it a gut feeling, intuition or spidey senses: for me the sensation of picking up on non-physical energy is like a breathy whisper through my conscious awareness. Like a gentle strum of fingers atop a still lake.

Time and physical reality froze. It felt like the very air was throbbing. Hyper alert, our eyes were locked onto that door as it slowly creaked open. When it stopped, the silence was profound. My aching eyes watered from the sheer awe of the moment. Just as whispers from my brain tried rationalizing that there might be an unbalanced frame needing a hinge adjustment, a small voice in the depths of my solar plexus screamed otherwise.

Darkness of the room within that door was as deep and foreboding as the vastness of space. Zane looked to me for instruction. I swallowed fear down with a calming breath, closed my eyes and focused.

Something pulled me forward. I was dragged–as someone with feet planted to the earth in resistance, with dirt spewing up around them. My eyes flew open just as I was pulled over the dark threshold. Bitter cold stung my face. Furniture and trappings of the room were as inconsequential as hollow doll house pieces. The lone window was the focal point here.

This was a portal. Again, my desperate, flailing brain jumped to movie images and situations with which I had prior experience. I pictured a single file chain of dead, somnambulant souls. But the truth was far more unnerving.

I heard Zane's voice as if from worlds away. Words were indistinguishable. One thing, and one thing alone, traversed this ethereal road. It would suffer no others. Any attempt by even the most malevolent of demons was unimaginable. For a fleeting moment, I felt the heat of a campfire on my face as my old mentor's words echoed through me. But this was no disgruntled wraith of trees and mountains. This was a motherfucking ancient elemental. Disturbed from slumber by God knows who or what on this property, it had risen from deep within the bowels of the earth. All the swirling fears of mankind harvested from midnight fever dreams crawled like roaches within its skin folds.

Zane crashed into me, sending me sprawling to the floor as the thing spilled in from the window. A single flashlight beam zigzagged over it in panic and then went dark.

"Get out if you can," I called to him.

There was no response. I smelled blood, or at least feared I did.

It took all the resolve I could muster to pull my flashlight from my pocket. The weak light struggled to illume small areas at a time. But the light was of no consequence. There was no shift to elude the beam, as I had hoped. I could not count on it as defense. A cosmic nightmare of infinite proportions planted itself with indestructible confidence before me, letting the light play along its gleaming membranes. Hundreds of small eyes filled with terror were trapped there, as if souls had been swallowed alive.

Without speaking, it communicated, its thoughts infiltrating my brain. I resolved not to listen, sure that to do so would signal the end of me. I searched with my hands on the floor for Zane, finding his sweatshirt and dragging him toward the door. The creature allowed me to do this. It wanted *me*. Once I managed to push Zane over the threshold and out into the faint light of the hallway, I was suddenly as helpless as a fly in a web. I could not move or speak.

Something with a texture that brought spores and lichen to mind wrapped around my left ankle. Its intrusive thoughts whispered through every fiber of my being. Its purpose was strictly to consume, but it had not done so for decades. It hungered. Intuitively, it savored the nuances of my psyche. As I struggled in vain to break free, it smelled the coffee I had brewed that morning; the thin sheen of soap lingering in the crook of my arm. Nothing eluded it. It knew my joys and deepest fears. It could taste the colors of my dreams.

As it pulled me closer, I relaxed, not succumbing, but remembering who I truly was. Remembering encapsulated moments when the universe had comforted, supported, and even saved me. Remembering that I was intrinsically the same essence as this being, as mind-blowingly impossible as that might seem.

Despite that knowledge, doubt flowed through me. Shutting my eyes against it I saw Elwyn Bale's face. Behind him were others not quite identifiable, ranging from massive presence to the smallest of creatures. They were mine, I knew, with me since the beginning. At their insistence, I willed myself to expand, energy surging outward. I felt myself merge with the night sky, moon, and stars. One with everything, powerful emotion welled within me.

Zane's weak voice split the silence.

In that moment the elemental released me and withdrew. Moonlight spilled in through the window when it had gone, highlighting things left on the floor in its wake. A random hairclip, a silver bracelet, several old coins, and a single baby shoe.

Zane required a short hospital stay, but he recovered. Others in specialized areas of the paranormal attempted to close the portal, but warned that the fix was temporary. I recommended the Devore house be leveled, but only time will tell if its owners opt to do so or are tempted to keep its museum and tour revenue going.

Before heading home, I followed Bale's intuitive suggestion to make an offering to the elemental. He led me to a series of hidden caves along the west end of the property. Jagged rock formations and cruel undergrowth were formidable, though I had no desire to get close. Afterward, in the safety of my own home, I scanned the walls, calculating the odds that spells and sage and salts would keep me safe. Something out there had tasted me, forever connecting us. That web of connection sparked a rush of emotion; I reached for my phone and called Dani.

To Libby!
Never eat the yellow snow!
♥ Cassie Marozsan

DON'T EAT THE YELLOW SNOW

By Cassie Marozsan

It's been five days. My backpack is empty. I ate the last of my food this morning so I could get up and move. I need to get as much ground covered as possible and hopefully find my way out of here.

Day One:

It was a simple hike through the woods. It was a nice day, chilly and gray—but nothing was on the radar that would cause any concern for a hike. I was following a trail that was made for the average hiker. My plan was easy: walk as far as I could, go off the path a little way, start a fire, make some dinner, sleep, hike back in the morning. So, that's what I started to do. The trail was dirt and there hadn't been much rain, so it was smooth to walk on. There weren't any signs or markers that stood out—it was just simple up and down, one trail, no smaller trails jutting out anywhere. I could hear voices in the distance but I didn't see anyone, nor were there any cars by mine when I parked, which was strange because there's no other entrance. Maybe they were cycling, so I really didn't think too much more about it.

I walked and took pictures until about 4:30 pm, then I wandered off the trail a little bit to find an open area to set up camp. It was still light outside, so I unpacked my small, one-person tent and set that up before starting a fire. I was by myself and I sure wasn't trying to impress anyone, so I grabbed the lighter and newspaper I brought so I didn't have to rub sticks together. After gathering an arm full of sticks, I opened my can of SpaghettiOs, put them in a pot, and warmed them up before enjoying my dinner and heading off to dreamland.

I had no idea what time it was when I opened my eyes, but I was freezing. I didn't want to get up, it was so cold, but I had to, even if it was just to see why my bones were stiff. I only got the opening to my tent a quarter way unzipped when the snow started falling in. As my brain transitioned to full attention, I saw the dark shadow wall about two feet high, all the way around the tent. "Shit."

After realizing how screwed I was, I gathered up everything in my pack to bundle up with to stay warm. I had a hat and I wrapped my hands with socks. I put on two hoodies, a light jacket, and my hiking boots, then gathered the courage to step outside the tent and pack up camp. As I was shoving everything inside my pack, I looked around and realized I had no idea where the trail was or even what direction it was in since the snow blanketed everything. Again, "Shit."

That's the gist of my situation. Now you're probably calling me an idiot and a bunch of other choice names that mean the same thing. I get it. But, in my defense, it's April, it's spring–I didn't think we would get hit by a freak snow storm. I'd checked the radar. Granted it was the *free* radar, not the one they try and charge $0.99 a week for, but you would think the free version would still show two feet of snow coming.

Day Two:

I'm lost. Yep, that's it. Day two: I'm lost. I've been lost the whole damn day and it hasn't stopped snowing.

Day Three:

I woke up freezing. I didn't even take my layers off last night. I still have no idea where I am and I haven't seen anyone. I can still hear faint talking somewhere, but even when I yell out for help, no one replies. I started to take this being lost thing seriously last night after the whole day was spent stumbling around realizing I was no closer to finding my car at the end of the day than I was at the beginning. My energy and supplies were being quickly depleted, so I decided I had to go through everything and make up rations before I started walking this morning. I filled a couple of empty water bottles with snow and wrapped them in my sleeping bag, hoping they would thaw in a little bit.

Another crazy thing: I haven't seen any animals. I'm in the woods, it's covered in snow, and I've seen zero tracks. I've heard some noises, but nothing crazy, I don't think. I feel okay—tired and cold, but nothing too bad. After evaluating my supplies again, I packed up and start walking. I can't find my tracks from yesterday, but I know which direction I came from because I pointed the opening of my tent to the direction I needed to keep walking. I thought I would make it back today. It was a full day walk to camp the first day, adding in the weather conditions and confusion, I should only have a few more hours today and I'll be back to my car. I think. I hope.

I was wrong.

I walked and kept walking until the sun started to go down. I'm hungry, and thirsty, and exhausted. My hands are freezing, my socks are wet. I need to lay down.

Day Four:

Nothing, Nothing new. Some trees. No people, but I still hear them. Am I going crazy? No clean water. Less food. More sleep. More exhausted. Still cold and wet. I'm talking more but it's to myself. *Crazy*. I am, I'm going crazy, no, not yet, it's only been four days.

Seems like I'm walking in circles because everything looks the same. It stopped snowing and the snow is melting. That could be a good thing, but right now all I can think about is the mud mixing in and not being able to find clean snow to fill my water bottles with. I was hoping I would be able to recognize something since everything wasn't blanketed in white anymore, but that was a false hope. It must be close to sunset now, so

I'm going to look for a drier spot to set up camp. After wandering around for twenty minutes or so, I found some snow to fill my water bottles with. It was muddy and the snow looked yellow. I couldn't help myself from laughing out loud, thinking of my parents always telling me not to eat the yellow snow when I was younger. I set up my tent and fell asleep extremely quickly.

Day Five:

It took all my energy to get up and moving this morning. As soon as I awoke, I ate the last few pretzels I had in my bag and drank a bottle of muddy water. I rolled everything up and put it in my pack and started walking again. I didn't make it far before I had to rest. I found a huge tree and slowly slid my way down the trunk until I was resting on the ground. I closed my eyes and easily drifted off with my back against the tree.

"Ms. Snow. Ms. Snow. Time to get up."

I tried to swat the noise away. I've heard people all week but no one has been real.

"Ms. Snow. Wake up."

My eyes slowly opened to the sound of someone saying my name. I blinked several times and took in my surroundings. I was inside, but it was still cold inside the brick room. Have I been rescued? Did someone find me while I was resting? I was still wet, but not from the snow or rain–it looked like I managed to wet myself. I must have been worse off than I thought after all those days in the cold. There were people standing around everywhere, but there was something strange about them. They looked like statues, like zombies, all wearing hospital gowns, mumbling, moaning, drooling. Honestly, *I* felt like a zombie, my bones were stiff and I couldn't open my eyes enough, or keep them open long enough to seem awake. I didn't even care that I peed my pants. Shouldn't I be embarrassed, or have an overwhelming feeling to want to be cleaned up? I'm just too tired.

"Ms. Snow, it's time to take your medicine."

"Medicine?" I slowly asked. "What day is it?"

"It's Monday Ms. Snow. Were you dreaming again?"

"Where am I?"

"Ms. Snow, you're home. You've been here the last nine years. Now take your medicine."

I reached in the little cup, grabbed a pill, and swallowed it with the little cup of water the lady gave me. I had no idea why I was here or what the "medicine" was for, but I didn't care. I didn't have the energy to care. I just wanted the voices to stop. Who were all these people, and why won't they stop mumbling and screaming?

"Don't forget to eat the yellow one, Ms. Snow."

I laughed quietly and I couldn't stop laughing. It grew louder as I kept thinking of my parents with their childish warning. The others must have heard me, because it started to sound like a full-blown comedy show with all the cackling going on.

"Don't eat the yellow snow … Don't eat the yellow snow … Don't eat the yellow snow… Don't eat the yellow one Ms. Snow… Eat the yellow Ms. Snow… Eat the yellow snow."

I drifted off to sleep again, cackling at the yellow snow.

Day One:

It was a simple hike through the woods …

SHE WAITS FOR ME

By Jason A. Jones

I'm trapped. I feel the ever-growing presence of the woman inside my head, inside my room, inside my house. This house is a tomb, a prison. I can't escape or she'll get me.

When darkness falls near my home, there aren't any street lights or any stars in the sky, just cornfields and gravel roads. A few howls from nearby coyotes pierce through the bleakness of it all, but other than that, nothing, just blackness. Old man Preston is usually out planting in his fields, but on this night, the fields are empty except for swaying cornstalks and a single solitary scarecrow in the middle, staring back at me with hollow, blackened eyes. A few years ago, you'd usually catch me sitting outside during a full moon on nights like this enjoying a cool breeze with a drink in hand. Duke, my chocolate Labrador, would be sitting beside me, occasionally barking at a car traveling down the road in front of the house.

But not on this night.

For a while now, I've only been able to observe from the other side of my window, in my bedroom on the second floor of the house. I have this unquenchable feeling I'm being watched, not by anything outside, mind you, but from within. My skin is utter gooseflesh and my pants are soaked from where I just pissed in them. I'm unable to move and I can't stop looking through my window. I don't want to turn around and see the thing that has haunted my dreams.

She's standing in the hallway in front of my locked bedroom door, I just know it! I can hear her breathing heavily and soon it will give way to laughing.

I saw them pulling up the gravel driveway, clouds of dust behind them, the car coming to a stop. I saw the trunk open, Dad getting out and racing back there, a huge grin on his face while Mom struggled to get something out of the back seat. I was in the kitchen preparing a sandwich when Dad called from the front door.

"Come outside and help us, James!"

I didn't hesitate. They were expert shoppers when it came to things like estate sales, yard sales, and flea markets, and I couldn't wait to see what they purchased.

"What ya got there, Mom?" I asked her as she furiously pulled at a rectangular object.

"Will you get this for me? I can't wait for you to see it." Mom's smile could be seen from the moon. She was always at her prettiest when she smiled.

Dad removed a box of trinkets from the trunk, sat it on the ground and closed the lid. Once inside, he put the box on the kitchen counter, its overflowing contents spilling over the sides like overgrown vines in a terracotta planter. I walked over to the living room sofa and laid the rectangle wrapped in butcher paper on it. Mom sat down beside it and began to reveal what was inside.

"I couldn't resist this. I paid a little too much, but I figured it'd be a nice addition to the rest of our vintage items." Mom caressed the object a little too obsessively. It was a portrait of an elderly lady cloaked in black with a fiery background. She was holding a skull. I didn't like it at all, but seeing the smile on Mom's face made it OK.

"Why though?" I asked, swallowing a lump that had formed in my throat.

"Why not?" She grinned.

The next day it was hanging in our hallway.

I've been stuck in this room, just waiting, biding my time until she can get in. I haven't been downstairs to survey the rest of the house. Good thing I have a mini fridge in here. I stocked it about a month ago with soda, but now there's just some cold fried chicken from the kitchen, some cheese, and milk. It's not gonna last long. I'm surprised it's lasted as long as it has. I've learned to eat smaller. I'm not sure if and when I'll get out of here.

She's banging on the door now. Make it stop! Dear God, make it stop! Thank you, Jesus, it stopped.

I'm like a laboratory rat, trapped inside a cage made of treated lumber, brick, and mortar. Mom and Dad's car still sits in the driveway, it doesn't move. It can't move. I miss them. I miss Duke. I know where they are though, I've known it for quite some time and every time I think of it, I shiver fiercely, knowing I'll soon be joining them. I've contemplated letting her in, letting her take me. My only comfort is looking through the window at the fields beyond. I've hoped for a passerby along the road but alas, no one has ventured through here in weeks. It's as if all time came to a standstill once *she* took possession.

Oh God! She's dragging a trash bag into the field!

Dad drove a semi for J&D Grain. Most days, he'd be gone for hours and wouldn't get home until Mom and I were in bed. Sometimes I could hear him downstairs, heavy steps upon the linoleum floor in the kitchen, opening the refrigerator door, probably getting a beer or something. A lot of times the TV would turn on and if it was a Friday night, he'd fall asleep in his chair. I'd find him curled up in it most Saturday mornings, the empty beer bottle on the floor beside him. On Saturday the 10th, he wasn't there.

I happened to look out of the kitchen window. It was seven o'clock and he was already sitting on a riding mower, making parallel lines up and down the lawn. I walked out onto the porch and sat on the swing. A gentle breeze hit me as I watched him. I could see a smile on his face as he mowed the grass, a huge set of ear muffs and a pair of safety glasses perched on his head. Eventually he pulled the tractor into the barn. I figured he was messing around in there awhile, because he didn't come out.

I heard Mom come out of their bedroom, sleep caressing her eyes, a strange look on her face. Her fingers were gently sliding across the old woman's portrait.

"Mom?"

"Yes, James." She didn't look at me.

"What are you doing?" I asked.

"You know, I did some research. The person in this picture was…a…wit—" She turned her head to face me and she screamed.

What I can see through this window is my only source of refuge. She's out there now, digging a grave, the shovel much too big for her bony, skeletal hands. She's scraping the ground, throwing dirt like a wild dog aggressively digging for its bone. The black trash bag is laying beside her. *How was she able to drag it?* I'm frozen, my eyes in a glassy stare. I can't look away as she starts digging more holes.

More holes.

She's creeping towards the house now. She's staring up at me in the window, smiling, and her stride is as graceful as if she's floating on air. I slowly creep up from a crouching position and lock the deadbolt on my door.

Mom raced out of the house and ran toward the barn. Within ten feet of the old hickory tree, she fell to her knees, her eyes staring up into it. What I witnessed that day is still with me, like a festering wound that will never heal. Dad hung from a rope, his mouth agape, blood and saliva fell from it. The rope was so tight, it cut through his skin. His dead, bleeding eyes watched as Mom started to hyperventilate. I grabbed onto her while she sat there and rocked slowly. Turning my head toward the house, I saw a glimpse of someone or something black standing in the open front door. My mind whirled like a tornado and my skin was clammy. Mom went into herself, and from that moment on she would get up every morning and kneel before the portrait, her eyes glassy and her mouth frozen into a smile. The words that came out of her mouth were ones of adoration and praise to the old woman. She went nuts. It wasn't too long before she met her demise as well.

While I wait, I try to sleep and it eludes me. I wish Duke was here with me. I hear his dead bark while I lie in bed. It haunts me.

Through the window, I watched as Duke ran frantically around the front yard, tail furiously wagging. He was darting from side to side, his mouth foaming. The bark was demonic and menacing. Finally, he laid down on the ground, his face looking towards me. I could tell his breathing was labored, his chest rising up and down like a bellows. My fear kept me from doing anything. It keeps me from unlocking this door and hauling ass downstairs to confront what has been destroying my family.

And the scarecrow in the middle of the cornfield was gone.

That was what Duke was seeing.

The scarecrow stood over Duke, looking up towards the sky, its straw-like hands hovering over him. The dog began to contort, his body writhing and bones cracking. *My God, I swear I can hear it!* Soon he was dead, his body twisted into a disgusting pretzel-looking thing. I screamed and banged my head on the window. It cracked and blood began to pool on the ground from a gash on my forehead. The scarecrow was back on the pole in the middle of the cornfield as if nothing had ever happened. It wasn't long before I saw the old woman dragging another black bag out into the field, this one a little smaller. She threw it into the second hole in the clearing, the shovel scraping.

Mom was worshiping the portrait like some crazed religious lunatic. It was removed from the hallway and placed in a shrine where the TV once stood in the living room. Small bloody carcasses surrounded the picture while Mom was on her knees, hands lifted in the air, her body swaying like a snake to the charmer's flute. I couldn't do anything now. She was gone. One night as I tried to sleep, I could hear her downstairs, talking to it. I swear it talked back to her. She was chanting something I didn't recognize and then I heard her cry.

And then suddenly, there was laughing...

In the middle of the night, I heard the tapping on my bedroom door.

"James, It's me." Mom's voice was gravelly. "Will you let me in?"

"No," I said with trepidation.

"Please come downstairs. She wants to talk to you." Mom started scratching on the other side of the door. I froze. My neck hairs went prickly and I could feel the dampness in my crotch.

"I'm not leaving, James, so you might as well come." I could tell she was getting agitated.

Then the banging began.

She slammed her body into the door with such force that the walls shook. I ran from my bed and cowered in the corner.

"MOM, STOP!!" Tears began to stream down my face and I tried to slink back further into the corner, hoping my body would disappear into the wall. Her hands were pounding the door like a hammer hitting nails. I covered my ears to no avail.

And then silence.

"James, I'm sorry. I know it's been a little rough since your father left." She said this calmly as if Dad had left for another J&D run. I bit my lip and I could taste the blood.

"Just leave me alone," I said, my hands balled into fists. I leaned into the corner and closed my eyes tightly, hoping she would go away. I could hear her cry outside the door. It drifted away as if she was heading downstairs. I slowly got up and walked to the bedroom door, and I noticed a faint light from underneath. I opened the door and peered out into the hallway. She was gone, but the light was more noticeable in the darkness. It was coming from the living room. I slowly began my descent even though I could feel my reluctance growing.

Candles were surrounding the shrine to the portrait. They were all lit and in the middle of them was Mom, her eyes were wide and her mascara smeared from her tears. She looked up at me and smiled as I stood on the bottom step of the staircase. In the far corner of the living room, in the blackness, where the candles allowed only faint shadows, stood the cloaked woman, her hands outstretched.

"Give yourself to her, James." Mom smiled as if she'd been given the keys to the kingdom, a queen sitting on a demonic throne beside this hideous monster. I couldn't move. My feet refused to step off the stairs.

"Get away from her, Mom."

"You don't understand. The cornfield is just the beginning. Duke and your dad were just the start of it. You and I are needed now." She bared teeth in a horrible grin. My skin immediately became gooseflesh.

"Our family's blood is what she craves. She's done this before. She is a living portrait and we must bow to her."

I couldn't believe what I was hearing. I stopped listening as Mom rambled on incoherently in the candlelight. The old woman stepped away from the darkness and stood directly behind Mom, cold steel gleaming in her hand. I screamed, but it was too late. The old woman ran the steel across it, slicing through. Blood began to pour from Mom's neck. She fell to the floor, the old woman knelt down before her and began to drink from her wound. I stood in horror and vomited. Mom's dead eyes looked toward the ceiling, a crimson pool beginning to form around her. The cloaked woman began licking the floor, running her tongue across Mom's body, now covered in blood. Suddenly the old woman looked at me. I closed my eyes as tightly as I could.

"Come here, boy. Take part in this wonderful gift." Her voice was childlike and gave me the creeps. She slowly began to rise from her position, facing me. A deep laugh came out of her throat and blood seeped from her lips. It was then my feet let loose on the stair step and I raced up the staircase, hitting my bedroom door hard, slamming it shut and locking it.

I'm still here, and she is pacing the hallway. I can hear her gentle footsteps crossing the floor. Occasionally I hear her whisper my name. She taps on the door, rapping her skeletal fingers, the nails scratching at the same time. She dragged Mom out into the cornfield like she did Dad and faithful Duke. I could hear the scraping of the dirt as she filled the hole. There's one more left. It's mine. I'll need to go to it soon. I'm scared to death. I don't have time to grieve though, she won't let me. My food is gone now and my room has the stench of shit and piss.

I guess I should go ahead and let her in. She's calling my name and it's driving me insane.

THE WENDIGO

By Heather Moser

There *It* goes again ...another bloody corpse. The hunt is over. I am safe another day.

I used to be terrified during this time of the year, right after the first snowfall. During the winter, I have to focus on finding the scarce food not already taken by the unending appetite of the frost. It isn't a simple task and it is made no easier by those creatures who walk on two legs. Hunkered down, motionless, lying in wait for me to be so focused on finding my next meal that I lose sense of myself and surroundings. I spent much of my time running from the stinging bites that fly out of their fire sticks. I have seen what happened to my friends; I could not let it happen to me.

You know what creatures I mean. They are out for my meat. Making me food for their bellies. Taking my head as a trophy and bragging rights. I used to live on the edge constantly. There were few moments of rest; my senses grew keen. They were honed for the scent and the sounds of footfalls on the snow. That was until *It* came. *It* changed everything.

When *It* came to my part of the forest shortly before the first snowfall of the year, *It* looked just like the ones who carry the sticks of fire, except *It* was weaker. Smaller. Unlike the ones who carry the firesticks, *It* wasn't alone. *It* had another with *It*. There were two of them. They seemed lost. They took some of my berries and a couple of squirrels, but that wasn't enough to sustain them. The snow and bitter cold set in shortly after they arrived. That was over a year ago now.

I remember when *It* changed. One day there were two of them. The next, *It* was all that was left. *It* was different. *It* didn't look weak and frail anymore. *It* moved faster. Faster than even I can run. *It* was stronger. Like night and day, the fear in *Its* eyes erased. But the hunger ... well, the hunger is insatiable. It is because of *Its* hunger that I no longer have to worry for my life. It may be difficult to see the carnage *It* leaves behind; the trails of blood crisscrossing through the snow. The pieces of raw meat and the smell as it rots. But it's a small price to pay to eat freely. I am protected now that *It* is here. For that, I am thankful.

CARNIVAL GAMES

By Loki DeWitt

The summer moon hung high in the sky, casting a warm glow over the field of cut grass. Jason led Charlie across it, gripping his little brother's hand tightly as they hurried toward the bright, multi-colored lights that highlighted the spectacle of the carnival. Charlie was running because he was excited to get through the gates and to all the fun things he knew were waiting inside. Jason was rushing because he knew that the quicker they got inside, the faster they would be done. His parents had decided that he needed to start showing more responsibility, and told him that the perfect place to start would be by taking his clown-obsessed little brother to the carnival while they had a date night.

Charlie's little legs carried him past Jason, which led to him tugging on his brother's arm.

"Come on Jason. Let's gooooooo!" As the brothers came closer, they were both slightly overwhelmed by the sights and sounds. Jason felt a small pull of childlike nostalgia wash over him; a small smile crept up in the corners of his mouth as they got closer to the ticket booth. Charlie cheered in excitement and somehow made his short legs pound even faster against the ground, dragging his brother closer to the fun.

Once their tickets had been taken, the carnival spread out in front of them in all its rainbow-colored glory. The scent of popcorn, funnel cakes, and cotton candy beckoned to them. The persistent tugging had stopped, and Jason looked down to see that Charlie had come to a full stop. His younger brother stood there, his mouth open, and his eyes wide with wonder as he took in everything around him. Jason leaned down and got right next to his brother. "You okay, bud?"

Charlie, his eyes wide in delight, didn't even look at him. "I wanna stay here forever."

Jason laughed and grabbed his hand as he stood back up. "How about we start with some cotton candy?"

Jason glanced down at his watch. Two hours had passed since the brothers had entered the carnival, and in that time, he could have sworn that they had ridden every ride there at least twice and had spent a small fortune sampling all the food options. While it had been more fun than he had thought it was going to be at first, that feeling had long since faded. He didn't want to ride any more rides, and he really didn't want to eat any more carnival food. In fact, all Jason could think about was how much he would rather be with his girlfriend, Allison. But as much as Jason wanted to leave, Charlie wanted to do more. It was a wonder that he had even let him sit down long enough to catch his breath. He had just enough time to do so, before Charlie grabbed his hand and drug him off toward another ride.

The carriage swayed and groaned as the Ferris wheel rotated and carried them toward the top. The noise and lights grew distant as they rose higher. Jason was intensely bored and wished that this was their last ride for the night, even though he knew his brother wouldn't allow it. He absent-mindedly let his eyes follow some people around as they moved around the carnival down below. As he traced their path, he felt a soft pat on his hand. He looked up and found Charlie looking back at him with the same enthusiasm that he had the entire time they had been there.

"Jason, look, a clown!"

"Are you sure?"

Charlie nodded enthusiastically and pointed out of the carriage toward the ground. Jason scooted toward his younger brother and looked outside. What stood there wasn't the clown Charlie had claimed it was; it was more of a jester, clad completely in black and white, from the bottoms of its curled shoes to the dangling bells of its hat. Its appearance wasn't the unsettling thing about it, though. It was the fact that it stood there, looking up at the Ferris wheel, waving at them. A small jolt of fear shot through Jason, making him move back, away from the bars. Charlie didn't back up though, he waved back.

"Hi, mister clown!"

Jason slid back over toward his brother and put a finger to his lips. "Shh!"

Charlie looked at his brother with sadness in his eyes, but did as his brother instructed. Jason looked back out between the bars, but the jester was gone. His eyes darted back and forth, trying to see if he could find where it had gone, but he saw nothing. Jason closed his eyes and shook his head. Maybe it was some combination of strain from the lights, all the carnival food, and his brother's overactive imagination that had him all riled up, but he knew jesters couldn't just vanish like that. To set his mind at ease, he looked back out one more time. He didn't see any jesters, but what he saw brought a smile to his face. Down below, making her way through the games, was Allison.

He turned and looked at Charlie, who was quietly sulking. He reached out and put a hand on his shoulder and offered a half-cocked smile. "Say, bud, you want to stay a little while longer?"

Charlie's frown quickly melted away, and he answered with a happy cheer. Jason looked back out the window at Allison. It looked like he was going to salvage his night, after all.

As they stepped off the Ferris wheel, Jason grabbed Charlie's hand and began making their way through the crowd, looking for Allison. Charlie caught sight of the jester that had been waving at him from the Ferris wheel. Seeing it made him smile, and he started to tell his brother, but decided against it because he didn't want to upset him. So, instead, he gave a small wave. The jester returned the wave before their path moved them out of sight of it.

The brothers continued onward until Jason finally saw her; she stood alone in front of the gallery of games. She wasn't playing any of the games herself, but watching others play. Jason smiled broadly as he got closer to her.

"Hey, Allison."

Allison turned and smiled at him. Jason did his best to look cool and confident as he stood there.

"Hey, Jason. What are you up to?"

Jason ran his fingers through his hair and smiled. He looked down at Charlie, who was watching the games.

"Oh, just hanging out with my little brother." He rolled his eyes a little as he looked back up at her.

She laughed and shook her head. Jason smiled. She knelt down in front of Charlie, who looked at her and smiled. She smiled back, and glanced up at Jason.

"Do you want to see your brother win me a prize?" Charlie thought about it for a moment and then nodded.

"Can he win me one too?"

She laughed again and nodded. As she stood up, she looked at Jason, who hadn't taken his eyes off of her.

"He sure can." She grabbed Jason's hand and walked him over to a target shooting game. Without a word, she lifted the rifle and held it out to Jason. "If he wants to score big, all he has to do is take his shot."

Jason took the rifle and gulped. He handed the game runner some money, put the rifle to his shoulder and took aim. While he loved playing games, and he really loved having Allison's attention, everyone knew that the games at carnivals were rigged. He looked back at Allison, who smiled. With a smirk on his face, he focused back in on the targets. He had skill and luck on his side, and that meant that nothing was going to stop him from getting Allison the stuffed animal of her choice. Jason fired pellets at the target, while both Charlie and Allison watched. After a few shots, Charlie's attention was snagged by a voice he barely heard.

"Charlie."

The voice was barely a whisper. He turned his head toward the sound and saw who had called to him. The jester stood there in full view, its black and white costume immaculate, its face covered by an expressionless mask in the same colors, the bells on its hat shining in the carnival lights. Charlie smiled as he saw it standing there and gave a little wave. The jester waved back, and then silently beckoned with a finger for Charlie to come to him. Charlie looked up at Jason, who was busy flirting with Allison. He looked back at the jester and frowned. He wanted to go to the jester, but also didn't want to make his brother mad. Charlie knew Jason had a crush on Allison, and as icky as he thought it was, he just wanted his brother to be happy. Slowly and quietly, Charlie slipped away from his brother, and made his way toward the jester.

Jason only had one shot left, so he knew he had to make it count. He took a deep breath and narrowed his eyes as he tightened his finger around the trigger. The shot found its mark and the glass plate shattered as the pellet hit it. Allison cheered loudly, and Jason looked at where the plate had been with wide, surprised eyes. Allison stepped forward and threw her arms around him. He dropped the rifle and smiled as he put his arms around her. With a confident smile, he looked at her and pointed toward the selection of large stuffed animals that hung above the game area.

"Which one do you want?"

Allison pointed toward a grey and white wolf. As the game runner handed Allison the massive stuffed animal, she hugged it tightly and made a cute squealing sound. She looked at Jason and she leaned in to plant a kiss on his cheek. Filled with confidence, he knew he could impress her by duplicating the feat and make his brother happy at the same time.

"Do you know which one you want, buddy?"

Jason glanced back, with a smile on his face, to get Charlie's answer. His smile quickly faded when he saw that Charlie wasn't there. Panic surged through Jason as he frantically looked around the area to see where his brother had gone. When he didn't see him after a few minutes, he turned to Allison.

"Go find security. Let them know Charlie is missing." He didn't wait for her to respond, and took off looking for his brother.

"Charlie!" Jason yelled his brother's name as he ran. He knew that as much room as he could cover with his feet, he could cover much more with his voice. As he continued his frantic search, his mind raced. *Why would Charlie leave?* It wasn't like him to run away like that. He had always looked up to him, and even though they didn't spend as much time together as they used to, he knew Charlie trusted him completely.

"Charlie!" He yelled his name again as he continued to navigate through the crowds of people. Mostly, people were moving out of his way, which made things slightly easier, but no matter how many people moved out of his way, he still couldn't seem to spot his brother. As he made his way past all the rides that they had ridden, his eyes stung with tears. All Charlie had wanted to do was enjoy the carnival with his big brother, and somehow, Jason had made something so innocent into an imaginary inconvenience for himself. His path continued to take him past the rides, until he finally reached the last one they had been on together: the Ferris Wheel. As he passed the massive steel structure, he remembered something. While they were up in the air, Charlie had spotted a clown.

That had to be where Charlie went.

Jason turned the corner and ran toward the food area. Now he wasn't just looking for his brother, he was looking for that jester that had been waving at them like a creep. He spotted something out of the corner of his eye—something black and white. He spun and ran toward it, but by the time he reached where he had seen it, it had disappeared. In the distance, he spotted something black and white again. Once more, he ran toward it as fast as he could. Again, it vanished from sight before he could even get close. His frustration grew as he continued to run. Then, down by the cotton candy stand, he spotted him. The jester stood there, out in the open, waving at him just like he had when they were in the Ferris wheel. Jason ran toward him, yelling.

"Grab him! He took my brother!" He shouted out the command to anyone who would listen. Several people turned to see where he was pointing, but most of them only returned a confused look, like they couldn't see what he was looking at. The gap between himself and the jester soon closed, and he dove at him to keep him from getting away. Instead of colliding with a person though, Jason slammed face first into the hard red dirt. He sat up quickly and looked around. There was no way that the jester had gotten away from him that quickly. He looked around frantically as he wiped the dirt off his face. He had to still be around here somewhere. Suddenly, he spotted him at the farthest part of the carnival grounds, where the funhouse sat all alone. This time though, the jester wasn't alone: he was holding hands with Charlie and leading him into the funhouse.

"Charlie!"

Jason knew he was close enough that Charlie had to have heard his name yelled, but his brother didn't even look back. Jason could not let that jester do anything to Charlie. Going into the funhouse would give them less room to run, and when Jason caught them, there was going to be Hell to pay.

Jason rushed into the funhouse and was immediately disoriented. The outside world had been brightly lit and multi-colored; the entrance to the funhouse was lit only by a dim red light. It took him a moment to gain his bearings, but once he did, he made his way through the red room and deeper into the building.

"Charlie!" He yelled his name again, knowing full well that his voice would carry through the entire funhouse.

"Jason?"

He froze dead; Charlie had answered him. Now all he had to do was find out where he was.

"Where ya at, buddy?" He moved forward as he spoke, listening closely for the answer. The silence he got in response filled his stomach with dread. He pressed on. The next room was filled with smoke and strobing lights, and again, it took Jason a moment to gain his bearings. When he did, he saw a small figure rush through the smoke at the far end of the room. As they ran, they let out a little giggle that sounded just like the way Charlie laughed. Jason ran toward the shape, but when he got there all that he found was empty space and smoke. The feeling of dread in his stomach grew stronger; he could practically feel it building up in his throat. As he stumbled through the rest of the smoke, he put his foot down in the next room. The floor moved as he stepped forward, causing Jason to go tumbling down. As he crawled back up to his hands and knees, he realized that the entire room was spinning. He looked ahead and saw that he was in a long cylinder. He remained on his hands and knees and crawled forward through the rotating cylinder, toward the blackness that awaited him at the end.

"Charlie!"

His voice carried down the cylinder with an eerie echo, and so did the laughter that rang back in response.

"Jason. We're waiting for you."

The voice wasn't one Jason recognized, but it was clear that they knew who *he* was. He tried to look forward to see if he could spot the speaker, but the strobe lights from the room behind him were still throwing him off.

"Who are you? Where's Charlie?"

Instead of an answer, Jason heard only maniacal cackling. The pitch of the laughter rose, higher, and higher until it was meshed in with the grinding noise of the cylinder turning. He continued to crawl forward, trying his best to ignore the whining in his ears.

"That's it, Jason. Just a little further. Then we can really start having some fun."

The anger he felt helped him push forward through the tunnel. He didn't know who was responsible for this, but once he got to them, he was going to make sure they paid for everything that they had done. At the end of the tunnel was a small flat platform, before a curtain decorated with a painting of a jester. He pushed the curtain aside violently. Stepping past it led him to a room in sheer darkness. Jason allowed himself a second for his eyes to adjust to the change.

"Almost there now."

Despite the absence of light in the room, suddenly all Jason could see was red. Without thinking, he jumped to his feet and charged forward.

His momentum carried him through the blackout curtain on the other side of the darkness and into the next room.

The room he stepped into was brightly lit, and the sudden switch from darkness to light played havoc on him. As his eyes fought to adjust to the sudden change, he glanced around and realized he'd stumbled into a hall of mirrors. And he wasn't alone. At the end of the reflective passage stood the jester.

"Where's Charlie?" He screamed the words as he charged toward the jester. The jester did not flinch, they did not move. When Jason reached the end of the hall, instead of finding the jester, he slammed hard into a plexiglass pane. He bounced off and hit the ground hard. The jester began to laugh. Eventually, the cackling form of the jester was all that Jason could see. The laughter echoed in his ears; he couldn't help but cover his ears to try and shut it out.

"Shut up! Shut up! Shut up!"

Suddenly, the laughter stopped. The silence was nearly as bad as the laughter. His eyes darted back and forth until he spotted them, the jester at the opposite end of the hall.

"So, Jason, Charlie tells me that you like games. Well, that works nicely, because I do too. This is what we are going to do, Jason, we're going to play a game."

Jason held up his hand and shook his head. "I'm not playing any games with you. Now, where's Charlie?"

The jester shook his head, making the bells on his hat tinkle lightly. "If you don't play, you will never see Charlie again."

Fear rose up in the pit of Jason's stomach. "What's the game?"

The jester chuckled sinisterly. "Oh, just a little game of hide and seek."

As angry as Jason was, he couldn't help but scoff and roll his eyes. "Hide and seek?"

The jester nodded. "Oh yes, Jason. It's one of my favorite games. Charlie's too."

Hearing the jester speak his brother's made his hands to clench into fists. The jester held up his hand, causing the lights in and around the hall to flicker. As much as Jason wanted to manhandle the masked villain, he knew that if he was going to have any chance of getting his brother back, he was going to have to play by his rules. He forced his fists to unclench, as he kept his eye on his opponent.

"Very good Jason. Now, seeing as this is a carnival game, there should be prizes on the line. If you win, you and Charlie get to leave here, like none of this ever happened."

Jason smirked. This was almost too good to be true. He shifted his stance and cocked his head to the side. "And if *you* win?"

The jester giggled and shook with glee, making the little bells on his hat tinkle.

"Oh Jason, that's easy. I have been here a very, very long time. This carnival has been my home since long before you were born. At first, it wasn't so bad, all the music, the laughter, the sights, the sounds. Eventually, though, it got old, it got tedious, and most of all, it got lonely. You see Jason, the carnival is no fun if you don't have someone to truly enjoy it with you. So, when I win, I get to fix that. I won't be alone anymore. Charlie will stay here with me, and together we will spread the carnival across the world!"

Jason could feel his confidence slip as the masked maniac made their decree. He knew that if he refused to play, that would be akin to forfeiture, and he would never see his brother again. With his back against the wall, Jason shook his head. "Alright. Let's play."

The jester laughed again, and as he did, the lights in the hall flickered. Jason swallowed hard. He knew that he could win, but he also knew that he was in for the hardest game he ever played. The jester began to flicker across all the mirrors, and Jason tried to keep an eye on him; that was when the laughter stopped and the lights went out.

The lights came back on and Jason immediately knew something had changed. What surrounded him now was a virtual labyrinth of reflection. The halls extended outward and didn't seem to end. Lights danced along the endless panes, making dazzling displays. Jason knew that the game wasn't going to be simple, and he also knew he had to win. He began to run down the twisting corridors, attempting to find the jester and end the game as quickly as he could. As he began to make his way through the maze, he heard something that caught him off guard: Charlie's laughter. His head snapped toward the sound of it. Charlie stood on the opposite end of the corridor. Jason turned heel and headed back toward his brother. He breathed a sigh of relief as he picked up the pace.

"Hang on, buddy. I'm coming."

His feet moved along the mirrored floor as he pushed forward, hoping to once again hold his brother tight and keep him safe from the jester who'd tried to take him. As he reached out for him, Jason instead slammed hard into the reflective wall, seeing only himself reflected back. He felt a mixture of fear and frustration rising up inside him, manifesting into tears as he heard Charlie laugh again. The tears stung his eyes and blurred his vision, and he continued to push forward through the mirrored halls. "Charlie! Where are you?"

His voice echoed against the glass walls. This time though, he didn't get laughter in response. "I'm right here."

Jason looked toward the voice; he didn't see Charlie. Instead, he saw the leering masked face of the jester. With triumph in his voice, he yelled out to the jester, "I found you! I win!"

He rushed toward the jester, knowing that in some games of hide and seek, you had to tag the person to get them officially. As he rushed toward the theatrically garbed figure, it vanished before his eyes, replaced with only the stunned reflection of himself. He spun around to see if he could catch a glimpse of Charlie or the jester, but all he could find was his own angered face looking back at him. "That's cheating!"

"Is it?"

The voice came from nowhere, but sounded close enough to be right in Jason's ear.

"Then you're going to hate this."

Jason spun around again, hoping that perhaps the jester would slip up and give him something to work with. Unfortunately, this time, when eh saw him, above the jester's head was lifted a large mallet, like one would find at a strength testing game. Before Jason could even respond, the jester brought the mallet crashing down into his head, causing the brightly lit halls to be replaced by darkness.

Jason sat up and rubbed his throbbing head. His mind flashed back to the last thing he remembered, and the memory only made his head throb harder. The jester had cheated; the game wasn't over yet. As long as he could still move, he could still find the jester and end this nightmare once and for all. Slowly, he tried to crawl back to his feet. He instinctively reached out, like there was something in front of him to grab ahold of. Jason's fingers collided with some sort of invisible barrier. Confused, he moved slowly in a circle and found that the invisible barrier completely surrounded him. Before he could say anything, he heard the sound of laughter behind him.

"Tag! You lose!"

Jason turned to see the jester, setting the heavy end of the hammer down onto the mirrored floor with a thud. The thud reverberated in his head, making him reach up and instinctively, touching the place where he had been struck. Earlier he had been yelling, but now when he spoke it came out as a pained groan. "You cheated."

The jester shook their head. "Now now, don't be a sore loser."

Jason shot the jester a glare, but his eyes caught sight of something much more interesting: Charlie. His younger brother stepped forward and took the jester by the hand, looked up at them, and smiled. Jason's stomach turned as the jester looked back down at Charlie.

"Leave him alone." In Jason's head, the sentence sounded defiant, but in reality, it was more of a sad croak.

The jester looked up from Charlie, and back toward Jason. "Oh Jason my boy, I don't see why you're so upset. I mean, if you think about it, you didn't even *want* to be here tonight. You would have rather been with your friends, or chasing Allison than having some good clean fun with your brother." A gloved hand rubbed Charlie's head, making the younger boy smile. "You see, that's your problem, Jason, you think you are so grown up. 'Old-fashioned fun' is something you try to tell yourself that you have gotten too old for. Charlie here remembers how to have a good time though, don't you Charlie?"

Charlie looked up at the jester and nodded enthusiastically. "Sure do!"

The jester knelt down in front of Jason, who was slowly regaining his bearings. "You tried to forget the spirit of the carnival, the spirit of *real* fun. Lucky for you, you are going to have a long, *long* time to remember how to have fun, Jason."

Jason looked right at the masked figure. "What does that mean?" The jester stood up and chuckled.

"Oh, you'll know soon enough."

"Hey Jason, can we go play some more games?" Charlie's request cut through the intensity between Jason and the jester.

Jason went to answer his brother, but someone else answered instead. In front of him was still Charlie, but the other person with him was no longer the jester. Instead, in the hall of mirrors he saw himself.

Panic shot through him as he looked down at his body. It was covered in black and white clothing.

"No. No, No!" He shook his head in denial, making small bells tinkle. He looked back at Charlie and he saw himself look down at his brother.

"I tell you what, Charlie. Instead of a game, how about we go on a few more rides?"

Charlie nodded enthusiastically. Jason watched as Charlie took the hand of the imposter. The two began to head toward the exit. The real Jason tried to chase after them but found himself stopped by an invisible barrier. It was then that Jason realized what he had truly lost. The jester was now free to spread the spirit of the carnival all over the world, just like he said. Not only had Jason lost, but he was going to be stuck in this kaleidoscope prison, all alone, forever. He wanted to cry, but no tears came.

As Charlie and the imposter stepped out of sight, the imposter shot one last look back at the one who had taken their place. With a big grin on his face, he winked.

"Besides, everyone knows that carnival games are rigged."

SURVIVING THE CHANGE

By Amanda Woomer

No one knows where it came from, how it started, or who was to blame. The older generation said it had to be the Russians ("Damn Commies," they muttered). The younger generation that was so focused on human rights, always holding their protests, blamed it on nuclear testing … the radiation had to have leaked out, like Chernobyl all over again, but so much worse this time. Maybe it was a sunburst or a disease that passed from rabid animals. People had their wild theories—it was the government or aliens, it was the end of days that the Mayans predicted thousands of years ago, it was the first stage of the rapture … or perhaps it was just Mother Nature sick and tired of the human race messing with her, and she finally decided to fight back. Whatever it was, where kids used to go to school and teenagers used to go shopping, where people would sit in church or watch a football game, where the humans once lived life, the Biters now roamed like an infestation that could not be exterminated.

Tess couldn't shake that thought from her mind—an infestation of vermin—as she waited for Brett to return with the blankets they needed to bring back to the camp. They had already run into six or seven Biters, but they were all too busy eating to notice the two teenagers on their bikes, and even if they did, they were far too slow to catch them. But something about standing in the darkness of the abandoned city street—a place that had once been brimming with life—set Tess on edge. She kept her back against the truck, standing by the wheel to feel protected while Brett rummaged through the truck bed, looking for the blankets the other camp had sent. Winter was coming, and their camp had no way to heat the tenants' rooms, so these blankets were their only ticket to surviving until the spring.

And not everyone would make it, she had to remind herself. So many of her friends had died last winter … How many more would she lose?

A bump shook the vehicle, knocking Tess back to the present—how could she have been so careless as to let her mind wander while out in the open? She could have been killed.

Or worse, she reminded herself of why she was alone in the middle of an abandoned city—practically an abandoned world—risking her life for a couple of blankets. She pushed herself away from the cold metal of the truck.

"Brett, what is it?" she called out, looking around for her best friend. "What the—"

She leaped back in a panic as she bumped into someone, or rather—she realized too late—something. She should have smelled the rot and decay before she even walked to the back of the truck; she hated herself at that moment for being so stupid.

"Jesus Christ!" she screamed as the milky-eyed ghoul grabbed hold of the nearest thing—her arm. Tess tried to reach for her gun tucked into her jeans as the Biter continued to squeeze her arm. She had heard stories of just how strong these things were, but as it tried to break her arm, she found herself less impressed and more terrified.

For an instant, it felt as though time slowed down. Tess always heard stories from Biter attack survivors—the moment one of them opens their mouth and bites down on human flesh, it feels as if the world has stopped to show you the exact moment that your life was ruined. But she never really put much thought into those stories … until now.

She watched in horror as the Biter's yellow, rotten teeth broke through the skin of her left arm. Layer after layer of skin was torn apart until its teeth hit the bone.

A gunshot filled the deafening silence as the Biter's head exploded, some of its blood raining down on Tess's cheek. She looked up at Brett, who stood in the truck, his pistol still held in his hands as he looked back and forth between the ghoul and the girl.

"Brett," she whispered in a panic as the pain suddenly swept through her, causing her legs to tremble and fall out from beneath her.

It was in that instant—from when the gunshot sounded to when she was sitting on the freezing cold ground—that time sped up to catch up with her.

The pain in her arm was unimaginable. Tess hit her head against the truck to try to make herself forget about the pain. She tried to silence her screams. She didn't want any more of those things to find them. One was more than enough and more than she could handle it would seem.

"Where the hell did it come from?" Brett ripped his scarf from his neck and wrapped it tightly around her arm. The blood was already soaking through. "We did a complete perimeter search. Can you feel your arm?" Brett placed his hands on her cheeks and looked into her eyes as if searching for something. But searching for what? An answer? The truth? Any signs of the Change?

"It tingles a bit, but I'm fine." Tess pushed him away, trying to blink away the dark spots from her vision. "We've got to get the blankets back to camp."

"Always the soldier." He patted her on the back, but Tess couldn't help but notice how he kept his distance. One of those things had just bit her—they both knew what that meant.

"We should try to get back as fast as possible," Brett said as they both climbed back onto their bikes.

And try to beat the infection, Tess finished his thought for him.

"We should get back before the ghouls and feds find us."

Tess shivered. If there was anything in this god-forsaken world more terrifying than hordes of Biters, it was the feds—the soldiers sent in to fight the infected. And right now, that included her.

"You can ride, right?"

"Yeah, of course," she sighed, kicking off and speeding down the road.

The world had significantly changed in the two years since the Biters appeared, and that changed world was eerie the moment the sun went down. The big city was silent, the avenues empty. The solar-powered street lights were the only illumination left in the city, guiding them along.

The silence frightened her most. Having always lived in the city, Tess didn't really know what to do with herself in the silence. Her thoughts still got the best of her, and right now, those thoughts revolved around the doomed sequence of events just after a bite. She glanced down at her left arm as she continued to pedal. Blood had already soaked through the bandage in the perfect outline of teeth marks.

How long does it take? An hour? She tried not to panic.

Her brother had been bitten about six months ago and had changed relatively quickly. Less than twelve hours later, he was gone entirely. Her older sister had killed herself from the grief. Just Tess and her uncle remained of their once happy family.

A blinding light pulled Tess out of her morbid thoughts from the past. She pulled back on her brake and swerved to the side, grazing the big white van that had appeared out of nowhere. Thrown off balance, she toppled onto the cement just as two feds jumped out of the car, armed from head to toe.

"Tess!"

She could hear the panic in Brett's voice. If the feds saw her bite mark, she would disappear into their van for good.

"I am so sorry!" the driver, who was the younger of the two men, called out. "I didn't even see you!"

"He's new—first night out," the older one explained, pushing his dark hair out of his face. He was at least a full head taller than Tess, an intimidating figure even without the gun strapped to his side. After a moment, his eyes went from the young man still panicking beside him to the girl sprawled out on the ground before him. The look on his face changed as he turned to ask her. "Are you hurt?"

He knelt down and helped to pull Tess back up to her feet. *Yeah,* Tess thought to herself. *At least twice my size.*

"I'm fine." She tried to shake the man off her arm, suddenly frightened—not by his domineering appearance, but rather the simple fact that he was her enemy ... and right now, she was outnumbered and out-armed.

"We're just trying to get back to our family." Brett was suddenly by her side to help explain.

"It's dangerous to be out past curfew," the older fed said before he glanced down at the blankets strapped to the back of Brett's bike. His heavy brow furrowed, a line appearing between his eyebrows. Tess and Brett held their breaths before the man smiled and innocently commented, "Pretty big family if you ask me."

Tess desperately wanted to step forward and point out to this man—whomever he was—that survivor camps should not be illegal these days. *If you ask me,* she added sarcastically to herself.

Brett smiled as Tess climbed back up onto her bike. He tried desperately to keep up the façade. "Tell me about it."

The two men stared at each other for a moment, tense, before the fed looked down at his hand, sticky with blood.

His eyes narrowed. "I thought you said that you weren't hurt." His gaze came to rest on Tess's arm with the loosened bandage and the infected bite peeking out.

Brett and Tess exchanged a glance.

As the fed moved to grab Tess, Brett threw out a punch and managed to hit the older man squarely in the jaw. "Tess, go!" he screamed at her.

She used all her strength and energy to pedal her bike down the street, suddenly wishing the lights would go out and help hide her in the darkness.

The van revved to life somewhere behind her, and a gunshot nearly gave her a heart attack. Whether the bullet was meant for Brett or for her, she wasn't sure, but Brett had not caught up with her, so that was enough to answer her question.

"Holy crap!" she screamed before chancing a glance behind her.

Another gunshot, and Tess knew this was no joke. She had to do something and fast or risk being another of the feds' nameless victims. She quickly turned down a small street, unsure where it led, but at least it was dark. The screeching tires and the glow of the headlights were gone just long enough for her to ditch her bike and start climbing up the fire escape of one of the old buildings.

She smiled from her perch as the two feds ran into the alleyway. Her smile faded when she spotted their guns. She froze and remained completely still, watching the two men, praying to whatever god might listen to an Infected that she would remain unseen. Her hopes were dashed when the young driver looked up and spotted her.

"Coop!" he called out as he shined his flashlight on her.

Without a word, Coop aimed his gun and fired, the bullet hitting the wall just above her head.

Panic.

"Oh my God! Oh my God!" she muttered to herself as she climbed the rest of the ladder and threw herself over the ledge, hiding on the roof.

"Stop running, kid!" She could hear Coop call out to her, his voice echoing in the alleyway. If he kept this up, there was sure to be a hoard of Biters arriving any time soon.

She scoffed at his request.

Pulling her handgun out from her waistband, she leaned over and sent down two shots blindly. One of them must have hit its mark because someone cried out in pain.

"Take that, assholes!" she screamed as she ran across the rooftops toward the only place she knew she would be safe in this world.

"And you're sure they didn't follow you?"

"Pretty sure," Tess winced as the doctor cleaned her wound.

"We have more pressing problems, Norman," the doctor interrupted. "She's been bitten. We need to put her in isolation for the next twenty-four hours."

"What about Brett?" Tess demanded. "He's still out there with those monsters!"

"And the Biters," her uncle tried to joke.

Why can he never take things seriously?

One of the three leaders of the camp, Joyce, placed her hand on Tess's shoulder. "We've sent some scouts out to look for him. If he's out there, they'll find him."

Tess didn't want to think about why he wouldn't be found. Anything could have gotten to him—dogs, Biters, the feds… if he was even still alive.

"The boy is most likely dead… or worse." The doctor finished wrapping her arm in clean white bandages.

"Oh, thanks. That's reassuring, Doc," she sighed, jumping down from the table.

Her Uncle Norman led her down the hall, suddenly all business. "We're not too sure about the incubation time—for some, it's minutes, and for others, it can be more than a day. Richard," they both stopped at the mention of her brother's name, "his Change was average: ten hours and thirty-six minutes."

"So you think I still have a few hours left?"

"In theory."

Neither of them wanted to mention the elephant in the room—by this time tomorrow, she would probably have a bullet in her head.

They walked down the isolation chamber's hallway to the clean, empty room. It was similar to a hospital room—cream walls, a bed, and even a toilet. There wasn't a need for much else. No one stayed for long. The events of the night finally began to catch up with her.

I am dying. This is my last night on Earth. My family is dead, my best friend is dead, and soon I'll be dead ... I'm going to die here, alone.

She turned to face her uncle. For the last two years, she had been a soldier, and he had been her commander. After her sister died, they were all each other had left in this world. Tears filled her eyes, and panic filled her chest as she threw her hands around him.

"I love you, Uncle Norm."

"I love you too, baby girl."

Tess tried to ignore the fact that this was likely the last time she would ever touch another living being without the irresistible urge to bite.

"Be strong." He placed a kiss on her forehead before locking the door behind him, leaving her once again alone with her terrified thoughts.

The doctor shook his head as he took back the thermometer from Tess. "I'm just dumbfounded. Three days is the longest anyone has ever gone without Changing."

"Could it be that she's immune?" Norman asked, still sitting next to Tess. She appreciated his courage.

The doctor sighed. "I don't think so. You told me you had stomach cramps, and you do have a fever, however slight it may be. Those are the early stages—the very early stages. Usually, they take minutes... But for you, Tess, it has taken nearly three days."

"So I'm still Changing."

Doc nodded his head. "Just very slowly." He watched Tess closely before venturing on, "This could be a good thing, though."

Tess furrowed her brow. "How?"

"It's just a theory, but I believe that we might be able to find a cure for whatever this thing is. If nothing else, we could study it."

"You mean study my Change?"

He nodded his head. "We might begin to understand it and then find a way to fight it," he added with an excited gleam in his eye. "We could put an end to all this."

For a moment, Tess allowed herself to hope that something good might actually come out of this nightmare. Norm wrapped his arms around her just as the message chime sounded over the PA.

"Attention: illegal campers—"

"What the hell?" Norm leaped up to his feet.

Tess froze in fear. He hadn't said much to her, but she could still recognize his voice. It was that fed—Coop—the man who was also probably Brett's murderer.

"I must say your little hideout was quite tricky to find, but it's time to go. We have surrounded you, and I am holding the register of every man, woman, and child in your little establishment. You have fifteen minutes to pack the things you want to bring with you to the reservation before we incinerate this place. Your time starts," he paused for dramatic effect while everyone in the building held their breath, "now."

"I thought you said they didn't follow you!" Norm turned to his niece.

"They didn't!" she defended herself. It had been three days ago. "I shot one of them, for God's sake!"

"It's too late for that now," Doc tried to calm both of them down.

"Well, what should I do?" Tess asked the two men nervously. She looked down at her bandaged arm. The right thing to do—the honorable thing to do—would be to let them burn her alive. But her very human mind still feared death. "Should I stay, or should I go?"

"They'll find you and put a bullet through your head if you stay." Norm shook his head.

"But we cannot risk infecting others." Doc shook his head in response.

"Everyone out! Now!" An armed fed appeared in the door, a gun pointed their way. The group raised their hands innocently as if they had nothing to hide. "Up to your bunks and get your belongings now!"

Terrified and thoroughly confused about what she should do, Tess lowered her eyes, pulled her hood over her head, and followed the two men out of the isolation chamber.

"What should I—" Tess tried to ask Doc.

She knew her leaving that room was a death sentence for everyone else in the building—her friends and what was left of her family—but as the fed followed behind her, continuing to shout orders, she found herself running from the safety of the isolation room, without even a second thought. The members of the camp were running through the halls, bumping into one another and trying desperately to avoid the feds.

Caught up in the moving sea of humanity, Tess realized that her uncle and Doc were nowhere it be seen, and she was being ushered away from her room. The camp Tess had called her home for the last two years was an old apartment building, four people in a room with a mess hall in the basement and the isolation chambers on the upper floors.

She slipped into the line of illegal campers and slowly began to make her way down the winding flight of stairs. Tess dug her fingernails into the palms of her hands, trying to ignore the guilt and terror pulsing through her veins as she watched the faces of the people around her. She was surrounded by terrified campers, arms filled with the few belongings they owned and determined feds, their guns raised and ready to fire on them if the moment arrived.

Very rarely did Tess look to her uncle for permission (you needed to be able to survive on your own in this world), but now she was like a lost little girl looking for help with every step she took. Something caught her eye as she stopped in her mindless march.

"Hey! Watch it!" Someone bumped into her.

Eyes wide, she looked down to the next landing and spotted the fed from the night of her bite—Coop.

Knowing her stillness would draw his attention, she quickly started to follow the line of people once more and pulled her hood down over her face, hoping to shield herself from his eyes.

The closer she got, the harder it was for Tess to breathe.

She closed her eyes as she brushed past him and dared to release a sigh of relief, but a hand firmly grabbing her arm made her scream out in pain instead. Everyone turned to look at the cause of such a cry. Tess spun around to find the fed holding on tight to her, his fingers digging into the bite wound.

"There you are."

His smile, slightly hidden by the scruff of his beard, sent a shiver down Tess's spine as she tried to pull away. His fingers just wrapped even tighter as he pulled her past the hoard of campers.

"No! Please!" Tess screamed, looking to her comrades—her friends—for help. "Please!"

"Out of the way!" Coop's voice boomed through the stairwell as everyone stood back and watched Tess struggle under his grip. "Move!" He continued to drag Tess behind him.

The crowd did little to help him pass.

Maybe it's their pathetic way of trying to help me.

Looking exhausted, Coop sighed before pulling one of his many guns out and sending a warning shot into the air. The staircase filled with screams, and everyone fell to the ground, their hands covering their heads.

"Everybody, *please* get the hell out of my way!" he ordered, pulling Tess along behind him.

Tess looked down at the people huddled along the banister, their wide eyes watching in horror as she was dragged behind the fed, and, with one final scream, she disappeared into their van.

THE BENSON
A NOVELLA
2.5 IN
THE EXPERIMENT IN TERROR SERIES
by
Karina Halle

I have never been inside The Benson hotel before. Looking back, it's kind of weird since I've lived in Portland for my whole life, but I guess there are a lot of things in your city you never see. Not the way the tourists do.

Tonight though, I decided I would be a tourist. Having a camera at my side would certainly help in that pretense. I smile up at the doorman as I make my way up the sidewalk, pausing briefly at the bronze plaque on the ground as I have many times before when walking throughout downtown, and then timidly walk up the steps inside.

"Good evening and welcome to The Benson, ma'am," the doorman says to me, cheery enough in his fancy, gold-gilded uniform. Still, I feel like he's judging me and what I'm wearing: my Doc Martens still muddy from the morning's rainfall, my maroon leggings with a hole in them and a scuffed leather jacket. I'm obviously not a guest here, not at one of the most prestigious hotels in the state of Oregon.

I give him a tight smile and walk past him into the revolving doors which sweep me inside. The lobby is surprisingly busy for nine p.m. as there's a line at the vast checkout counter a few people deep, and the bar/lounge to the right of me is crammed full of swanky patrons swilling martinis. I barely have time to take in the understated grandeur and opulence of the lobby—which totally reminds me of the golden age of Hollywood—before a waving movement brings my attention to the bar again.

In the corner, swilling what can only be a Jack Daniels and Coke is Dex. Actually, he's not swilling it. Rather, downing it in fast gulps and as soon as he sees he's caught my attention, he waves the prim waitress over and orders another one.

I swallow hard, feeling all sorts of strange feelings rush up in my body. I'm nervous, I already was, but I'm excited too and though my breath catches slightly when I see him, it eventually flows out all hot, ragged and sparkling with nerves.

I haven't seen Dex since we parted ways at the airport in Albuquerque. It wasn't long ago, but it still makes me feel like I'm going on a first date all over again. Not that we ever were dating and not that (with his girlfriend Jenn) we ever would. But I can't help the way I feel. Stupid. And in love with my partner.

I smile, broad and completely natural for him, and make my way to where he is sitting, at a small, white clothed table just big enough for two. Before I reach his side, I wonder if he's going to hug me and before I can finish the thought, he stands up, stepping around the table. I am quickly enveloped into his arms. He smells like Old Spice and a bit like the hand-rolled cigarettes he picked up in New Mexico. His arms are strong and firm around my back. The hug is close, tight and genuine. I relax slightly, wishing we were somewhere else and not this busy lounge where people watch us with disinterest.

I am the first to pull apart, though I could have stayed in his arms all night. I give him the once over now that I am up close.

He looks pretty much as he did in New Mexico. The cuts on his face from the shapeshifter's attack are faded. His moustache has been trimmed, almost gone, as is the scruff beard under his chin. His eyebrow ring glints from his black brow. His cheekbones are high, perhaps higher than before. I take another step back and see that he's lost a little bit of weight. It shows in his face most of all.

"Checking me out again?" he says, his voice low, his lips snaking to the side in a smirk. There's something off about him, but I don't know what it is. Maybe it's because, despite the closeness of the hug, there's an awkward distance between us, like we aren't sure how to act around each other now that the skinwalkers and Maximus and sharing a bed for a few nights are gone. We both almost died in New Mexico–I know it had an impact on us, but it doesn't seem to have any bearing here in the swanky Benson hotel.

And then there are his eyes. Dex's eyes are his focal point, the part of him that wins people over or drives them away. Dark chocolate, enigmatic and emotive. Sometimes they are ruthless, sometimes seductive. They are a mystery as much as he is and the one thing I can't help from drowning in over and over again.

But here, tonight, they are clouded. No, that's not quite it. Not clouded but subdued. The sparkle and zest that roam in them, no matter what his mood, are gone. They are handsome, beguiling eyes, but not his.

I think back to Red Fox and how he had gone so long without his anti-psychotic medication that he began to actually feel again. It was scary for him, no doubt (and for me, let's not kid ourselves) but in the end … he was free. Or so I thought. Now it seems that sparkle and life, the manic highs and lows, are gone. As destructive as they were, they are an important part of him.

"Sorry," I mutter to myself, dropping my eyes quickly to the table just as the waitress comes by and puts down his drink.

"What would you like, Perry?" he asks me. I look up at him and the waitress. Her name tag states her as Prudence. She has white hair and a friendly smile but a stance that says I better be quick with an answer.

I don't drink normally, especially not on the job—which is what I am doing here tonight with Dex—but I say, "A glass of the house red, thanks."

It's the cheapest and will relax my nerves. Prudence leaves with my order after Dex gives her a quick wink. He then turns to me as we sit down.

"So how are you, kiddo?" he asks, peering at my face, trying to read me before I say anything. "Is it nice having me in your neck of the woods again?"

"It's just nice to see you again," I say honestly. With Dex living in Seattle and me in Portland, I only ever see him when we film. And in the between time, I miss him.

A blush starts to creep up my neck. I can feel it.

He gives me a smile that reaches his eyes and shows perfect teeth that are quite white for a smoker. "Well, it's nice to see you. Too bad you're not bunking with me tonight at my motel."

I give him a sharp look, not sure if he's kidding or not.

He smiles again, almost leering. "I'll probably be shaking in my boots after tonight with only my pillow to hug."

The waitress comes back and gives me my wine. He gives her the same kind of smirk. This is how I know he's messing with me.

I roll my eyes. "So, what is our plan for tonight anyway? Are we just going to sit here and drink and wait for the ghosts to show up?"

"Patience, Perry," he says and takes another gulp of his drink. He gestures to the wine and nods at it. "Have some of that and relax."

I take a sip of the acidic merlot and look around me. As gorgeous and old-fashioned as the hotel is, there are so many people about, and I can't imagine how on earth the place could be haunted. But apparently it is. In fact, Portland has a few ghost tours that come around and poke their heads in the hotel a few times a week. I doubt anybody ever sees anything, though.

"Are we the first ghost hunting show to come inside here?" I ask Dex.

He coughs on his drink and shakes his head. "Fuck no. We're a bit behind on this one. I think just about every ghost hunter has been in this hotel at some point or another."

"Do they ever find anything?"

He gives me a wry look. "What do you think? Of course not."

"What makes you think we will?"

He smiles again and reaches over with his hand to pat me softly on the head. "Because I've got you, kiddo. You're my little ghost bait."

I think back to Red Fox, to a moment when Dex said I might be offered up as bait to the skinwalkers. The idea bothered me then and it bothers me now. I take a longer sip of the wine this time.

He's watching my face closely, as usual, and he still keeps his hand there. I'm not sure if he's trying to comfort me or what. I shoot him a deadly look from the side of my eyes.

"I'm joking you know," he finally says, his voice less rough, less gravely. "I just mean, well, you know there's something about you, something that attracts these things. You're like a secret weapon."

"Some weapon," I scoff and look down into the glass, my vision becoming a blur of deep reds. "What's the point of just attracting these ... things? These people? If I could use this ... power ... whatever it is, for good ... that would be a different story."

He shrugs and takes his hand away, his attention back to his own drink. The back of my head feels vulnerable without his hand there. "You never know. There's supposed to be a shitload of ghosts in this hotel, maybe you can help one of them."

I raise my brows at him.

"A shitload?" I repeat. "Where do you get your information, Mr. Foray?"

"Wikipedia. That thing is never wrong," he says without irony. He looks around him and takes in the scene. "We're supposed to meet the night manager, Pam, in a couple of minutes. She said she'd find us. She'll give us a tour of the place; hopefully give us the real story. I want that on film."

"And what do you want me to do?" I ask. Once again, we're going into a film shoot more or less blind. And by we, I mean I. Dex always knows what's going on and I'm always in the dark. I did research The Benson before biking over here and all that, but I have no clue what to do or say. There is no storyboard, no script. We just wing it and I usually end up looking like an idiot.

"Just be yourself. Ask her questions. I'll film both of you. We'll wander around the hotel. Then we'll probably be allowed to go off on our own and do some exploring. I'll give you the infrared camera this time so we can see if we pick up any hot or cold spots."

I shiver at that thought. Using the infrared meant we'd be wandering around in the dark. Whether I'm in a lighthouse on the coast or in the New Mexican desert, the darkness still gives me the creeps. Especially now that I know there are things out there that want to hurt me. That know I'm a sort of "bait."

By the time Pam shows up, I have finished my glass of wine. It has only left me anxious, not relaxed. Pam is on the overweight side, similar to the way I was in high school, but unlike me, she seems to bustle with confidence. Or bustle with something. Her wide, cheery face gives her the appearance of being younger than she probably is and she speaks a mile a minute.

"You must be Perry and Dex, I recognized you!" she exclaims, beaming at us and holding out her hand. We both give it a quick shake. She points to the name tag on her black suit. "As you can see, my name is Pam. Pam Gupta. I'm the night manager here at The Benson."

"Thanks for having us," Dex tells her sincerely, reaching under the table and bringing out a backpack and a camera bag.

"No, thank you," she says putting extra emphasis on the words. "As soon as you told me who you were, I looked up your ghost show and immediately fell in love with you guys."

Dex and I exchange a quick look.

"I mean," she corrects herself and lets out an awkward clip of a laugh, "I was scared witless at the Darkhouse episode and the one in Red Fox but I was so drawn in by you two. You're just so … so …"

"Handsome?" Dex asks, flashing her a smile and stroking his chin scruff.

She blushes and giggles. "Well, yeah I guess you are."

I roll my eyes. Dex doesn't need any more encouragement.

"But," she continues, "you're both just so … lucky!"

We look at each other again, even more confused.

"Lucky?" I ask.

"How about I explain as we walk? I don't have much time to show you around before I start my shift."

We get up, Dex giving the backpack of equipment to me, and we follow Pam through the lobby. For a larger woman she walks like a sprite, moving quickly between people and showering her big smile on all of them. The guests eye Dex and I curiously, intrigued by the camera he has placed up on his shoulder.

We stop before a grand staircase leading up to the second floor. I eye myself quickly in the mirror on the landing. My floral dress is sticking to my leggings in static cling, and my black hair is a mess from my motorbike helmet (and Dex's hand). I don't look camera-worthy at all. I shrug helplessly at my reflection and look to Pam who is pointing up at the stairs.

"There's been many sightings of one of ghostly guests walking up and down this very staircase," she says, sounding like a chipper tour guide talking about museum pieces and not dead people.

I look at Dex beside me and see the camera is going, picking up everything Pam is saying. Sensing I'm staring at him, he reaches out and pushes me toward Pam, into the frame. I know he wants me to start acting like the host I am.

I smooth down my hair and clear my throat, stepping into the shot. "Have you seen any ghosts, Pam?"

She shakes her head quickly and looks wistful. "No, I haven't. Come on, let's go to the next floor."

Not exactly the answer I was hoping for. She scurries up the stairs and we follow, my short legs straining to keep up with her quick busybody motion.

We walk toward the elevators and as we are waiting, she says, "I think you two are lucky because I've always wanted to see a ghost. I believe in them. So badly. But I've never seen one. Weird, right, considering that I run The Benson. At night."

The elevator dings and the doors open. There's a couple inside who eye the camera with trepidation, but we step inside with them anyway. Pam makes small talk with them as she pushes the button for the 8th floor and doesn't mention ghosts again until the couple get out at the 5th floor.

She tilts her head at us. "I don't like to discuss the ghosts around the guests though. People can be pretty strange about things like that."

"I don't blame them," I find myself saying.

"I guess you'd know," Pam says as the elevator stops at the floor, and she leads us out into the hallway, past a rotary phone resting on top of an antique table.

She notices me eyeing it and gives it a quick wave with her hand. Her bracelets jingle with the motion.

"We try to keep all the original furnishings from the hotel. Adds to the class and elegance of the place, don't you think?"

I nod, not really needing to be sold on the hotel as a whole.

Pam takes us to the right, and we walk past the rooms down to the very end of the hall. Dex keeps filming, even though he takes his head away from the camera.

"So, if we show The Benson in a good way," Dex says to Pam, "any chance we can score a free hotel room for the night? I'm staying at a roach motel outside of the city, and I'm getting itchy just thinking about it."

Pam turns around briefly and smiles at him but then spins around and keeps walking without missing a beat.

"We'll see. Would you two be sharing the room?"

Dex automatically grins and looks down at me as we walk. I shake my head, not amused.

"No, Perry snores and kicks in her sleep," he says.

I smack him on the shoulder and the camera shakes.

"I do not!" I protest.

"Oh, and drools," he adds quickly.

"So, you two are a couple?" Pam asks, not looking at us this time but slowing down as she nears the end of the hall.

"Only in certain situations," I mutter under my breath.

"No, we are not. Perry is far too good for me and I am forced to make do with my Wine Babe girlfriend."

Finally, Pam stops walking and looks at him. "Wine Babe? You're with someone from that show?"

"You've seen it?" Dex asks, his eyes wide and hopeful.

"Yes," she says slowly, and for once her chipper look is gone. Her cheeks sag a bit. "My ex-boyfriend used to drool all over that skinny, exotic one."

"Yeah, that's his girlfriend. Jennifer Rodriguez," I inform her. She eyes me and sees that I'm none too thrilled about it either. Nothing like a hot woman to make two chubby girls feel like they're having a bonding moment.

"Well, I'm just glad some women watch it," Dex says, turning his attention the camera, perhaps feeling the animosity and low self-esteem just reeking from our pores.

Pam laughs and the cheery façade returns. "Don't be silly. I don't watch that dreadful show. They pair shiraz with Kraft Dinner. Only an idiot would watch that. Like my ex-boyfriend."

Dex opens his mouth to say something, but I know he completely agrees. That's the reason he quit doing camera work on Wine Babes and started up Experiment in Terror with me instead.

"Anyway," she continues, "here we are."

I look at the door we've stopped in front of: Room 818.

"Where are we?" I ask.

"This was Parker's room," she says ominously.

"Who is Parker?" Dex asks. I'm surprised that he doesn't know something for once.

"Parker …" Pam starts and then trails off. She takes her keys out from her pocket; the noise of them rattling fills the hallway. It suddenly seems very empty and hollow and a weird, familiar feeling washes over me, causing the hairs on the back of my neck to stand up.

The lock turns, and the door slowly creaks open. Only blackness and dust come billowing out of the room.

"After you," Pam says.

Dex shrugs and then nudges me in front of the camera, indicating that I am to go first. Of course. I always have to be the first to walk into everything when I'm on camera. And sometimes when I'm not on camera. It depends on how sadistic Dex is feeling.

I take in a deep breath and push the door aside. It slowly swings open with a low groan, and I walk blindly into the swirling dark.

"Should I be putting on the night vision?" Dex asks no one in particular. I hear him fiddle with the camera settings but before anything happens, I am blind. Pam has walked in beside me and switched on the lights.

"No sense in scaring ourselves yet," she chirps, and I can barely make out her round face.

Dex comes in and Pam shuts the door behind him. Once my eyes adjust to the light, I see that we are in a hotel room that probably looks the same as any other hotel room, albeit a large and very pricey one. Aside from a heavy chill that seems to hang in the air, there's nothing too off-putting about the place. The bed is made, there seems to be a separate room with a living area, divided only by a Japanese-type paper partition, and I can just see a rather opulent looking bathroom jutting out to the right.

"As I said, this is Parker's room," she says. "Well, it was his room. I say this because some guests who stay in here say they still see him. But it happens very rarely."

"And once again," Dex repeats, sounding bored, "who is Parker?"

Pam walks over to the king-sized bed and sits down on it. It sags a little from her weight; the mattress is not as springy as it was back in the day.

"We have a lot of ghosts in this hotel. Parker isn't the most well-known of them, but he is the most real. Because he was a real person and his story is terribly tragic. Tragic, but all too common."

I go over to the bed and sit down beside Pam. Suddenly, that slightly see-through partition between the bedroom and the living area is giving me the creeps, like I can sense someone standing behind it.

Dex looks like he picks up on the vibe too. Although he is standing in front of Pam and I, with the camera in our faces, his eyes keep flitting over there and his head is cocked slightly as if he is listening. I stifle the urge to shiver—I don't want to look like an amateur—and keep my attention on Pam.

"What happened?" I ask, trying to keep my voice light, trying to ignore the goosebumps I can feel rising underneath my jacket.

"Parker, Parker Hayden, was a ship owner in the '30s. Back then, Portland was a very different city. The ships were its lively hood. There was a lot of money, a lot of crime, a lot of … well, scandals, I guess. Think Vegas, but on a river. Anyway, Parker was just one of the many wealthy ship owners. He spent half his time here, half somewhere on the east coast. He rented a room, this room, spending an obscene amount of money every night. He was a ladies man too, no surprise there! He was also a bit nuts. But because he was rich, you called him eccentric. There were rumors he was having an affair with a maid or two; sometimes he'd be caught stealing tons of toiletries and hording them in his closet. In this day and age we'd call him a weirdo but back then, he was just rich and powerful and you let him do what he wanted."

"Doesn't sound too much different from nowadays," Dex says softly, keeping the camera focused on Pam. He's paying less attention now to the other room, which makes me feel a smidge better.

Pam laughs. "You're right about that. And it was the same kind of outcome. Back in 1934, Portland was hit hard—really hard—with this strike. I think it was called the West Coast Waterfront Strike? Anyway, there was the strike, his ship was basically inoperable, and he lost a lot of money. Really fast. According to the records, he was kicked out of the hotel because he couldn't pay his bills. Not for this room, not for any room here."

"And what happened?" I push.

She sighs and rubs her face quickly, looking uneasy for the first time tonight. Lines appear on her youthful face.

"He wouldn't leave. He was kicked out several times, out on the street even. Publicly humiliated. All unshaven and messy, like a vagrant. He said people were after him, wanting money and that he was afraid for his life. Then the hotel staff found him. Dead. Hanging in the maid's laundry room, from a noose made out of towels. The strike ended two days later. How is that for irony?"

She smiles at me, but it is forced and I can't be bothered to return it. The story stirs something in my gut.

I look up at Dex and see that his attention is back on the other room again.

"What is it?" I ask him. I can't help myself.

Pam's attention goes to him, and we all look over but see nothing.

"The guests who have seen him," she puts in, her voice low, her eyes on the partition, "they say they see a man pacing anxiously in the other room there, muttering to himself. Once he notices you, he tries to say something or write something down. But no words come out and as the guests get more scared and confused, the ghost gets frustrated. Sometimes he disappears, sometimes he rushes at the guests and then ... poof."

"Well doesn't that make for a memorable stay," Dex comments underneath his breath.

Pam giggles nervously at his lame joke and then gets up. "I'm afraid I will have to leave you two now. Duty calls."

Dex lowers the camera and touches her arm lightly, causing her to pause mid-bustle. It's obvious she wants nothing more than to get out of the room. I have half a mind to join her.

"Where is the laundry room?" he asks.

Pam looks down at her feet quickly. "The laundry room? Why?"

"Well, we aren't ignoring the place where the man hung himself. With towels, mind you. I mean, I can make a swan out of towels, but a noose?"

"I'd show you, but I really must—"

She looks at me for support as he reaches forward and plucks the keys out of her hand.

He holds up the keys in front of her face. "Just tell us which key will get us into the laundry room and we'll have no problem finding it on our own."

"Dex," I begin, not wanting him to step out of bounds. He can be relentless sometimes.

He ignores me and flashes Pam a smile that usually makes me weak at the knees. "Come on, Pammy, you know you want our little show to succeed here. Parker would want us there. Give the man some closure."

Her mouth twitches while she thinks it over. Dex gives her a quick wink and she blushes slightly. I can't help but roll my eyes again.

"All right," Pam mumbles and takes the keys from him. She goes through them in a blur and pops one off the ring and into his outstretched hand. "It's in the basement. This will open the freight elevator at the end of the hall and take you right there. But I want this back, OK?"

"But of course." He grins and closes his hand over the key before she has a chance to change her mind.

She looks at me and I give a little shrug.

"We won't wreck anything or scare the guests," I say. I want to add, "We promise," but I know we can't promise anything. Destruction and fear seem to follow Dex and I wherever we go. That is the nature of the ghost hunting business, even one that's only on the Internet.

I can see Pam isn't comfortable with the situation, but she doesn't say anything else. She just leaves the room and shuts the door behind her. The movement causes the dust to fly off of the nearby lamps.

I slowly let out my breath and look at Dex. He's watching me carefully.

"What?" I ask.

"Do you want the lights on or off?"

He raises his camera a bit and I get it. Are we going to shoot this in the dark or in the light? I know what I'm going to say, and I know what he's going to say.

"Leave the lights on," I tell him.

"I think we should have them off."

I knew it. "Why do you even bother consulting me if you're just going to do what you want anyway?"

"I like you to feel like this a partnership," he says, and sounds strangely sincere. He tucks the key into his cargo pants and gives me a quick smile. "And you know that shooting in the dark adds to the tension."

"It also adds to my ever-building threat of dying young," I point out.

"Twenty-two ain't so young anymore, kiddo. I mean, you've almost surpassed James Dean. If you kick it now—"

I raise my hand in the air. "That's enough. Let's just get this over with."

"Perry's famous last words."

"Dex. Shut up."

It's his turn to roll his eyes. I feel a cold waft come in from the living room area, and I automatically rub my hands up and down my arms. There's definitely something going on in this place, and I am in no hurry to find out. But of course, it's my job to find out.

"What if we just leave this light on here?" I say, pointing at the lamp. The rest of hotel room, including the bathroom and the living area, are only lit by residual light. It's just dark enough to be spooky over there, but it's not so black that I'd be having a panic attack.

"If you wish," Dex says and I hate how unafraid he sounds. Then again, he always gets to view things through the lens. He never has to be the one seeing the horrors face-to-face.

It's a catch-22 with my job. On one hand, I'm often scared shitless at the slightest thing and pray that I don't bump into a ghost (or a skinwalker, now that I know those things exist). On the other hand, if I don't run into anything, it makes for a pretty bad episode. I mean, most ghost hunting shows don't have much to show for themselves, anyway, but that's also the point: We don't want to be like most of those shows. We are above and beyond that, at least that's what Dex rattles off half the time. I don't even know if he believes what he says, but the fact is that when we do capture some unexplainable stuff on film, the views go up and we look good.

It's too bad our looking good comes at the cost of me nearly peeing my pants every time.

"So …" I begin.

"So, just come here." He places his strong hands on the sides of my arms and physically moves me over so I'm right in front of him and the camera. I don't want him to let go but he does. "I'll roll it, you give a quick spiel based on whatever Pam just said and then walk into the other room. I'll be right behind you."

"Don't I get a flashlight?"

"I'll be your eyes. Ready?"

I nod, square my shoulders and take a deep breath. We usually go in just one take and I give a very quick overview of what we are doing in The Benson hotel and what we hope to find in room 818.

Then I turn around and face the darkness of the living room. I don't know how it's possible, but it seems to have grown darker in the last few minutes. Before I could make out a couch and a table, as well as the entrance to the fancy bathroom. Now, I can't see anything at all. Just the partition with its slightly transparent sheets of fabric paper and that terrible feeling that there is something, or someone, just beyond it, waiting for me to enter its clutches.

Dex clears his throat, a signal that I need to move. I feel frozen on the spot but will my legs to step forward, even though every part of me is screaming not to.

Somehow, I do it. I step into the void and feel a rush of frigid air flow around me. No, flow is too gentle of a word. It slams into me like an invisible hand.

I pause and take another step, trying to pick up where the bed should be. I still can't see anything, but Dex says in a low voice, "Move to the right a little. The bed is right in front of you."

I do as he says and stop. Dex sucks in his breath in one sharp motion.

"What is it?" I whisper uneasily. I wish I could see what he is seeing.

"Do you not see it?"

I turn around and see his silhouette against the light. "See what?" I feel the symptoms of a panic attack poking around my spine.

He doesn't say anything but keeps the camera trained on me while reaching into his backpack. He pulls out what looks like the small infrared camera.

"Here, turn the switch on, it's on the side," he says and hands it to me. I fumble for it, feeling around for the button.

It comes on and then I can see again. Well, kind of. It's aimed at the floor and I can see the shape of my feet and legs glowing a hot red against the blackness. I feel a lot like I'm in Predator.

"Now turn around and aim it straight in front of you."

I hesitate for a second, afraid of what I'm going to witness. Then I turn on the spot so I'm facing the black room and look through the infrared camera. I nearly drop it.

Right in front of me, to the side of the bed, is a tall, long shape of pale blue light. A hazy silhouette. The outline of a man who isn't there.

"That's unbelievable," I hear Dex say from behind me. I can't form the words to agree. The fear is overpowering my fascination. There is someone standing right in front of me. Parker Hayden.

"Talk to it."

"What?" I whisper hoarsely, my eyes flitting from the screen to the blackness in front of me. If I walk forward, will my hands grab onto a desperate dead man? Or will they pass through them, like no one is there at all? Do I even want to know?

"Mr. Hayden," Dex speaks in a gentle voice, void of any self-consciousness. "Mr. Hayden, we can see you. Would you like to talk to us? Would you like to tell us something?"

The shape on the camera shakes vigorously on the spot, like the picture on a television that's being hit from the side. Then it stops and in a blink of an eye it bursts out of the screen, screaming past us in a blur of cold, miserable energy.

And just like that, all the lights in the room come on and it's just Dex and I left staring at each other, cameras in hand, feeling cold and dumbfounded at what we just encountered.

I manage to shut my mouth so I don't look like a drooling fool on camera and look back down at the infrared.

"We need to follow him."

I look up at Dex with the most incredulous stinkeye I can muster.

"We need to follow him? We don't even know what that was. Or who that was. Or where he went. Or if he wants us to follow him…"

Dex turns around and heads to the door.

"Dex!" I yell after him and grab onto his sleeve. I look up at his eyes but I can see he's already gone, thinking in the mind of a ghost, plotting where Parker would have gone next.

"Perry, we can't just leave it at that."

"I don't know, I think what we just captured is some pretty awesome stuff. Maybe that's all we'll get for tonight. Maybe it's time to go home."

The side of his mouth twitches and before I know it, he's grinning at me. "Why Perry, I thought you'd turned into quite the little fearless ghost hunter back in Red Fox. Getting cold feet, are we?"

I wish I had a snappy rebuttal for that, but I don't. The truth is, I'm scared. It doesn't matter how many times you've seen a ghost; it's still scary. And considering how often these supernatural beings have tried to kill me in the past, I think I have every right to fear each one I encounter. Every chance I get to get out of the shoot alive is a chance I want to take. I mean, deep down inside, I'm just an ordinary, 22-year-old girl who likes to listen to metal and dreams about chocolate on a nightly basis. Just because I'm ghost bait, doesn't mean I have to exploit it.

But I don't say any of this to Dex. Even though he's just my partner (and I'm usually the sane one), I can't bear the thought of losing face with him. He took a risk by creating this show and by putting me in it. I took a risk by giving up my old job to make something of my life. I want to be the person that he thinks I am, that fearless, brave girl—woman, even—who laughs in the face of danger. Something more than ordinary.

"Cold feet?" I repeat, my voice hard. "You're the one who is showing up all icy on my infrared."

He studies me for a second, sucking slowly on his full lower lip, trying to read me. I hate it when he does that. But instead of looking away as I often do, I hold his gaze, challenging him.

"OK, kiddo. Glad to see you're still up for the challenge," he finally says.

"I deal with you every weekend, don't I? Anything after that is a piece of cake."

He flashes me a quick smile and opens the door. I follow him into the hallway, take in a deep breath and try to calm my nerves, which are firing all over the place and causing me to shake internally. My bluff worked. Now all I need to do is keep up appearances.

As we walk down the hallway to the freight elevator, I already know where Dex is planning on taking us: the laundry room. I don't want to think about the horrors that might lie there, so I ask him, "You told me you saw something, before I turned on the infrared ... what was it?"

We stop in front of the elevator and Dex inserts the key, giving it a turn and pressing the down button. The elevator purrs loudly, as if it hasn't been turned on in decades. I'm reminded of The Shining for a brief instance and hope a river of blood doesn't come flowing out of it.

"Just some really weird lights dancing around. You know how you can get those orbs on screen, like the ones we saw at the lighthouse? Same kind of thing but they were jumping up and down, like balls in a lotto machine or something."

The elevator button light goes off, and with a loud metallic groan, the doors slide open to expose a larger than average elevator behind them.

"Ladies first," Dex says, but I shove him forward. Not this time.

We get in and press the button for the laundry level, which is marked, thankfully. It's also below the first floor and the first two parking levels, which is a slight cause for concern. Just how far down are we going?

I give Dex a nervous smile, which he returns with a mischievous one. An agonizing minute later, we lurch to a stop on the laundry level.

The doors shudder slightly, then open as if being pried by invisible hands. In front of us lies a long hallway, poorly lit by buzzing overhead lights, casting shadows on the few doors that lie along the way. Not the most welcoming place.

Dex steps out first. He grabs my hand, his grasp on mine firm and warm, and I let myself feel the momentary wash of comfort that only he can provide for me. I let him lead me into the hallway. The elevator doors remain open and waiting for the next passenger, only on this empty, quiet floor, there is none to be found.

Dex hoists the camera onto his shoulder again and motions for me to turn on the infrared.

"Might as well start filming this now."

"Where is everyone?" I ask. "I mean, the hotel runs around the clock, doesn't it?"

"But which clock?" he answers in a statement, not a question.

I sigh and flip on the infrared again. My body glows a vibrant red but when I aim it over at Dex, he only comes up orange.

"What?" he asks as I purse my lips, thinking.

"Seems I'm a lot more hot-blooded than you are," I say and quickly show him the screen, placing his hand in front of the lens.

He chews on his lip briefly and then places his hand against my forehead. It feels cool.

"Well you're not hot…"

I shoot him a wry look.

"I mean, not internally hot. Outside is another matter." He winks at me.

"Are you flirting with me again, Mr. Foray?"

"Again? Whatever do you—"

He's interrupted by a wall of sound as all doors down the hallway suddenly swing open and bang against their walls. Simultaneously, the elevator behind us powers up with a thunderous whir, the doors closing quickly.

"It's go time," he says and we're off down the hallway to the first door.

Dex is just about to enter the room when the door slams shut in his face, almost smashing his nose back into his skull. He gives me a scared look I don't see on him too often. Probably the thought of having to get a nose job.

He goes for the handle and I'm right there at his side as he jangles it back and forth vigorously. It's locked.

We dash for the next door and the same thing happens. Same with the last door after that. All doors locked. Nothing to explore.

"Now what?" I mumble, feeling a familiar wave of cold snake around my feet and ankles. I point the infrared down at it, but it doesn't register anything out of the ordinary.

Dex doesn't say anything for awhile so I look up at him. His eyes are focused above him, at a loose-looking vent on the ceiling.

"Perry," he says slowly, carefully.

I shake my head. "You've got to be kidding."

He looks back at me and shrugs. "What's the harm? I'll just boost you up there. If you crawl around for a bit, you'll probably end up in one of the other rooms and then you can open the door from the inside."

"I... don't even know what to say to that."

"No? You usually have some sort of witty one-liner."

"You go up there, Dex. There's no way in hell I'm going."

"You can't hold me up and it's too far for me to jump. Short man syndrome, remember?"

"You can't hold me up."

"Perry, for the last time, stop acting like you weigh one million pounds. You don't. You're as light as a feather."

I let out a laugh. I can't help myself.

"I'm not …anyway, even if you could push me up there, do you think I'd fit?"

"Again, Perry–"

"And if I do get up there, do you think that aging duct would hold me? I'd come crashing through like a bag of bricks."

"Stop using your non-existent weight problem as an excuse, just because you're too chickenshit," he challenges.

My mouth drops slightly. I am not chickenshit. And my weight problem isn't non-existent.

"Fine," I say and walk toward him. "If you don't think it's an issue, then away I go."

He steadies his gaze at me, sussing me out. I cross my arms and give him an impatient stare.

He nods quickly and lowers his hands joined together. I step on them unsteadily and before I can even question just what the hell I am doing, I'm boosted into the air, one hand on the camera, the other reaching for the vent.

Once Dex has me steadied and I can stand, albeit wobbly, on his hands, I climb to his shoulders and push the vent aside. It pops up and slides out to the side with an easy clatter that rattles down the hallway. Up close, it is big enough for me to fit through. But it's also black and fathomless and hides a wealth of things that could frighten me to death. It's a vent, for crying out loud. Since when did this show turn into Mission Impossible?

"You OK, kiddo?" he asks from beneath me, his voice shaking slightly, either from apprehension or from the strain.

"Not really. Have you ever been in a dark vent before?"

"Several times," he answers seamlessly. "Once you get up in there, I'll hand you the flashlight so you don't have to be in the dark."

"How thoughtful of you," I mutter and reach for my hands into the vent. It's cold and I fear it will be icky inside but the bottom of the duct feels mercifully dry.

"On the count of three," he says and once we count down, he pushes me up further and I'm waist deep. I feel his hands slip away and with a groan I pull myself forward until everything except my calves are inside the dark air duct.

I'm scared as hell. The sides of the duct have me unable to turn around and I can't see what's in front of me. For all I know, there could be a giant rat in front of my face, ready to gnaw it off, starting with the little tip of my nose. I am starting to panic and an attack in this tight of a spot would be a dangerous thing indeed.

"Uh, Perry," I hear Dex say. His voice is comforting but the tone isn't.

"What?" I say as quietly as I can. My words reverberate around me.

"I guess you can't turn around and reach for the flashlight…can you?"

I close my eyes and let my head thud against the cold bottom. "No."

"That's OK, I'm just going to stick the flashlight inside your boot. That way, when you get a chance to move around a bit more, you can grab it."

I feel him grab my leg, undo the laces on my left Doc Marten and shove the flashlight inside.

This has to be the stupidest idea ever. Some ghost hunters we are.

I sigh and then cough loudly from all the dust.

"Perry, I'm going to try and talk you through it. Just move forward until I tell you to stop. And when I tell you to stop, see if there's an opening off to your right. If there is, go down that way and it should place you in the laundry room. At least, I hope it's the laundry room."

"OK!" I yell, hoping my voice will scare off any hideous creatures that are waiting for me up ahead.

You can do this, I tell myself. One movement at a time, like a snake. Remember if you need to escape, you just need to back up and you'll be free.

I repeat this to myself as I slink forward, feeling more and more like Tom Cruise. Or Garth from Wayne's World when he keeps landing on his keys.

After what feels like a lifetime of wiggling and trying to refrain from vomiting on the infrared, Dex yells for me to look for a space going off to the right. I feel for it but though I still touch the same cold metal walls, there's a bit of a breeze up ahead, flowing down the right side of me.

I continue, hearing Dex's babbling from below becoming more and more muffled, until my hand doesn't slam against the side as normal. I found the opening.

I take it, maneuvering like a rat in a maze and wiggle down in a new direction. After a few beats, I can't hear Dex at all anymore and that realization fills me with dread. If I need to get out, I'll have to not only back up but make a turn going backwards as well. In the pitch dark, the idea is terrifying and disorienting.

But I continue, because I'm determined to see this through. And soon enough, my eyes start to pick up something ahead of me. There's just a little difference of light up ahead and then my hands come across cool air and a vent covering.

My fingers wrap around the metallic grate and pull it up with ease. It rattles as I push it to the side and I stick my head down below, taking in deep breaths of fresher, non-contained air through my nose. I don't know what's below me, all I can see are a few red lights, which I guess are the on-off buttons of machines. There is some other light, though, spilling in from under a doorframe and with hope I realize that Dex and the hallway must be on the other side of that.

I carefully slide across the opening, distributing my weight on each side until I'm just past it, then I lower myself down, my legs dangling helplessly. I have no idea what the hell is below me but I'm just going to have to hope for the best. I take a deep breath, wiggle myself out until I'm hanging what must be a good few feet off the ground, and let go.

I land on solid ground, though the impact makes me stumble to the side and my body goes flying against a desk that makes an impression in my hip.

"Fuck!" I yell. That's going to leave a giant bruise.

"Perry?" I hear Dex call out from the hallway. I scurry over to the door, careful not to trip over anything in my way, and feel for the doorknob. I yank at it to open, but nothing happens. It appears to be locked from the inside and the outside.

"Are you OK?" he asks and I can hear the worry in his voice. He likes to surprise me by acting human from time to time.

"I'm fine," I say, rubbing my hip where the desk went into me. "But I can't open this fucking thing."

"Are you getting any reception on your phone?"

I tuck the infrared under my arm and bring my iPhone out of my jacket pocket, while reaching down for the flashlight in my boot. It works but the bars are gone. No service.

"No, are you?"

"No," he answers with a sigh. "Look, I've been trying the key she gave me and it won't open any of the doors here. I can't call her either. There are some stairs at the end beside the elevator. I'm just going to run up to the lobby and grab Pam."

"Dex, don't you dare leave me!" I yell and pound on the door for impact.

"Well, what the hell do you suppose we do then? Hang out like this until a maid shows up? What if they are done for the night? Do you really want to spend a night locked in there?"

No. I don't. But I don't want him taking off and leaving me alone in this scary, dark room either.

"Look," he continues, "I'll be right back. And I mean, right back. I'm not going to let anything happen to you."

That's kind of hard to do when you aren't here, I think but I know I have no choice. Either he goes or I'm locked in here all night. That thought is too terrifying to fathom.

"OK," I say hesitantly.

He taps the door lightly. "I'll be right back."

I hear his feet scurry off and a door at the end of the hall open. And then silence again.

I put my back against the door and face the darkness of the foreign room. I flick the flashlight on and slowly graze it across the black.

In a creepy, fleeting light it illuminates a few laundry bins, laundry machines, a makeshift office consisting of a whiteboard, a file cabinet and the desk I ran into.

And a dead man hanging from the ceiling.

I scream bloody murder, dropping the flashlight and camera in the process.

They fall to my feat in an outburst as loud as my wail, and as I quickly fumble for them, the light in the room goes on.

I raise my hand to my eyes to shield them from the light and try to get a glimpse of what's going on. The image of that dead, bloated man hanging by his neck is seared into my brain.

The laundry hampers, machines and office are all still here.

The hanging man is gone.

There is an African-American woman who stands to my far left, her hand on a light fixture, giving me a quizzical stare. She's young and thin with large eyes and is wearing a plain grey dress with a white ruffled apron across it. A very classic-looking maid.

"Good heavens, child," she exclaims in a thick Southern accent. "What on earth are you doing in here?"

I blink hard, trying to make sense of the situation. The maid looks at my hands and what I'm holding.

"Are you filming me? Who are you? What is this?" she demands, her voice growing higher with each question.

"I … I'm Perry Palomino," I stammer, my voice squeaking.

"Am I supposed to know who you are?" she asks and puts her hands on her hips.

"Uh, no," I say and give her an awkward smile. "I'm here with my partner Dex. Dex Foray. We are, uh, we doing a project here. We have permission of the night manager. Pam … something. She said we could come down here and film."

"Just what are you filming. Charlie Chaplin?"

Hmmmm. How to explain the next part without seeming batshit crazy.

"Well …" I begin.

She cocks her brow at me and folds her arms. She's in no hurry.

I let out a burst of air through my nose and say, "We're ghost hunters."

She smiles, her teeth blindingly white. She doesn't sound as amused as she looks. "You're pulling my chain."

"No, no sadly I'm not. We have a show, Experiment in Terror. It's on the Internet."

"The Internet?"

"I know, it sounds lame but we've been doing quite well. I mean, we have advertisers and people actually tune into watch us. Well, watch me. Since I'm the host. Just not a very good one. Actually, I think people tune into laugh at me, but whatever gets me a pay check." I'm rambling now.

"This is a radio show?" she asks.

"No, just on the web."

She frowns and walks toward me, eying my hands. "What kind of camera is that?"

Though there is nothing menacing at all in her voice, I flinch a little and back up into the door. She pauses and gives me another disbelieving look.

"You never seen a black woman before?"

"Huh?"

"I know we aren't too common out West here but you best be getting used to us."

Now it's my turn to frown. I study her more closely. She's at least in her early thirties, her pretty face is unlined but she has this authoritative air about her. Everything sounds like an accusation but one that's filled with a hint of doubt. Though she's trying hard to hide it, I can see she's as afraid of me as I am afraid of her.

I raise the infrared to her, slowly, as if she is a skittish cat, and show her the screen, flicking it on.

She looks at it and shakes her head, not getting it.

"It's infrared," I explain. "It picks up heat energy."

"Well, my oh my," she says. "That's the dumbest thing I've ever heard. You trying to make a motion picture?"

"No, ma'am," I can't help but say. "Much less than that."

"And you what? You hunt ghosts?"

"It sounds ridiculous when you put it that way," I admit.

She snorts and turns around, heading back to the machines. "It sounds ridiculous anyway you put it, child."

"We've just been told the ghost of Parker Hayden is known to haunt this room."

She stops in mid-stride. Her whole body is tensed up. It makes me tense up too. I must have hit a nerve.

"Have you seen him?" I whisper, making sure the camera is running but not pointing it in her direction just yet. I don't want to scare her and just getting our dialog recorded would be more than enough for the show.

"Seen who?" she repeats slowly. She still doesn't turn around.

"Parker Hayden. The ship millionaire. He lost all of his money during the strike and then killed himself–"

"Don't you dare speak ill of him," she threatens in a low voice so raspy and ragged that it almost sounds demonic. "He would never kill himself."

I bite my lip, unsure of how to proceed. I have no idea what is going on but those hairs are standing up on the back of my neck again.

"Do you know who he was?" I ask carefully.

Finally, she turns around and looks at me with tear-filled eyes.

"He was ... my friend."

I don't know what to make of that. "Pardon me?"

"He was ... my lover. I haven't seen him for days, not since they threw him out."

Oh. Dear. God.

"He wouldn't have killed himself though," she continues, her voice warbling with emotion. A tear spills down her cheek, leaving a dark trail. "He has troubles but he wouldn't have done that. Not Parker. Not my Parker."

"Ummmm," is all I can say to that. I slowly raise the infrared camera and aim it at her.

"You're filming me now?"

Yes, I sure am, I think and look at the screen. My breath freezes in my throat. Through the infrared, I can see my own hand in front of me burning a deep red. The shape of the maid though is coming out a steely blue, like the blue I saw in the hotel room.

I look back at her. And I realize I'm talking to a ghost.

"I said, are you filming me? Answer me, child," she says, her voice angry. She wipes away a tear with a rough swipe of her hand.

"No," I say quickly and lower the camera. "Sorry, I … what did you say your name was?"

"I didn't. It's May," she answers. "I'd say I'm pleased to meet you Miss Perry Palomino, but I'm afraid I'm a victim of some terrible joke."

There's one thing I've learned about the dead: they don't like to learn they are dead. Things kind of go crazy when they do, like their entire existence is shattered and they go along with it. I mean, imagine you think you're alive and someone tells you you're dead. Then you start putting together all the pieces and *BLAM*! Your entire world is ripped apart. The very realization can make most ghosts simply disappear. The acceptance pushes them on into the afterlife, or whatever the next step is.

But for selfish reasons, I don't want to lose May. I don't want her to realize she's dead. Because while I've got her here, in this room, I can use her. I can use her to get to Parker.

"When was the last time you saw Parker?" I ask her innocently enough. I still keep the camera aimed at the floor.

"Five days ago," she says. "He said he'd come by the next day. I was here waiting. He never did. I reckoned … I don't know. I feared the worst. The very worst."

"Which was?"

"That he was dead, Miss Palomino. But not by his own hand. No, he that was murdered."

"By who?"

"The sharks. Who else?"

My face must have contorted into a look of pure confusion because she continues, her voice and demeanor more impassioned by the second.

"The sharks are the fellas who he owed money to. You just don't lose a boat without losing a few friends. These fellas meant business and I seen them threaten him more than a few times. Parker went and told the police but they do nothing. They don't have no control. Parker would tell me he was scared. So scared. He's a man who don't get scared, you hear that. So if he's scared, I reckon there's a reason for it. They are after his life."

The idea of Parker being murdered by men he owed money to is just as believable as suicide. I don't know what to believe but I choose to give the ghost the benefit of the doubt.

"Did Parker leave any proof, any records, that these men were after him?"

She closes her eyes for a second and it's then that I notice a strange transparency about her.

"There was his diary," she tells me. Her eyes open slowly. "It's his checkbook. But he would keep a log on the back of the checks he couldn't write anymore. Most of it doesn't make much sense to me…if I could talk to him, hear from him, he could tell you himself. I just need to talk to him. Can you find him for me? You said you knew the manager?"

"Yes … but I don't think it will make much difference."

"Why is that?"

"Do you know where he would have kept the checkbook?"

"On his person. Where else? What aren't you telling me? What are you really doing here?"

I look down at the screen and aim it at her. She glows a translucent blue. It's beautiful, for once, and not scary.

"What happened to Parker?" she goes on, her voice cracking over his name. I don't say anything but I meet her eye and I know, in one look, that she knows the truth. Maybe not that she's dead. But that he is. Her face crumbles. She puts her hand to her head and stumbles backward.

Out of instinct, I go after her, my arms outstretched, hoping to reach her in time before she goes over.

I almost reach her when she smashes against the floor with a sickening thud. The world goes black. The lights go off and I find myself on my knees, my leggings ripping open on the cold hard floor.

"May?" I cry out and raise the camera, hoping to see her blue form through the darkness. I only read my own heat and no one else's.

I slowly get to my feet and try to flick on the flashlight with my own hand.

Cold fingers reach over my elbow in a stealthy grasp. I can feel the ice through my jacket.

I am yanked harshly to the side until I crash into a wheeled laundry bin and another hand grabs me by the face and pulls me over the side and into it.

All I can think about is the painful cold that comes from the grasp, as if permafrost is entering my veins and creating a sheet of ice on my face. And then I find myself face first in a laundry bin, smothered by a million towels and pulled deeper and deeper into them until I can't breathe and I can't scream and I can't move. I can only drown here.

The blackness behind my eyes grows darker somehow, as if the dark has a million different shades and nuances and I was only scratching the surface. It's a different kind of obsidian, one that signals the end, finality. I don't want to succumb to it, but all I can see is this blackness, and all I can feel are these hands that won't stop pulling me deeper, that won't let go, and my thoughts become less … and less … and less …

"Perry!"

I think I hear my name but it sounds too far away to be real. I think of May and wonder where she came from.

"Perry!"

My name again. It sounds familiar.

There is a rush of noise and light and commotion and I feel more hands grabbing me. Only these ones are warm and though they are strong, I can feel the care seeping through them.

I think of Dex. And remember where I am.

I put my hands at the bottom of the bin, and push myself off. As I do so, they come in contact with something beneath one of the towels. I'm afraid it's the remains of whoever was pulling me down before, but I still close my fingers around it as Dex yanks me out of the bin and into the harsh fluorescent light of the room.

I cough wildly, trying to find my breath as Dex keeps his hands on either side of my shoulders, steadying me. As the air hits my lungs and my wincing subsides, I notice Pam standing beside the door, a key in hand, her face in a look of absolute terror.

"Perry," Dex says. "Perry, look at me."

I manage to look at him. His dark eyes are searching mine relentlessly, his brow furrowed, his stance tense.

"Are you OK?" he asks.

I nod, feeling relieved and embarrassed all at the same time.

"Was I sticking out of the laundry bin?" I ask with trepidation.

He nods and I see a hint of a smile tug at the corner of his mouth. It would have been a comical sight, my giant ass in the air and all.

"I leave you alone for five seconds …" His tone is light but he knows there is more to the story. And that I'll fill him in on it later.

"What's in your hands?" Pam asks, looking at them with curiosity.

I glance down and see I am holding a rectangular cover of well-worn leather. I open it carefully and see what I thought I would see. A checkbook filled with writing. The possible proof that Parker Hayden was murdered and not a victim of suicide. I walk over to Pam and place the item in her hands. She looks up at me surprised and confused.

"You may want to run this by a historian. Or even the police," I say. "There's a chance that Parker Hayden didn't commit suicide after all. It could be a cold case file. A very cold case."

I feel extremely cheesy as I tell Pam that. No surprise, Dex says, "Wow, I leave you for one minute and suddenly you're CSI: Portland."

I give him a tired smile. I'm ready to go home.

A few days pass when I get a call from Dex. We're not at the point where we call each other just to talk, but every contact I have with him is still important and I still get stupid butterflies every time I see his name pop up on the call display. This time, he's calling to talk about our episode at The Benson.

"How's it all looking?" I ask as I sit on my bed, listening to my younger sister Ada argue with my dad downstairs.

"Oh, it's looking fucking fantastic, kiddo," Dex says, his voice coming in low and smooth over the line. "I just want to hug you for keeping that camera rolling while May was talking. I'll have to run it over some other footage and do that little subtitle thing underneath but it really helps our case, especially when you get that blue shit on screen. That really is something."

"Best show ever?" I ask, amused at his praise.

"Well," he says slowly, "it probably would have helped had I been around but you did OK on your own."

"I'll take that as a compliment."

"There's something else, too, you should take as a compliment."

My eyes perk up and I sit up a bit straighter, putting down my Spin magazine. "What's that?"

"Pam just called me. She said she handed over the checkbook to the police who are having a division look into it or something. Anyway, the point is ever since our visit, all the haunting in the hotel has stopped."

"What do you mean, all hauntings?"

"Well, she says she usually gets some sort of feedback each day. Since our shoot, there hasn't been any. I don't know what that means but she seems to think that whatever you did down in that laundry room...well, I guess you cleared the place."

"So I'm an exorcist now?"

"Don't flatter yourself, kiddo. You're miles away from being Father Merrin and for all we know the haunting could start up again. I'm just saying...next time you feel like being hard on yourself because we aren't making a difference and there's no point to any of this...I dunno. Don't. Because you did good here. You did good."

I let Dex ramble on a bit more to please my ego, and then we hang up. Like the other times before, I still don't know what to make of my ghost hunting. I don't know how I got roped into doing the show, how I ended up being a magnet for the supernatural and what on earth it has in store for me. The only thing I do know is that it's dangerous and I'm compelled to keep doing it.

But I also know that even though someone is dead, it doesn't mean they're beyond help. And for every ten ghosts that try and kill me, if I end up saving one of them, it might be worth it after all.

Though you may want to remind me of that, next time I'm locked in a coffin or something.

BODY BOX

By Shawn Proctor

When I woke up and heard the high-pitched ringing, I knew a part of my middle ear was missing. She had stolen the malleous or incus—hammer or anvil. I shook my head, but the sound remained, along with the memories of my daughter, Chandra, in our bedroom. Chandra's footsteps padding across the carpet. Her thin fingers touching my hair and skin. Her nails picking through my flesh to touch the organs underneath.

That morning I asked my husband Allan about a lock for her room.

"At five years old? Don't you think she's a little young to be able to keep us out?" he asked. Allan had one eye on the television, one of those drug intervention shows. His cell phone buzzed. He glanced at the display and tossed the cell aside.

"I don't mean for locking *out*," I said, leaning against the wall. My balance had been off since last night.

Allan paused the show. He looked at me, probably noticing the worry lines across my forehead, the sadness that sagged the skin under my eyes, and the slump of my stomach. He opened his mouth three times, half-formed words caught. "It was jewelry. Try forgiving her, if only for yourself."

I swallowed hard.

"I love her, but," I said, "she's stealing again, Allan."

"Stealing?"

Parts of my body, I thought and picked at the cuticle around my thumb. "Things only I would know about."

"I'll talk to her." Allan picked up his phone and began typing.

The day the jewelry had turned up missing, I had tried not to blame her. I had asked Chandra again and again whether she had taken them. I used a sweet voice, one a four-year-old would understand. I explained the difference between right and wrong, that you shouldn't take things that aren't yours. Finally, I begged—"You don't understand what they mean to me. They are the only things from my family I kept."

She just smiled, wrinkled her upturned nose, and said, "No, Mommy."

I had found the jewelry in her closet, hidden in a small purple box in the back. I screamed at her then. Threatened. Shook her by the arms. Allan snapped Chandra up before I could do anything more. Chandra was crying so loudly her voice disappeared for three days.

I would have done far worse had I known what would come later.

The first time I noticed a body part missing, we were at a butterfly conservatory. Chandra had been sick the weeks before with a two-week fever that broke overnight, and Allan suggested we take her out, just to relieve her isolation. Chandra knew to never touch the wings, which would remove the chitin, the tiny scales that made them shine iridescent.

Allan walked her to a box where chrysalides hung with the next generation of butterflies ready to emerge. The hard mountings looked like tiny shells. "They only live for a few days once they emerge," he told us.

"The butterflies die so soon?" Chandra covered her mouth. Fat tears gathered in her eyes.

"That's not true," I said, knowing that most butterflies live for weeks.

Chandra began to cry. She pushed me away and started to run. I tried to grab her arm, but my leg buckled and I fell to the pavement. Allan helped me to a bench and went to bring her back.

"I hurt Mommy?" Chandra asked, stepping from behind an exotic fern.

"No," I lied, clasping my knee, pain surging down to my ankle. I felt a strange scar and hole in the joint. "You scared us."

A butterfly flew past and Allan's eyes followed its erratic path. He sighed.

Chandra's eyes narrowed when she touched the scar. She ran her finger pads run along my purple flesh until her nails cut the knotted skin. "I hurt Mommy," she said, her gaze locked on my eyes. She licked her dry lips.

It felt as if the ligament had never been attached, it had vanished so completely. Of course, Allan didn't believe me when I said my limp was because of Chandra, that I knew from her reaction that she had pulled strands of ligaments from my knee.

I haven't eaten much more than a crust of bread or drunk anything stronger than tea in months, since she cut a rope of intestines from me, leaving a nickel-sized dent in my stomach. Chandra grew despite eating little of what was offered at dinner. "She never touches her fork," Allan said.

When Chandra was at school, I sat at the kitchen table. I couldn't walk much further than the bus stop, so I made up logic puzzles to keep my reasoning sharp. Angels on the head of a pin. One hand clapping. If I screamed and no one heard it, I wondered whether it would make a sound.

The night after Chandra cut a nerve from my eye, ruining my peripheral vision, I had to talk to Allan. His eyes, even while sleeping, remained open, the vitreous gel like set gems. In the seven years we'd been married, he had never remembered anything after he fell asleep—it was like talking to his naked inner thoughts. I needed him to have no memory of our conversation that night.

"My life since Chandra feels compressed. Small house, small desk, small bed. Small body, too. I calculated that I lost ten percent of my weight in the last three months." I sat up, my back to the headboard.

"Compressed?" His voice was raspy, barely a whisper.

"I can't walk anymore. I'm scared I will lose everything," I said.

He took a deep breath, as if settling to sleep. "She will replace you, piece by piece."

My heart raced, and I pushed my hands against my chest, feeling something odd: an asymmetry under a thin scar. Chandra had plucked a rib from my chest. *Was she going to rip out my lungs, fiber by fiber?* I wondered.

"When did you realize that?" I asked, but Allan didn't answer.

The house was still, except for the endless breathing cycles of my husband and the shallower patterns of Chandra. I limped to her room. For an hour, I sat and watched her, tucked inside the covers. A poisonous butterfly of my own creation.

By the dim hallway light, I searched her closet. I felt the small outline of her special box, where she had hidden my jewelry. I felt an edge, but of a much bigger box than I remembered. It had grown heavier.

Taking it to the hallway, I found what I had hoped, what I had feared. Inside was a tiny organ, which I recognized as the hammer of my ear, along with a splinter of rib, intestines like knotted yarn, a shred of nerve, and a cut of tendon.

Beneath were parts I didn't expect, parts that were not mine. Tucked at the very back, were the blackened shreds of Allan's seminal vesicles. Our bodies, the parts that were taken, had shriveled like apples left for months in the icebox. Lost to me, the way my youth had been. *We will both be replaced*, I thought.

I promised to myself then never to confront Chandra. Not to yell or threaten or tell her I had learned her secret. It had become our family's secret.

I looked closer, and what I saw made me slam the box and tremble, hoping not to wake the child nearby. A child who would most certainly come again in the night. There, on my intestines, were garlic dust, a drop of olive oil, and petite spiraled teeth marks.

THE CUTTING OF THE OUROBOROS

By E.E.W. Christman

A woman travels alone. She takes the 5:15 train from Saratoga Springs to New York City. She is the only passenger without any bags—the rest are tourists leaving the mineral springs and returning to their apartments and brownstones. Designer luggage rolls down the aisles and lines the overhead compartments in neat leathery rows. The woman takes only a backpack she bought at Goodwill three years ago, ratty and patched. Her shoes are muddy. They stand out among the clean Louboutins and Versaces.

The train crawls through the New York countryside like a slithering silver wyrm—not a pink garden buddy *worm*, but a great monstrosity vanquished by a knight on a horse in a high fantasy novel *wyrm*. It wriggles between golden apple orchards and highways thick with fumes. It's dark when they arrive. The woman steps out of Moynihan quickly, not slowed down by the labor of luggage. She walks with a familiarity that isn't hers. The woman has never been more than twenty miles away from where she was born. But she doesn't need to know the streets. She just needs to follow the thread in her chest, dragging her forward and sideways, down avenues lined with scaffolds and alleys warm with the steam from kitchen windows. It grows taut the deeper the woman travels into the bowels of the city. She reaches for her sweater and clutches. *It's around here somewhere ...*

Despite a population of eight million, with apartment buildings climbing up for stories all around her, the woman finds herself alone. The streets, so busy moments before, are quiet. The thread grows warm between her ribs. She comes to a street somehow devoid of sound in a city that never ceased its screaming. Everything is damp, as if the concrete's sweating. At the corner—the thread is tight now, twanging eagerly, painfully—is an old theater. The faded sign reads "Charon's Carnival" in a once festive, now putrid yellow. The intersection is impossibly empty, save the mist and steam.

The woman walks to its center, her internal string practically dragging her across the pavement. She tries to ignore it and pulls the supplies from her backpack, placing them beneath the blinking streetlight. The three skulls are arranged in a row—raven, rabbit, fox—with candles made by the woman's own hands, the wax mixed with her blood, sweat, and piss. Their flames dance in the fog. The woman looks at her phone. It's nearly midnight. The thread hums excitedly. She sits and counts down the minutes. The seconds seem to stretch on and on. They swallow up the fog, the light of the streetlights, the distant sounds of people, until there's nothing but the foul candles, the skulls, and the woman. She waits, the string strangling her beating heart, the seconds yawning into eternity.

The empty eye sockets begin to glow softly. Looking into them, the woman can faintly make out the flickering tongues of weak flames. Their jaws move up and down. They speak:

"Life," cries the raven.

"Fear," whispers the rabbit.

"Waste," growls the fox.

"These are my gifts three," the woman responds. "And with them, I bind you to me."

"Life, fear, waste." The three skulls say in unison. "Ask us your boon, make haste!"

The woman takes a shaky breath. This is it. After this, she couldn't turn back. But what she was about to ask seemed less impossible than turning around, walking back to the train station, and buying a ticket home. *No.* The only way out is forward.

"Take me to Death."

The nameless street opens beneath the skulls and the candles. The pavement doesn't crack, nor does the ground shake. Rather, it is like a great mouth yawning wide, revealing a bottomless esophagus and teeth made of dirt and stone. The woman stares into the earthy maw, but sees only darkness. She takes one of the candles, ignoring the heat of the wax on her fingers, and steps down. *No way but forward* ...

The woman descends. The streetlight's glow fades. She's scared to look back and see the hole where the world waited. The woman thinks, even now at the brink of realization, she could still turn back, climb out of this pit, and leave. So she keeps her eyes forward, and temptation at her back until she climbs so deep that there's nothing behind, and nothing ahead. Nothing but the candle's flame to light the way, and the thread twanging in her chest.

The skulls bounce along next to her as the tunnel drops into the bowels of the earth. Not bounce, she realizes. Sway (or fly, in the raven's case), walking with ethereal bodies. The three keep pace, but don't speak until finally—how long has she been walking?—there's *something* ahead. The woman hesitates to call it light. There is simply illumination. The darkness is no longer all-consuming, all-encompassing. It is merely shadows, and in the folds of those shadows, the woman can see a gateway.

"Be quick," says the crow, hovering by her left shoulder.

"Be wary," says the rabbit from between her legs.

"Be cunning," says the fox, prowling against the wall.

The gateway's an arch of roughly hewn stone and bone. Ribs and jaws jut at the woman; empty eye sockets leer at her hurrying steps; curling fingers and toes reach for her earnestly. She crosses the threshold and for a single wretched moment, the air is sucked from her mouth. She walks through the briefest of voids, and the woman feels her blood boil, her veins engorge, and her hands swell. She resists the urge to scream for fear of the nothing creeping down her throat and into her already expanding lungs.

It's the worst second of her life. It's nothing but pain and the rising tide of death. But when the woman lifts her foot to take a second step, it's over. She takes a beloved breath. Even the thread seems to slacken in relief. This is just the preamble; the real test lies ahead.

The woman is no longer descending. The tunnel evens out. The earth is slowly replaced by beams of wood and wall-mounted oil lamps. The glass ends in blackened tips. The woman looks down and sees hardwood floors instead of dirt. A narrow carpet, too moth-eaten and rotten to be considered beautiful, runs to the end of the hallway-that-was-once-a-tunnel to a set of double doors, once fine and beautiful but now deteriorating. Its glass panels are opaque with grime, and the brass doorknob shines with greases. When the woman opens it, the hinges groan as if the act of opening were more than it could bear. But the string feels ready to break; she's close.

Beyond the door is an opulent home in the throes of decomposition. The marble floors have a thick layer of dust; the woman could look back and see the trail her sneakers had left. Paintings and mirrors framed in gold and platinum cover the walls, but their contents are too faded or filthy to make out. Motes hang in the lamplight, their movement the sole activity in this beautiful tomb.

Light flickers from a nearby room. The raven flies through the open door, closely followed by the nervous rabbit and the cautious fox. The woman takes the rear and enters what appears to be a library. The meager light from her candle and the scattered lamps doesn't penetrate the murky shadows above, and shelves ascend into black pits. Who knew where or if they ended. The spines are too faded to make out. There are hardcovers, leather bound books, pulpy paperbacks, books so new they could have been bought at an airport and scrolls so ancient a single touch would turn them into dust. There's a single armchair, under-stuffed and uncomfortable-looking, and in that armchair is Death.

Of all the cosmic entities that have taken up the mantle of managing mortals, Death has the most faces. So many that as they look up at the woman, they have no discernable features. One moment, they are feminine, the next masculine. They are pale followed by dark, thin followed by fat. They are the most exquisite and beautiful amalgamation the woman has ever seen, and somehow repulsive. Their smile makes her want to weep in joy and dread.

"You're early." Death's voice creeps like mold into the woman's ears. The sound of it fills her brain and makes her body grow heavy with exhaustion. Nothing sounds more pleasurable than lying down on this dirty carpet for eternity. But the woman came prepared. She dug her nails into the warm wax, pain and heat bringing her back to life, and she says the words she'd rehearsed so many times:

"Death, God of Many Faces, Harbinger, Doom-Bringer, Peace-Seeker, the Keeper of All Souls Great and Small: I have come for the one who comes for all, seeking the unseekable, longing for that which is beyond the mortal realm. Hear my challenge."

Death nods. "As it was, as it is, as it shall be." Then they lean forward conspiratorially, as if they are the woman's oldest friend. Perhaps they are. "What do you ask?"

"Give me the soul of Hazel Knight."

Death's grin is so wide, their impossible lips threaten to rip through their cheeks. "What do you offer in trade for ownership of this soul?" The woman shakes her head.

"By virtue of bravery and witchcraft most foul, I demand the chance to win my prize."

Death stands. Their robe flutters around them like a great, threadbare curtain. Its color, once a bright blue or possibly purple, is now faded. Their arms are too long; their legs are too tall. They stand over the woman like a great silken tower, and for a moment, she wonders if Death won't simply squash her as easily as one might squash a gnat. But they extend a starved arm and gesture for the woman to follow. She does, her ghostly companions in tow.

The quintet passes through an enormous pair of double doors made entirely of glass so filthy the woman briefly mistakes them for wood. In the dark room beyond, the air is thick with putrescence and humidity. As the woman's eyes adjust to the darkness, she sees they're in a greenhouse, although it's unlike any greenhouse she has ever seen. It's vaulted ceiling gives the impression of a cathedral of glass, though little light shines in (and where does the light come from, the woman wonders). The garden boxes and planters are full of dead or dying plants, gray fronds curled and starved beyond recognition. Others have a cloying sweetness, like fruit that has just gone off. The trees and brambles bear no fruit, however. Any such byproducts have fallen to the ground in blighted heaps of fleshy rot. This place is less garden, and more mass grave.

Death guides their uninvited guests—if they objected to the presence of the woman's ghostly companions, they didn't say so—to what must be the center of this gangrenous garden. There's a raised dais of broken tiles. Scattered across it are the tools one might use in a living garden: empty pots, bags of soil, trowel and scissors covered in rust. Death hands the scissors to the woman.

"All you must do to claim the soul of Hazel Knight," Death takes a seat upon a stool on the dais like a grim king overlooking their ruinous kingdom. "is find her."

"Here?"

Death nods. The woman turns left, then right, then back the way they'd come. She can no longer see the door to the library—they had only walked ten yards—nor can she see the edges of the greenhouse. There is only the murk of the ceiling and the canopy of dry leaves surrounding them. If the garden has boundaries, an end and a beginning, a place where floor meets wall, they're too distant to see. Death is unreadable, but if the woman had to ascribe an emotion to their ever-shifting visage, it would be confidence.

No way but forward...

The stagnant garden is a senescent maze. If not for the divine thread pulling at her heart, the woman would be hopelessly lost. As she walks between the rows of spoiled plants, the invisible string gets hotter and hotter. The dais is no longer visible, but the walls aren't any closer. The dead garden is endless.

Mostly endless, the woman mentally corrects herself. The longer she stares at the gray stalks and crumpled leaves, the more she notices the intermittent splashes of life. Every now and then, an emerald vine or thick stalk climbs from the corpses in stark defiance. When the woman looks into the boxes, she can see little green sprouts clawing their way every upward toward the sparse light. Little living souls, forever outnumbered by the dead.

The thread *burns*. The heat spreads like wings from her ribcage. The woman pants slightly, sweat dripping from her forehead. But she keeps walking. She looks down at her companions who have remained silence ever since they'd entered Death's domain. There is no time for rest. Be quick …

She knows the plot as soon as she lays eyes on it. It's at a fork in the mossy path. The only currently-living plant is a withering tree at the plot's center, its long roots cracking the nearby tiles. From its barren branches hangs a single sanguine apple. She's drawn to it like a magnet. The thread sings …

Be wary. The woman resists the urge to pluck the cartoonishly perfect apple from its stem. It's too easy, like the tree's wearing a giant "touch me" sign. A trap from Death, then; a honeypot to catch wayward flies. But her guiding string isn't a trap. It's an ethereal organ, an extension of her will. And it's pulsing rapidly, as if filled with feverish blood. The soul is here. It has to be.

Be cunning. Stringy dried brambles surround the tree like gnarled hands. The woman pushes them away with her feet. There's nothing but gray branches and fallen leaves.

No. Those aren't leaves. The woman bends down. The thread is scalding now. Huddled beneath the brambles are dark velvety spears. Black earth tongues. Mushrooms, not dying, but thriving. She caresses their bodies, and the thread suddenly snaps. The greenhouse falls away. Tiles and soil and panes of glass drift away, and the woman falls. The skulls hang in the air, orbiting her like osseous moons. Their ghostly figures are gone, but the flames behind their sockets remain. She hears Death's voice:

"A deal…"

"Is a deal," echoes the raven.

"Is a deal," then the rabbit.

"Is a deal," then the fox.

"The soul of Hazel Knight is yours."

There the sound of rushing air, then blackness, then—

"Oomph!" The woman's lungs punctuate the thick night fog as she hits the asphalt. The familiar sounds of the unfamiliar city surround her once more. She is alone at Charon's Carnival once more, and the skulls on the ground are merely skulls once more. The disgusting candles have burned down to stinking puddles of wax, their flames barely flickering.

The woman stands. Her body feels the same as it did before. Her feet still ache and she shivers from the cold. But there is a lightness there that was absent before, as if an iron weight had been removed from her chest that she hadn't even known existed before. That place in her soul—in every soul—where death lurked and waited, where every struggle and anxiety stemmed from like a great tree, is gone. She is untethered. Unshackled from her own demise.

Hazel smiles. For what does a deathless witch have to fear?

THE MIDDLE OF NOWHERE

By Stacey Ryall

"Eye spy, something beginning with 'M'."

"Moon?" I answered.

My little brother threw himself back in the seat, beaten.

"Well, it's not a great game for the middle of the night in the middle of nowhere," I offered him.

Dad always turned off the high beams when he saw a car approaching us. So, he groaned when a car came from behind us, its blinding headlights beaming through the rear window. I had already marked it down as the first car we had seen in the two hours since we had left the highway.

"Pass me if you're in such a bloody hurry!"

He slowed and pulled over to the side of the gravel road. He waited for it to pass, but suddenly the lights clicked off. I turned to see that it had gone. Dad continued to drive slowly, looking out the windows, searching for its headlights traveling down an invisible back road. But there were no traces of it, not even the flying dust that it had appeared to be kicking up. It had gone, like the clouds that had disappeared to reveal the circle of moonlight beaming down on the sparse plains.

I had worn out all the songs on my MP3 player in the first five hours of the drive. The only radio channel we were getting reception from was 86.6 FM, easy-listening at its worst. *Crooners from Hell.* Dad tapped his fingers to 'Black Magic.' To me, it would have been more appropriate if the frequency was 66.6.

Like staring out into the dark nothingness wasn't daunting enough, my mind was now plagued with the idea that we'd just had an encounter with the 'Ghost Car' of outback New South Wales.

"Oooh...ghost car...ghost car... GHOST CAR!" Jack taunted as if he had read my mind. Dad chuckled under his breath. I pretended I didn't see him frantically looking everywhere for the 'disappearing car.'

"Gazza told me that once he was followed home from the pub by a UFO," he said, turning to Mum.

"Gazza would have been rolling drunk. He probably thought it flew out of his arse-hole too, didn't he?" she replied.

Jack laughed hysterically, and at the pointy end of a long trip, his laughter was contagious. I giggled along.

"Come on, I know you've heard the stories too, haven't you?" Dad continued. Mum went quiet again.

"What stories, Mum? What stories?" Jack and I had stopped laughing.

"It's okay. People get bored living out here. They make stuff up to entertain themselves, to scare city-folk."

So it wasn't a ghost car. It was a perfectly normal car full of a perfectly normal family, like us, *and it was sucked into oblivion by a UFO.* I was even more eager to make it to Grandma's farmhouse now. I could feel relief just anticipating the moment we saw the huge ancient gum tree that signaled the entrance to the farm driveway.

It was a clear night now that the clouds had parted. The full moon shone through the trees to make peculiar patterns on the gravel road. Every now and then I would see a lone tree standing out in the middle of a sparse paddock, its few leaves blowing with the night breeze. I thought about how lonely and afraid I would be if it was me standing there. If suddenly a beam of light picked me up out of the car and dumped me somewhere all alone, leaving me to find my way home. Dad opened his window, and let the cool night air swirl in. He poked his head out and sucked in the fresh air.

"You don't want me to drive? You've been driving for hours … you look tired," Mum offered Dad.

"I'm fine. We're nearly there."

We had made this trip up to the country many times before. Mum and Dad tried to visit Grandma at least twice a year, though it was a far drive and that wasn't always possible. Someone else my age might have found it quite the imposition, but I'd rather have been stuck in a car for seven hours with my family than with my girly friends—wasting our school holidays at the shopping mall or something.

But I *was* getting anxious to make it to Grandma's. I couldn't sleep in cars now, like I had when I was little. I was too alert, too attentive. The trip was taking longer than usual. Although I had enjoyed taking in the scenery during the day, it was now pitch black and my over-active mind was in fine form. I wondered how well Dad remembered these narrow roads. As I looked ahead of the car, all that was visible was the dirt road as far as the head lights reached. The moon was again covered by clouds.

But Mum saw something else.

"What's that?" she cried, interrupting the silence.

I looked in the direction she was pointing and saw red and blue lights flashing in the distance. As we got closer, Dad said, "That's the turn off to the farm."

I could tell in his voice that he was worried. So was I.

"It's a crash," said Mum.

"Grandma?!" I shrieked.

Dad picked up speed, then slowed down as we approached the flashing lights. I could see from a fair distance that it was a sedan, just like ours, and it was wrapped around the old gum tree.

"Oh God." Mum gasped.

"There's Grandma!" Jack yelled as we all turned to see her leaning on the front gate, saddened, propped up by police officers, and a blanket wrapped around her.

"She's okay," Dad sighed.

"Then who …"

We slowly drove past, all staring at the wreck out the side windows. It was a mess, hardly anything left of it. Mum urged us to turn away. I did, though I saw Jack try to peek over my shoulder. I quickly put a hand across his face. By the time he knocked my arm away, we had passed it.

"It looks like the driver was probably suffering from fatigue. In a hurry to arrive at his destination, he probably took this corner a little too fast. I'm terribly sorry for your loss ma'am …" the officer sighed, shook his head, and decided there was no more he could say.

The little old lady stood quietly. She would ask no questions.

Who could ever answer them?

As we moved further away from the wreck, the road and the countryside went dark again. Mum and Dad hadn't spoken a word. We didn't stop. We just continued driving into the night. The announcer on 86.6 introduced another old classic; 'Black Magic' by Sammy Davis, Jr.

Dad began tapping on the steering wheel, and Jack poked me in the side.

"Oi, wanna play eye-spy?" He smiled.

GOOSEBUMPS

By Joy Johns

It started when she was little.

She learned pretty quickly that no one would believe her, not about this.

It didn't matter if she had good grades and brushed her teeth every night, if she kept her church dresses clean, if she said 'Yes sir or No Ma'am 'and was always perfectly polite.

She had been good, clean, polite, articulate, all the things that generally made adults listen.

She knew what grownups were like about Santa Claus and the easter bunny … but she figured that they believed in angels and God and a holy ghost, they said they believed in demons, and they believed in the Devil, so why wouldn't they believe her about this?

The first lesson was that there was no help. She would have to deal with this by herself.

The nuns at the orphanage would wash her mouth out with soap and call her a liar, and it would be in this surprised, disappointed tone that hurt so much more, after all she was their good girl.

The other kids had never really liked her much; she had never really fit in. The other girls never understood why she wanted to play with fire trucks or dinosaurs and wasn't interested in dolls. Honestly, she thought it was weird that they wanted to be mothers when they had never even had a mother. What was so great about dolls anyway? They stared at you with those eerie perfect faces, and their eyes always looked like they were following you around the room. And they had the most annoying fake crying and some of the dolls wore diapers and wet themselves. Honestly, what was fun about cleaning up fake pee?

She wouldn't trade her dinosaurs or her fire truck for a hundred stupid dolls. The fire truck could put out fires and save lives and the dinosaurs were like dragons, but they were real, or they used to be a long time ago. Her games of pretend were never about making dinner or changing babies, they were daring rescues in collapsing buildings consumed in raging infernos or they were the earth millions of years ago with T Rexes and triceratops on an Earth so different from the one she knew. It was a strange world with strange creatures.

The boys sort of half accepted her, but that was in some ways worse than the eye rolls and the gum in her pigtails from the other girls because they would let her in sometimes and for a little while she would feel like she had real friends, but then they would sneak off to the cafeteria or go play baseball and a hundred other things that they never let her go along to and she would find herself once more a stranger, an outsider. That somehow stung so much worse than just outright dislike.

She was an alien. Something that just never fit, never really belonged. It was why she tried so hard to make the nuns happy, they at least were caring.

So, she put her head down and done her homework and kept her dresses clean even though she thought dresses were dumb because she just wanted so desperately to feel like she belonged somewhere to somebody.

She was quiet about her too-tight shoes and the blisters on her heels, she bit her lip and sat still when sister Anne brushed both her hair and her ears even though it hurt. The sisters told her she was a good girl and that she would get adopted someday.

But that was before she knew about Rule 1 and Rule 2.

Rule 1: *They won't believe you. No matter how good you are.*

The night she learned Rule 1 had been terrifying. The streetlights were snapping on one at a time and she was running back to the orphanage, racing the darkness and the electric pop of the orange soda coloured light as they snapped on like giant flashlights.

The Nuns had a lot of *rules that could not be broken.* But the biggest one was always be back inside before dark, before the streetlights came on fully. She had been out further than usual, nearly to the edge of the woods at the end of the property; the other kids had been particularly mean that afternoon, so she got as far away from everyone else as possible. She had her favourite book in her pocket and who needed those jerks when she had daisies and dandelions and a book she loved?

She had been so lost in the adventures of the children in Narnia that she missed the creeping darkness as it closed over her like deep water, slowly drowning the day. She had had to race so hard for the doors, she felt like something was watching her the whole way, just on her heels and her arms came up in goosebumps. She was absolutely sure that if she turned to look there would be something there, in the darkness, just behind her and waiting to devour her. Her heart pounding, she crossed the threshold, slamming the door shut on the night behind her as she panted in the bright safety of the well-lit hallway.

That night, she couldn't shake the feeling that something was *off.* After bedtime, she stayed awake staring up at the ceiling, listening to Chrissy's snoring and the creaking of Laura's squeaky old bed, which made noise every time she moved on it.

Snap thud. Snap thud.

Something moved under her bed. An icy chill covered her body and all the hairs on her arms stood up. Her breath fogged in the dark as the temperature dropped. With a growing terror, she watched as her blanket was slowly, menacingly pulled off of the end of the bed and underneath. A clawed hand reached up for her ankle and she was sure that it was going to drag her under the bed.

She screamed bloody murder, and as Chrissy and Laura were staring to wake up, the light snapped on and Mother Superior was there asking what had happened. She described the awful hand that had tried to reach for her, and Mother Superior told her it had just been a bad dream.

She explained its pale grey skin, how it had just looked so *wrong*. The long black nails, the jagged points of them snagging in the fabric of her rainbow blanket. the way it had searched for her ankle.

She had argued and cried, and Mother Superior had been gentle, but firm that it wasn't real. Night after night it came, and the nuns' tolerance began to fray.

Eventually, they took her to a doctor who made her look at ink blots and take tests. There were so many questions, and eventually the nuns had taken her home. They told her that she had night terrors. But as things got worse, as she kept insisting that the *thing* was real, they seemed to think that she was lying for attention. After the second time they put the bitter, burning soap in her mouth, she realised that they would never believe her.

She was truly alone. That was when Rule 1 was born, on the night she spat soap in the sink for the second time. *Don't tell them, they won't believe you.*

That Sunday she stole a holy water vial from the store that the nuns used to help fund the church. That night she waited, sweat on her palms and in her armpits as she clutched the vial to her chest. When the monster pulled her blanket down and began reaching for her ankle, this time she let it find her. She watched as its bony, sharp, clawed fingers wrapped around her foot, and she tipped holy water on it. The skin hissed and bubbled, cracking and burning. The creature pulled its hand back and she scrambled like lightning under the bed after it, fueled by pure adrenaline and the stupid bravery of small children who haven't yet had the world beat common sense into them. She saw it then, the monster under her bed, and she snarled, "Take it all, bitch" as she dumped the rest of the vial on it. She had no idea what the words meant; she had overheard some of the older kids say things like that when the nuns were out of earshot, and it just felt right.

The monster scuttled, crab-like, from under the bed across the room and the up the wall. It moved like a spider, from the wall to the ceiling and then through the open window to the outside, running away, screeching into the dark with strange jerky movements.

After that she pulled out her hello kitty diary and started writing her *Rules of Survival*.

Under Rule One she wrote: *Always keep holy water nearby.*

Then there was Rule 2: *If you can see them, they can see you, and they will come for you.*

It was Halloween. The nuns did not approve of the holiday, calling it a pagan travesty. But the social workers that liaised with the orphanage had suggested that they have an open day for prospective adoptions; she promised it could be a bit of a fundraiser too.

So now, for the first time, the halls were decorated with pumpkins, fake spiderwebs, and bunting in crimped black and orange paper, and she felt a thrill at it.

"Sarah! Come here!" The social worker, Jen, waved at her from across the room. She had her natural hair pressed into perfect thirties waves. She wore a red dress and red lipstick that set off her warm, brown skin perfectly. She looked so glamourous.

"Who are you dressed as, Miss Jen?" She asked, her eyes wide in wonder.

"A star called Josephine Baker," Miss Jen answered with a smile.

Sarah was in awe and Miss Jen smiled. "You know Josephine Baker was a real Hollywood star who moved to Paris and had a pet cheetah named Chiquita, and she adopted 12 children."

Sarah was in complete awe. Miss Jen bent down and said, "Come with me. There are some nice people who want to meet you."

Sarah put her hand in Miss Jen's and let herself be lead through the crowd, taking solace in the warm coconut smell of her one familiar through all the years of her life. Miss Jen who was always kind and who always had time to listen to every child, but especially to Sarah, who never seemed to be able to make friends. She was, Sarah believed deeply, the best grown-up in the world.

The nuns had refused to dress up for the occasion, but someone had persuaded them to let the face painter add a dash of whimsy, and even Sister Mary Margaret sported a purple butterfly wing design that looked almost like a super hero mask.

Sarah was ushered over to a nice-looking couple who were dressed up as Dorothy from *The Wizard of Oz* and a pirate with an eye patch and a real, live parrot on his shoulder.

They were Mr. and Mrs. Ming, and they were kind and fun and they really listened to Sarah, even when she wanted to talk about dinosaurs. Their parrot was named Max because Max Ming sounded cool to Mr. Ming, who liked comic books.

Weeks went by and Sarah started to really believe that this time would be different, that she might have a real family. She had gone to sleepovers with the Mings and Miss Jen, and those nights were her favourite. She got bath bombs and special snacks, and Mrs. Ming sang her lullabies at night. For the first time, she felt seen and loved, just for herself. At night, as she was drifting off to sleep, she practiced in her imagination, for the day when she could call them her mama and daddy. She would look up into Mrs. Ming's warm brown eyes and run into her open arms saying "I knew you would find me someday, Mama. I knew I belonged to someone. I waited for you my whole life." And her mama and her daddy would tell her that she had always been theirs and that they had waited for her too.

Tonight was the first night she would stay overnight with just the Mings. Miss Jen said they were ready to try a sleepover without her. Sarah was practically a livewire of excitement. Soon, she was sure they would tell her that they were going to keep her.

It was midnight when she woke up to the sound of tapping. She thought at first that it was a tree branch; it was the same sound during windy nights when the old oak tree lashed its branches into the glass window. But then its too-long fingers spread out and its face pressed against the glass, and she saw it. And worse, it saw her, *and it knew*. It had a milk-pale face and eyes like a spider, black like small dark ink blots which sat in small groups around its head. Its mouth was full of row after row of teeth, some like needles and others more like sharks' teeth. Sarah felt the icy cold fingers of real fear spread through her as the thing reached with elongated fingers into the casement and unlocked her window, sliding it up. She had let her guard down. She had thought that she had finally found the happily ever after, the storybook part of her life.

New rule: If you see them and they see you, they will know, and they will come get you because you can see them.

New rule: there's no place like home. I don't get that. I can't have that and thinking that I do will get me killed.

Sarah thought of the Mings sleeping downstairs and how much she loved them. She thought of how much danger she was to them. She understood that she couldn't afford to believe that they could save her from the monsters. It wouldn't go away if she turned on the lights. If she ran to them, scared, asking them to save her, she knew what would happen. It wouldn't stop, not now that it realized she had seen it. She could run into the arms of her would-be parents and it would follow. If she were lucky, it would only kill her in front of them, and they would scream as she was eviscerated in front of them by something invisible. Assuming it didn't kill them too, they would be accused of her murder. *It was invisible, your Honour,* would not fly as a defense. She saw now that she couldn't get adopted. Wherever she went, they found her; at least in the church it was harder to get at her and she was surrounded by holy weapons. She could control it better at the church. If she survived this, she would make sure she never got adopted. For tonight, she needed to save the family she could never have.

Sarah watched as the demon began opening the window slowly,· inch by inch. She had to stop being scared. Now wasn't the time to be frozen. Now was the time to protect. It was toying with her, drawing out her fear. She saw its nostrils catch her scent, and it opened its terrible mouth. A thick, forked tongue darted out like a snake through its rows of wickedly sharp, glinting teeth.

No fear. She slapped herself hard and the pain cleared her head, her fear replaced with a cold rage. She fed the rage, letting it simmer into something feral. She ripped the hair tie from her wrist and shoved her long blonde hair into ponytail. She looked around the room for her backpack and pulled out the stash she always kept for emergencies.

The demon slid into the room, tall and bone-thin. Its clawed fingers were deadly-looking, but spindly. It gave her an evil smile as it climbed the wall and scuttled toward the ceiling like a spider. Sarah figured it thought she was just another stupid kid, the same mistake the others had made. She would be ready. She faked fear while she doused the sewing shears in her pocket with holy water. They were big, sharp, old steel things that she had swiped from the crafts room. Social services and the nuns searched for weapons, but scissors, which she kept bundled with stacks of craft paper and rows of paper snowflakes, she could claim were art therapy. Sarah faked falling and she let out a muffled cry of pretend terror. The demon dropped, its claws reaching for her. She played helpless.

"You can see me. It's been so long since I ate the tender flesh of a Seer. Your eyes will be delicious." The words hissed over her skin and into her mind. It lunged.

Now she screamed to herself. She smashed a vial of holy water into the monster's face as she brought the shears down with all her might on its bony wrist.

The demon screamed as she severed its right hand, the holy water glowing on the shears' blades and heating them a molten white. It was like wielding a sword, she realized, as she watched them burn and cut through the demon like it was made of butter. It scrabbled backwards away from her, blinded by the holy water in every eye except for the smallest one furthest to the left on its head.

"What are you?" the demon hissed, and she smiled at the hint of fear.

"Not helpless," Sarah replied. The demon lashed out like lightning, and she was thrown backwards, hard. The shears went flying from her grasp. The blow was enough for the demon to get its remaining hand around her neck.

"I will carve you up and eat you slowly."

Sarah kicked out and felt her toes connect with the scissors. She pulled the rosary from her pocket, the one carved from olive wood from Jerusalem that Sister Mary Margret had on display in her office. It had been blessed by a priest; Sarah had stolen it after her mouth had been washed with soap for the third time. She stabbed the crucifix into the demon's hand, and it shrieked and let her go. As it recoiled, watching in horror as the crucifix burned its way through its hand, it tried to pull at the wooden beads with the stump of its right arm and then its teeth. But the sacred olive wood set small fires when it touched them, its skin boiling and bursting in the way of the worst kind of burns.

Sarah gripped the shears with her toes and slid them backwards towards herself, her fingers closing on the cold steel handle. The demon's face was a mess. The skin around its mouth had burned away, leaving it with exposed jaw and teeth. It lashed out blindly and managed to scrape Sarah's scalp with a grazing blow. Blood welled up as pain sliced through her. She blinked hard as the blood trickled down into her left eye. She heard voices. The Ming's were waking up, coming to check on her. She had to kill it now if she was going to protect them. Her eyes welled with tears as her heart broke for the family she had dreamed of, with lullabies and hugs, a pet parrot that learned her name and followed her everywhere. A dad that never raised his voice or his hands. A mother that wanted to tuck her in every single night.

She loved them, and she couldn't keep them. She was heartbroken. Rage at the unfairness of it fuelled her, and a red haze descended as she let it carry her on a wave of violence.

Sarah gripped the shears and stabbed them through the demon's remaining hand, pinning it to the desk to her left. She climbed the dresser in a flash and used the rosary like a garrotte. Planting her foot into the demon's back, she leaned all the way back, until the rosary cut through the neck, severing its head. The remains of the demon vanished into Sulphur-scented black ashes and bones, which disintegrated in a matter of seconds.

Sarah quickly wiped the blood from her face and shoved her beanie on to disguise the injury. A second later, the Mings burst in, turning on the lights, blinding her. They were greeted by the sight of Sarah by an open bag as if she were packing, surrounded by a trashed room, a pair of scissors stabbed into her desk and strange black smears on the floor.

They hugged her and asked her if she was OK. Then she did what she had to: she made it look like she was mentally unstable, a flight risk, which in the aftermath, was not a hard sell.

She was back in the orphanage before the sun rose, crying herself to sleep for weeks in the secure wing with bars on the windows and only the nuns for company.

Ten years later.

At eighteen, Sarah finally made her legal, legitimate exit from the institution, she spent a full year faking therapy sessions so that they could diagnose her with a disorder and "treat" her successfully. She faked diaries and learned to hide the small blue pill in the gap between her back molars. By the time she aged out of the system, they absolutely believed she was just a nice girl who had overcome a disorder. She was free at last.

She tilted her head up to the warmth of the sun, her closed eyes filling with the orange haze of amber light that shone down on her upturned face. Her sneakers were thin-soled, and she could feel the bumps of the gravel under foot. This was the furthest she had been outside the walls in years. Her backpack was full of stolen relics and holy water. Anything and everything she thought she would need to stay alive on the outside.

The rich, soothing smell of the pine trees filtered through on the breeze and she felt a warm, wet feeling at the corner of her left eye… a tear, she realised. At last, she was free.

BUILD-A-TWIN

By Torrence Bryan

It grew out of loneliness, as most ideas do. Good or bad. For better or for worse. Of course, I couldn't tell you which this ended up being. I'd have to leave that up to you to decide. But in the beginning, I was lonely, and there was the idea.

I had spent most of my life alone, and I was tired of it. It was time for me to change that. But if I were to find someone who would appreciate me for all of my quirks and idiosyncrasies, I couldn't just *procure* them. I wasn't a savage. I wouldn't force someone to be my partner if they had no interest in doing so. But *creating* a partner? Now there was an idea that just might work.

They wouldn't be just a partner then. They would be better than a spouse, more perfect than a sibling. They would be what I had craved all along: a twin.

I started with the right arm. My bank teller had the most beautiful skin, tawny and freckled, with long fingers, and nails she liked to paint in bright colors. I loved those nails. They made my day every time I saw them. And so, I decided, she would be the first.

I invited her out for lunch, and she accepted. A drink, a light meal, one more drink–please, I insist–and a tablet I had placed at the bottom of her glass. She grew drowsy, and I helped her back to my car. When she passed out in the passenger seat, I drove back to my house, dragging her down to my perfectly prepared basement. She slept through the whole thing, even when I brought out the bone saw, slicing through that perfectly tawny skin as smooth as butter. I tried to cut around the arteries as best I could, not wanting her to lose any more blood than necessary, and wanting to preserve the longevity of the arm with the brightly painted fingernails while it waited in my freezer. And still she slept, while I bandaged her stump, and brought her back to the bank, resting her in the quiet alley behind her place of work.

Like I said, I wasn't a *savage*. I had no wish to cause her pain. I just wanted her right arm. The newspaper reports said she had been attacked on her way back from lunch, and I smiled, pleased I had gotten away with it. Of course, I never returned to that bank, either.

I hoped to find the left arm next, but as most plans do, it went awry. Instead, I found myself eyeing the thick, muscled leg of my taxi driver.

"You look like you work out," I offered. *You look like you would be willing to hike with me to places never before seen. You look like you could dive off a cliff without any fear. You look perfect.*

He grinned, flexing his thigh in his (too-short) shorts. "Never miss a session."

And ever since my plan was in place, I never missed a chance. I whipped out the chloroform I had rolling around in my bag, soaking the tea towel next to it, and stuffed it over my taxi driver's face.

Luckily, we had been approaching a stop, and the car harmlessly rolled to a standstill. I took this as a sign from the universe that I had made the right decision. I jumped out of the backseat, and shoved my taxi driver and his (muscular) thighs across the console into the passenger seat.

Another short drive to my house, another quick return to my basement. The bone saw and I were like old friends by now. I prepared my taxi driver, said a quick thanks for what his body was about to provide for me, and dug into the flesh and through the bone. Blood splattered onto the waiting sheets, pooling where the tarps collected. It was kind of pretty when you looked at it.

Blood. The life force that propelled all of us, and would one day propel my twin. I couldn't wait, smiling as I stitched both sides of the artery back up. The jagged edges of my cut on the leg would need to be cleaned up, the meat on the inside a rich red, dripping, but it wasn't anything I couldn't fix with my sewing kit.

And then it was back to the cab for my taxi driver, neatly packaged up, sans one leg. At least his taxi was an automatic. He wouldn't need two legs to make a living–like I said, I wasn't *cruel*.

Of course, not all of them were successes. I lost the donor who gave me the right leg–an older man I passed on a quiet trail near my house in the evening. He was about the same height as the taxi driver, and obviously an avid hiker. He would be perfect. I couldn't miss the opportunity. The trail was secluded enough, but I didn't have the tools to get him back to my house. I had to make do and perform the surgery in the woods. Unfortunately, he lost too much blood and didn't survive. I left his body hidden in the trees while I dragged my prize back to my house, desperate to get it in the cooler before it rotted completely.

They found him the next day. The cops called it a fucked-up kind of killer, taking prizes to mark his victims. Of course, they didn't understand. How could they possibly understand? It was beyond comprehension to them, because what I was doing had never been done before.

The left arm was uneventful, coming from a swimmer at a gym a few towns over. I painfully befriended them before inviting them out for a drink. A sweaty evening full of empty beer glasses later, and I was the proud new owner of a left arm. I stood in my freezer, admiring my twin coming to life. Soon. Soon, we'd be together.

The torso was harder. Not wanting to maim someone that badly–like I said, I wasn't *crazy*–I began to attend funerals for people I didn't know. And then one day, weeks later, everything fell into place, like it was meant to be.

An open casket. A blood clot in the leg that had killed him. But the body itself was in its early thirties, in great condition, and ripe for the picking. So, I hung around the funeral, pretending to dab at my eyes when really I wanted them all to shut up and leave so I could have my torso.

Eventually we made our way to the graveyard, they quit their whining, and we all went home.

And that night, I snuck back out to the freshly dug grave. It was peaceful, being in the graveyard at night. There was nothing else but me and the bodies. Kind of what it would be like once my twin was here. And after hours of digging, I reached the casket. Since this body was already dead, there was no point in dragging it back to my house to make sure the surgery was clean.

I brought out my knives, and began cutting through the thick, clammy flesh. It was harder to cut through a dead body than a real body. Wasn't as alive. Wasn't as malleable. But I did it, sweat and blood dripping down my face and down my arms. I did it for me. For my twin. For *us*. And by the time the sun began to rise, taking the place of the moon, I had my torso sitting in my freezer.

But the hardest was the head. I couldn't take a dead body for that one. They needed to be alive for as long as possible when I cut into them, so that I could detach their head and their brain, and immediately stitch it onto the body of my twin. It would require some planning, and some choosing. And someone with a damn good brain if I was going to be stuck with them for a lifetime.

First, I prepared my twin's body, painstakingly stitching the body parts together. It wasn't easy, as each piece had a different trail of veins and arteries, but eventually I had them all together, a headless body sitting inside my freezer, waiting to come alive.

Then I sought out the perfect head. I needed a willing sacrifice. But after weeks of searching—*too boring, too self-centered, too ugly*—I turned to the want ads.

And there she was.

Looking for a good time, not a long time. Cindy. 555-0189.

I called the number, my fingers trembling. Could this be who I was looking for? A sweet voice answered, announcing herself as Cindy. And when I told her exactly what I was looking for—*a lifetime partner, the perfect brain, selfless*—she was all too happy to come to my place.

I was so excited, setting up my place for Cindy's arrival. I stalked her social media eagerly, wanting to know everything about her. She was everything I had been looking for and more. She was just ... lonely. *Perfect.* The day arrived, and I flew around my house in a frenzy. I wanted everything to be perfect. I wanted her to see what we could be together.

I had hoped to woo her into understanding what I wanted, to make her a willing participant, but when she arrived, I was all too excited to grab her by the throat and drag her downstairs to my basement. This time I had two tables waiting. One with my twin's headless body on it. And the other, for Cindy. I let go of her throat so I could strap her into the table.

"What the hell are you doing?" she cried.

"I can't wait to show you." I was so happy. "Just wait and see!"

I brought out the knife first, not wanting Cindy to die too quick and lose all that precious blood in her brain. I began slicing through the tender skin of her neck, and Cindy screamed.

I stopped slicing, looking at the rich, red blood dripping from the gaping wound I had made. I needed to be quicker. "I need you to stay quiet for me, Cindy. Quiet and still. Otherwise, this won't work."

Except Cindy didn't stay quiet or still as I cut, carefully cutting out veins and arteries, avoiding the thick spinal column. She stopped screaming when I cut through her vocal cords, a strange humming coming from her instead. I brought out my bone saw for the spinal column, slicing through it as efficiently as I could. It was thicker than it looked, and all the while Cindy watched me. I couldn't tell if it was horror or excitement in her eyes. Maybe both. Cindy's eyes closed as I finally snapped through her spinal cord. It was okay. I knew my twin would come back to life in minutes.

With bloody hands, I carefully raised Cindy's head up off the table, and carried it over to my twin's body. I couldn't believe this was happening. I was so excited. Too excited, if the growing cock in my pants was any indication. This was everything I had ever hoped for. With a careful touch, I began to attach Cindy's head onto my twin's body. Except now it wasn't Cindy's head anymore. Now it was my twin's, and they were about to be born. I was going to give birth to my twin. First, I reattached the veins. Then the arteries. And finally, the spinal column, reattached with a thick sinewy twine.

I stepped back, eyes wide. I had done it. I had really done it. Here was my twin, ready to live life with me. It was beautiful, and I'd never be alone again. My twin blinked its eyes. It rolled its head from side to side. It got to its feet, staggering, getting used to its new body. Its new form.

I had never seen anything more perfect in my life. The different skin tones all neatly stitched together, fusing different lives, different forms, different souls together in all of their beauty. Here it was—my twin.

I loved it immediately.

Except the way it was walking towards me, malice in its eyes, didn't seem like love. It seemed hurt. Traumatized. Like the different body parts were remembering everything I had put them through. I took a step back. Surely, they could understand this was for the best. Once they had been just a piece of a normal person. Now they were an essential part of something new. Something special. Still my twin stumbled towards me, arms outstretched, moaning as their vocal cords sprang to life.

Like I said. Good or bad. For better or for worse. I'd have to leave that up to you to decide.

SCYTHE AND SICKLE

By Mae Dexter

BANG! I nearly tore the back door off its hinges as I threw it open, running out like a woman on fire. Which I nearly was. *They* were nipping at my heels. I had to make it to the gate and into the cemetery. Behind me, I caught a glimpse of bright neon eyes and the shadow of what looked like … dogs?

But no dogs I'd ever seen. I also realized just how out of shape I was. If I survived this, I swore I'd join a gym or at least try to cut back on the snacks.

Missing the last step off the porch, I nearly lost my footing. But through some kind of Gods' given miracle, I carried on unscathed. The gate. I had to … make it … to the gate. If I could make it, I'd be free. My family would be safe. Tonight, I had been smarter and warded the house— save for the dining room and kitchen and back door. The previous night I had only warded the upstairs bedrooms and stairs. Tonight, I had thought ahead in case those fuckers came for me. Now as I ran, I realized it would be even better if I could get them to cross the gate and maybe take out one of them. That was my hope, at least.

Seeing the old gate tucked into the overgrowth of plants, I held out my hand. *Please let it work!* With mere inches to spare, the gate swung open on its own. I'd made it. I dropped my head down, breathed, and didn't look back. I'd made it. I was safe and so was my little family. The yelp and sulfur smell filling the air meant I'd taken at least one with me.

Good.

Drawing in another breath, I turned around to find the two remaining great beasts staring at me. I managed to flip them both off before they vanished. *Safe for another night.* While I desperately wanted to go back in the house, to check on my spouse and daughter, I couldn't. Not yet. I had to talk to *him* first. It was a rather cold night for October, but it didn't bother me; it never had. And it certainly didn't bother *him*.

He had better fucking be there.

Normally, I would slow down and enjoy the walk. I would enjoy the quiet cemetery after the living had departed for the day. Now was the time of the dead. But not tonight. My steps slowed past the rickety fence that surrounded my favorite headstone and twisted old elm tree. If the fence was there to keep me out or its resident in, tonight wasn't the time to find out.

I lifted a heavy arm to wave to the spirit leaning against the towering elm growing behind the stone. I was careful not to use her name, though I knew it. *Mathilda.* She'd been tried as a witch centuries before. I also knew that names had power and made a point of never using anyone's name in the cemetery.

After my father died, and I was old enough to understand, my grandmother had taught me many things. She had become my guardian after my mother had fallen "ill."

In reality, she was in a mental health facility, though I didn't understand why as a child. As an adult, I knew she'd been driven insane by grief after her husband, my father's, death.

I should visit her. If I survived.

Anyway, this valuable lesson about names came about on one of our many picnic visits to the cemetery, visiting my father and grandfather's graves. I'd just begun to read on my own and started to read aloud a name on a headstone. Her hand covered my mouth so quickly I thought for sure I had cursed.

"My girl, you must *never* utter names you see here."

I looked at her, puzzled. "But some of them have such pretty names."

"They are, but names have power, my sweet. You must only use them when you need them. And right now, you don't need them." She reached into the worn basket and pulled out a pint of raspberries. "Now go on and leave these by that old fence, would you?" I took the container and did as she said.

I snapped out of the memory as I looked towards the grave again. She floated hopefully toward the fence for her favorite treat–fresh raspberries as an offering of respect, though she could no longer consume them. "Sorry, not tonight." I moved on towards the pond. I didn't see *him*, but that didn't mean he wasn't there. He was always watching, waiting. Protecting what was his.

"Come on. I know you're here. My spider senses are tingling…" He materialized a few feet away, his pitch-black cloak billowing in the night and a hood over his head. I approached quietly. I may have been pissed off and scared, but respect for the dead and all. And for Death himself. He turned and spoke.

"Hello little one, you're out rather late."

My voice shook. "Dad."

I watched him consider me and how I must look to him. There were bits of greenery in my short, cropped hair, sweat stains under my arms, and my new jeans were torn–*fuck*. And I stank of sulfur.

You must be confused. It's OK. I was too. Death has a daughter? I was nearly six when I found out. I only knew that the man who had played with me in the yard, chased the monsters from my room, and sung me to sleep each night of the first few years of my life had died. A heart attack, they said. But even then, something had seemed off to my young, inquisitive mind. I had always been a little different, even then. I'd lived in the house by the cemetery all my life. I'd played with my friends no one else could see or hear.

But my parents and grandmother never treated me differently.

They told me to keep all of it between the four of us. Other people wouldn't understand. They would ask questions. Call us names. Some people inherited corporations, or chain retail locations, but Death, as it turned out, was our family business.

Lucky fucking me.

Thinking back, it wasn't all bad. My dad had lived longer than his father and his grandfather before him. Grandmother attributed his longer life to having a daughter rather than a son. I had been the only firstborn girl in at least six generations. Other girls had been born in that time, but always the second or third child. Until me and then my own daughter.

Before I was born, all iterations of Death had been male. My birth changed things. My father didn't drop dead right after my birth, as had been tradition. And my own daughter was thirteen and I was still kicking. A good sign. So, I didn't fear Death, like most, because I would become Death.

My father spoke, bringing me back to the present. "What was that?" I asked.

"I said you look like Hell."

I laughed. A wisp of grey came out of his robe where an arm and hand should be. It brushed a bit of dirt off my nose and pulled leaves from my hair. It cupped my cheek as my father spoke again. "Care to explain?"

I took a calming breath. "I was just chased into the cemetery by three Hellhounds. At least, that's what I think they were." I hadn't had the time to stop in my escape attempt to snap him a picture. "Huge dogs with bright neon green eyes, reeking of sulfur."

He didn't say anything. The grey wisp rested near where his face would be, and I could almost hear his finger tapping at his chin. "Is this the first time it's happened?"

I nodded. "The last two times had been in my dreams—nightmares." I shuddered. At least in my nightmares, I'd been far enough away from the beasts that they never caught me before they gave up and vanished. "I don't know what made tonight different, but I had an indication it was coming."

"You did? From whom?"

"The spirit fenced in with the old elm tree." It had been an odd thing. I had been trimming the vines and other greenery away from the gate in the yard yesterday. Why I bothered, I'll never know, as they were always all back in the morning. The spirit's voice had suddenly in my head telling me, *They're coming, be ready to ward and run to us.* I told my father all of this and he chuckled. "I don't know what's so funny, Dad, but I've had a long night." *And life,* I added silently, dropping to the bench behind me.

"I'm sorry. It isn't funny. In fact, it's incredibly serious. I just thought I was the only one she talked to."

Like knows like, I thought.

"She's an ancestor of ours." He looked towards her grave and gave her a small bow. "That fence is there to protect her. Did your grandmother never tell you? It's heavily warded. Her spirit is too valuable for us to lose to Hell."

Clearly there was a lot Grandma had omitted in my education. "Cool history lesson, Dad. Look, I need to figure what they want or how to fight these assholes."

He chuckled again. "I'll let the language slide this time." Still my dad. I'd sometimes taken to calling him Steve Rogers, but he didn't understand the reference. "They want you. They know you've exhausted your time on earth and it's time to go. And they don't much like us having a monopoly on the business of death."

You'd think they'd have a bigger issue with funeral directors.

I considered this. "You also lived longer than you should have," I added, as though this was a new bit of information.

He sighed. "I did, but I shouldn't have. I was supposed to die the week after you were born. But you changed that, gave me time. Not much, but more time than any of us had been granted before you." Death paused then. "Look, I don't know why you changed things. But something about you is special. Hell doesn't like that, and Heaven doesn't care. We're an independent contractor, if you will, my girl. Separate from Heaven and Hell. We take people when it's their time and we tell them where to go." He went on to explain that souls were still being sent to both, but Hell took issue with the old ways not being upheld; they wanted the power.

I bit my bottom lip as I tried to piece together what he told me. *What did this have to do with me?* But then it clicked. "They don't want me to take over as Death, do they?"

"Clever girl. They do not. They want to install one of their own. Which won't happen, but they're going to try."

As if this night couldn't get any worse. Maybe it will start raining and put a cherry on this shit sundae. "Tell me you have a plan." He didn't speak. Instead, a grey wisp reached inside his robe and pulled out what looked like a battered old sickle. The wisp handed it to me and when I took it, it hummed in my hands. The curved blade was rusty, and the handle warped and chipped in spots. I looked at him as understanding finally struck. "This was hers, wasn't it?" I jerked my head towards Mathilda. "Let me guess…I-I have to kill them before they kill me?" He only nodded. A moment later his own long scythe appeared in his hands, and I snorted. "That one would be more helpful, you know. I wouldn't have to get so close to them." It's not that I was scared.

I was fucking *terrified*.

"You've got to inherit this one."

Figures.

"I know you're terrified of what could happen if you aren't successful. But you'll have help. You only have to ask for it." I watched as a wisp pointed to the spirit inside the fence. Our relative, Mathilda.

And then he was gone. Fan-fucking-tastic.

I walked back towards the gate, leading to my still-sleeping and safe home. I paused a moment at Mathilda's fence. "I don't suppose you can tell me?" I asked hopefully. She only shook her head. I put on my best smile and waved to her as I moved on towards the gate and my bed. Just before I passed through, a female voice popped into my head: *He's right, you know the answer.* I turned back to her grave, but all I saw was the stone marker and old elm.

The next morning, my husband noticed the sickle above the door. He had never noticed my haircut or a new perfume, but this this he noticed, of course. "What's with that, Old McDonald?" he teased.

"Halloween is never over in this house. You know that." I mean, our house *was* decorated as though an oddities shop had exploded. Our daughter also noticed it when she came down for breakfast.

"Cool! can I try swinging it?" *Like knows like.* Even though she'd already started exhibiting some familial tricks of our trade–talking to ghosts my husband couldn't see, opening doors without touching them–she didn't need a crash course in this. I shook my head no and tossed her an apple, rushing her out the door to catch the bus.

That night, after I had checked on my daughter and husband, I made my way downstairs, setting up wards as I went. Again, I had left the doorway between the dining room and kitchen untouched, as well as the back door. I had discovered the smell of sulfur coming from that room when I had returned last night. They were coming from inside the house. *Spooky.*

The furniture in the dining room was old, at least 100 years according to my grandmother. I was clearly missing something, but I hadn't had time to research it further. If I survived the night, I swore to myself I would. Something about the furniture wasn't right.

I removed the sickle from above the back door and waited on the back porch. Last night, I had waited in the kitchen, which had nearly cost me. So, the porch tonight. Maybe I could pick one off as it came through the back door.

I smelled the sulfur and readied myself. I still had no idea how I would be helped, or by whom. I didn't have much time to think on it before one of their large heads appeared through the back door. The sickle was already raised above my head and I brought it down as hard and as fast as I could. It took the beasts head clean off…the stronger smell of sulfur now turning my stomach.

I jumped off the porch, tucking in a roll so as not to lose my hold on the sickle. Another Hellhound howled into the night when it found its dead friend on the porch. Saliva dripped from its enormous mouth as it snarled at me.

"Come and get me, fuckface," I taunted, swinging the sickle wildly. It leaped off the porch and landed not far from me.

We circled one another, swiping as we could. I managed a nasty cut along its side. Some of its acid-like slobber landed on my arm and felt like a thousand bee stings. I worried about where the last Hellhound was. There were always three of them...always.

The Hellhound took another lunge toward me, and I swung the sickle into its neck, cutting its jugular. The creature dropped to the ground and burst into a cloud of sulfur. But where was the last one? As I turned in a small circle surveying the yard, a large shadow leapt out from its hiding spot behind the bushes lining the fence, knocking me to the ground and the sickle from my hand.

I was so *fucked*.

The sickle was out of reach, and the Hellhound's jaws were far too close to my face. I needed help. *Now*. "You won't win this, bitch," I hissed. If I'd known its name, I would have used it. After all names had power, didn't they–Then it hit me.

Names. Had. Power. And I knew a name that had wielded a lot of power when she was alive.

"Mathilda, I need you now!" I screamed both aloud and in my head. Best to cover all my bases. I didn't see her, but boy, did I feel her slam into me! It took us only a moment to get oriented, but with her extra boost I was able to throw the beast off me and grab for the sickle. I hardly had it in my hands before the beast was back on me.

With one final swing, I sent the Hellhound back home. "And fucking...stay there. Please and thank you." I stood and brushed myself off. "Thanks for the help, Mathilda. Uh, you can leave now too, um, please."

She didn't put up a fight. But I imagined doing what she had done took more out of her than she let on. Her usual bright appearance was grayer now and less solid. She slowly floated back through the gate into the cemetery, where she vanished. I knew I should probably follow her, have a few words with my dear father. But I was exhausted. I slumped to the ground.

It felt like the end of Hell's pissing contest.

Well, at least it was for me. They would come for my daughter next. It was time to fully prepare her too. She'd be thrilled to find out that her goth phase wasn't actually "just a phase."

As I finally pulled myself back up, I heard another voice. But this one wasn't in my head. Turning towards the gate, I saw my father. "You did well, my girl. I'll see you and my granddaughter tomorrow. It's high time we had a proper introduction."

I just smiled at him as I turned back towards the house. He was right, of course. After all, *Father knows best*. At least that's how the saying goes.

Walking back into the house, I closed the door to the porch and placed the sickle back above the door. I needed sleep and a shower. But something about the dining room nagged at me. I followed my nose to the old curio cabinet. The smell of sulfur was strongest there. I wasn't surprised to find the door to the cabinet open.

I made to close the door when I noticed some of the wood was lifted just inside the cabinet. This is why we couldn't have nice things– Hellhounds. I lifted the piece further and felt a laugh bubble up in my chest.

"You've got to be shitting me," I muttered. There was a maker's mark of sorts. It read 'Morningstar Woodworking.' Family heirloom, my ass. More like Hell's welcome mat. I slowly started emptying the cabinet.

We were going to have one hell of a bonfire later.

DAISY, DAISY

By Bethany Drillser

ore rain? she thought irritably, hearing it pelt the windows. The weather this summer had been awful. Instead of playing in the sprinkler and catching fireflies, they'd been inside, watching movies and playing video games most days. Always with music blasting off the walls. It was fun and all, but childhood summers really should be spent in the grass and dirt, skinning your knees and making memories outside. *Oh well*, she thought. At least it was evening, past Daisy's bedtime; maybe tomorrow would be sunn– *KABOOM.* A clap of thunder rumbled the house, just as the power went out. In the sudden darkness, she closed her book, set down her beer, and sighed. She stood and walked toward the stairs, already anticipating, mentally counting down. *3 … 2 … 1 …* "Moooooom!"

"Coming, baby!" she called to her daughter, who she'd just tucked in for the night twenty minutes ago.

She thought about Daisy as she climbed the stairs in the dark, hearing the rain die down. She'd hoped this summer her daughter would finally make friends with the neighbor kids. At Daisy's age, she'd spent from dawn 'til dusk riding bikes and causing mischief amongst the houses in her neighborhood on summer break. In the spirit of optimism, she'd loaded up on popsicles and bought a pack of 64-color sidewalk chalk. She'd texted the other Moms and let them know Daisy was free most days.

Nothing. She wondered if it was the near-constant rain, or something else that stopped the Moms from sending their kids over to play. Daisy had always been what you'd call an "old soul." She often preferred the company of adults, and she didn't even need a nightlight in her room to sleep. And of course, she was positively obsessed with loud music–but not the pop songs girls her age gravitated toward. Daisy played heavy metal and hard rock all day long–her mother had allowed it despite the curse words peppered throughout the lyrics. Hell, she liked this kind of music too. And Daisy was mature enough to hear words like that but know to not repeat them. *At least I think so*, she thought, second-guessing herself with a cringe.

She sighed again, pausing on the stair. Apart from the music, sometimes Daisy *did* say an odd thing or two, bordering on macabre. Violent news stories or headlines about death tolls from natural disasters always caught her attention, even as her mother tried to turn the TV off fast enough. And there was that time her teacher had requested a meeting after Daisy had created that awful bloody drawing in red crayon. Or when she carved those angry-looking little figures into her bedroom door, cutting up her hands and forearms as she worked until she dripped blood on the carpet. Her mother had been shocked to find her curled behind the door the next morning, tucked into a tight, bloody ball. She'd had to make an emergency call to the carpet cleaning company that day, after emptying a box of bandages for Daisy.

Odder still was a few weeks ago, when Diasy went absolutely feral after her headphones broke–she only calmed down when her mother agreed to drive to buy a new pair that same afternoon. But… Daisy was just unique; she was hitting her "goth phase" early. She was smart and special, and she was her daughter; nothing she could do or say would stop her mother from lov–"Mooooom, *hurry!*" she screamed.

Wrenched from her train of thought, she hurried the last few steps and flung Daisy's door open. Daisy launched herself out of bed and into her mother's arms. She was sobbing and shaking with stark fear. Her mother was shocked at Daisy's terror and immediately felt guilty at not hustling up here faster.

"My fan! It's off!" she wailed. Her mother blinked, hugging her tight. Both she and Daisy had always slept with a fan blasting all night; they both enjoyed a breeze as they slept.

"Oh," she said, relaxing slightly. "Yeah, honey, the power went out, but that thunderstorm already passed. The power will kick back on soon. Did the thunder wake you?"

"No, Mom," she cried, looking up at her with wide eyes. "It's quiet. It's *so* quiet!" She began sobbing anew. Her mother hugged her tight, caressing her back soothingly. She leaned over and clicked the little battery-operated desk light on.

"There, does the light help?"

"No, Mom. It's not the dark … it's the quiet." She buried her face in her chest. Her mother wrinkled her brow in confusion and opened her mouth to say something more, when she heard a scraping, scratching sound from the direction of Daisy's closet. Daisy gripped her harder, trembling.

"I'm not afraid of the dark," Daisy whispered.

A low growling sound raised the hairs on her mother's arms. Her mind went blank with shock and fear, and she looked from the door down to the top of Daisy's strawberry-blonde head against her. The scrapes and heavy breathing sounds were growing ever louder.

"I'm afraid of the *quiet*." She lifted her tear-stained face.

Her mother's eyes were on Daisy's terrified face, but her ears were on the closet door, listening as it began to slide open on its track. Daisy pressed her face back against her mother's breast, clutched tight to her body, her next words muffled:

"If I can hear them … they can find me.

They're coming."

A SHELTER

By Jordan Heath

Winter. The bitter cold settled upon the city, as icy wind swept through the desolate streets, chilling everything in its path. Not too many people knew Samuel, but those who crossed his path mostly thought of him as nothing more than another local vagrant. He had been on the streets for just about as long as he could remember, but this year, winter came early. He was unprepared, and on that night, he found himself wandering aimlessly, his tattered clothes offering little protection against the biting chill. Desperate for warmth, having checked all of his typical safe havens to no success, he found himself downright desperate. As a last resort, he ventured into a part of the city where people in his position rarely go. The street was lined with beautiful historic homes.

Most windows were dimly lit by bedside tables or the glow of TVs that he couldn't imagine having the cash for these days. He hoped against hope that he could find a backyard shed unlocked or even a doghouse big enough to climb inside. Anything to block this brutal wind that he shouldn't have been contending with for another few weeks. To his surprise and initial delight, he seemed to have hit the jackpot. There it was, hemmed in on either side by million-dollar homes, what appeared to be an abandoned house. On some level, he knew immediately that this was unlike the slew of derelict properties that seemed to be a dime a dozen in other neighborhoods. This place seemed to call out to him, like an old friend promising warmth and protection from the frigid air biting at his fingertips.

With a mix of trepidation and hope, he cautiously approached the dilapidated structure. The home loomed before him, its windows shattered and its once-grand facade now crumbling under the weight of nature. His weary body yearned for respite, and despite the ominous aura that surrounded the place, he couldn't resist the allure of temporary solace from the unforgiving cold of winter.

He tentatively stepped up on the porch and crossed the fingers on one hand while using the other to push open the creaky front door. He took a step into the desolate house. Inside, a thick layer of dust covered every surface, as if time itself had abandoned this once-beautiful space. The only sounds on the air were the distant howling of the wind and the echoes of his oversized tattered boots slapping against aged maple floors.

As he ventured further into the house, the hint of unease that had developed in the front yard began to feel more and more like an impossible weight on his shoulders. He could feel it pressing down on him. He could feel it in his joints. Strange, indistinct whispers seemed to drift through the air, sending shivers down his now-aching spine. He wanted to leave. Every fiber of his being screamed it in his head, but it was so cold outside. He could never forgive himself for passing up such a find just because he had caught a case of the spooks.

And so, he shoved down his intuition, the one that had saved him countless times since his life fell apart, and sought refuge in a secluded room near the back on the bottom floor. A bedroom, he thought, though there was no closet. Maybe a parlor. These fancy old houses often had so many rooms that they had to make up new names for half of them. The air hung heavy with an eerie stillness, as if the house held its breath…as if it was waiting for something. But again, his intuition about this place was pushed aside, this time by pure exhaustion. He curled up on a thin mattress, his eyes heavy with fatigue. But the solace he sought, as he feared, was not in the cards for him this evening. Any chance of restful sleep was quickly dashed when he found himself living out some kind of twisted nightmare.

Haunting whispers seemed to seep from the very walls. His dreams were a harrowing procession of phantoms and grotesque apparitions that clawed at his mind and pressed against the boundaries of his sanity. The shadows around him elongated and contorted, crawling toward him with malevolent intent. The air was heavy and thick. It was suffocating, as if the house itself was closing in, suffusing him with an overwhelming sense of dread.

In one long, ragged gasp for breath, he thought he jolted awake, his heart pounding so hard in his chest that he could swear he heard his dog tags rattle. He could taste the salty sweat dripping down his face, despite the frigid temperature of the room. He knew in his heart that this was not just a nightmare. It was this room. It was this house. He had to leave. He had to do whatever it took to escape the clutches of this Hell house; he felt the panic overtaking him. He dragged himself up off of the filthy mattress and jerked the bedroom door open, but as he scrambled toward what he thought was the exit, the house seemed to conspire against him, its corridors shifting and twisting, leading him deeper into a labyrinth of despair and anxiety.

The whispers that he thought were in his head grew louder. Haunting cries now echoed through the halls, and the walls themselves seemed to breathe with a sinister pulse. Panic seized his mind as an insane realization, or delusion, took hold of his mind. This house was not abandoned; it was a *creature*, a malevolent being that fed upon the souls of those seeking refuge.

He tried. He wanted nothing more than to feel the biting wind that he so desperately needed to escape only hours before. Hours? Minutes? Days? How long had he been here? If he was honest, he had no idea. Every corner that he rounded in his frantic search for the front door seemed to unveil another space unfamiliar to him. Eventually, his limbs started to feel heavy, despite the relentless urgency pounding in his brain. His boots were filling with sweat. He had to stop. He leaned against the corridor wall and felt the sting of the cold plaster against his sweat-soaked threadbare sweater.

The shock of cold was just what he needed. In a moment of clarity, he realized that he was only around the bend from salvation. He could see the frail shafts of kaleidoscopic moonlight shining through the stained-glass transom. He forced his aching muscles into motion and nearly made it to the corner when it hit him. Like a lightning bolt, he felt something that made him think of a giant's hand crushing the inside of his chest. A pressure inside his ribcage he never would have believed was possible. He went down hard on his knees; the impact shot bolts of pain up through his hips. He reached out for a wall that wasn't there and fell forward, catching just a glimpse of the open front door, before the lights went out.

OBSCENE

By Phil Rossi

"Not tonight, Linda. Sorry," Barry said, already feeling a pang of guilt. "I'm really tired. Let's do it tomorrow night."

"But I might not want to have sex tomorrow night, Barry. It's like we can never be in sync. Remember when we used to have sex all the time? You couldn't keep your hands off me," Linda replied and then added after a pause: "It's okay. I can just use one of my toys."

"Now I feel bad," Barry said, the guilt deepening into an all too familiar sense of self-loathing. As a result, he wanted to engage in sexy time even less.

It wasn't a matter of attraction—Barry was and would always have the hots for his wife. That fact was indisputable, as sure as the sun rose in the east and set in the west. Physically, there wasn't a thing wrong with his plumbing; Barry could achieve an erection–with great success–and he was as horny as he was when he was eighteen.

"Now you're upset. This is why I can't share with you. You don't understand me," Linda said, turned off the TV, and then rolled over so that her back was to him.

"Linda..." he began, and then stopped. *It feels obscene,* he wanted to say aloud, but Barry knew he'd never be able to share or make Linda understand.

Obscene.

His skin, pale and like putty, sliding against Linda's toned and perfect flesh. His barrel of a stomach resting on the curve of her ass in a vain attempt to do her from behind. Barry had become a monster in the last several years, courtesy of stress eating, poor sleep, and an increasing lack of physical activity. He didn't recognize himself anymore. He was fucking gross and his wife didn't deserve that on top of her. The very thought made him want to gag.

And just as Linda had needs, Barry had needs, too. For a while, porn had done the trick—but more recently, even porn couldn't get the job done. He longed to feel the sexual touch of another human being. The lack of intimacy had turned him into a grumpy, and sometimes even a mean bastard. Arguments occurred almost every day now.

I can do this for her, he thought. *She wants this. I can do this for her tonight.*

"Linda…" he said and put his hand on the small of her back. Immediately, Linda shied away, and Barry rolled onto his side to face the wall. He cried silent tears until sleep brought a temporary respite from his misery.

Something has to give. Sleep deprived, with a headache from crying all night, and contemplating day drinking, Barry had decided it was time to take extreme measures.

He sat in his office with the door locked, staring at the computer screen where the mouse pointer hadn't moved from where it hovered above the "Rub Ladies" Subreddit link for the last twenty minutes. The forum was dedicated to "safely" sharing massage parlors that offered "Happy Endings." Was an adult massage considered whoring? On one hand, the very thought appalled him, on the other hand, it was so absurd as to be amusing. *Whoring.* Barry broke into a fit of nervous laughter.

Barry didn't think a happy ending massage was categorized as adultery. *Denial, Barry. Denial is the devil himself.* Linda would surely feel betrayed to her core. But wasn't there prostitution in the bible? He'd never been religious, so he wasn't sure. He was sure that he loved his wife and the last thing he wanted was an affair. He just needed release before the goddamn Chernobyl-level pressure building inside his nuts went thermo-nuclear, blowing his prostate right out of his body.

The thought of release–sweet, sweet release–brought about a stirring inside his boxers. Linda was asleep in the bedroom and wouldn't be up for another hour or two. All he had to do was go to her, pull back the covers, and slip her sleep shorts down over her hips.

Barry's stomach did a wet somersault, and he closed his eyes. He was a stranger to himself. He wouldn't let a stranger do *things* to his wife.

In spite of the blasting AC, Barry's cotton polo shirt clung to his back and armpits. He glanced in the rearview, his brow was shiny with sweat, and noticed the black sedan–the vehicle had been behind him pretty much since he'd pulled out of his driveway–was still there. Barry had convinced himself he was being followed. Maybe Linda had hired a private detective. No. That was ridiculous. As if on cue, the sedan turned off and disappeared, and then it was just Barry driving up the empty road past increasingly dilapidated buildings. The "good part of town" was already miles behind him. Waze took him past abandoned homes with sagging roofs, hanging gutters, and boarded windows. Small lawns were engulfed by weeds and trash. He drove by a liquor store where bars protected the windows and doors. A neon sign with proclaimed "Pen" with the "O" having gone dark. *Pen for the pig*, he thought and really wanted to park and get a bottle of something stiff. Barry continued to drive and continued to sweat while the neighborhood only seemed to get shadier.

No whorin' in the nice part of town, Barry old boy, a voice in his head told him. What if he got car jacked? How would he explain to his wife what he was doing in that neighborhood? According to Waze, he'd arrive at any minute—but all the buildings were abandoned now. *I should turn around.* Instead, he accelerated. *Nothing ventured, nothing gained.* And it was very possible that there would only be a massage and nothing funny. In fact, didn't he have control over that? He'd have to consent. Maybe just the touch would be enough to set him on the path to healing.

Moments later, a modest apartment building appeared at the end of the road. In stark contrast to the neighboring buildings, the three-level structure had intact windows that reflected the fading sunset in a dazzling light show. *New construction?* He thought, a little surprised. The exterior siding was crips and white. The fact that the place looked brand new somehow made him feel better about everything. And while Barry hadn't been aware they were restoring this part of the city, he was glad for it. Maybe it was a sign that he too could be restored. Another thought occurred to him too–the blocks beyond the apartment building had to be nicer than those he had driven through to get there. *I'll gladly take the long way home,* he thought.

Per the instructions in his confirmation email, he parked two streets down from the building in front of an abandoned condominium. When he got out of the car, his eyes were immediately drawn to the empty condo. Gray, weathered plywood was nailed over the windows and there were dark holes around the edges where industrious rodents had chewed their way inside. Maybe to the feast on the bloated corpse of some dead drug addict that had chased their last high behind those rotten walls. Where the front door had been was only a gaping opening filled with shadows so thick the possibility that only nothingness lay beyond was strong. A pure void just like the one that was devouring him from the inside.

He couldn't tear his eyes away from the blackness, even as a chill of primal fear rattled through him.

A rustling came from inside the building, and the sound was impossibly loud on the otherwise quiet street. He wanted to run, but it seemed as if his feet had been Gorilla glued to the cracked sidewalk. He was physically incapable of looking away. Moments from now, the dead drug addict would appear in the doorway, spent hypodermic dangling from a black vein. The face would be rotten and caved in like an old pumpkin, half-eaten by animals and dried vomit, blood, and rat feces would cake the front of addict's ripped tee shirt. *Any moment now.* The shambling ghoul was about to appear on the front doorstep, urging Barry to come inside, to join him and the rats in the void.

Barry shuddered and found his feet. He hurried up the sidewalk, only pausing once to look back at his Subaru. For a heartbeat, he considered moving the car, but he didn't want to draw any attention to himself because at the other end of the street he could see a cluster of youths throwing glass bottles at a dumpster. Each shattering caused his already strained heart to skip a beat. The kids didn't seem to have noticed him and he wanted to keep it that way.

He jogged up the sidewalk toward the fresh apartment building that rose like an oasis amongst the decay. Beyond the building, Barry glimpsed a beautiful grass field where daisies appeared to be made from pure gold in the sunset. He hadn't remembered there being any kind of park in this part of town. Even still, the sight of it made him feel calmer, made him feel like he could go through with this—whatever this was. He checked the apartment number on his phone—313—and then headed up the central stairwell. Once he reached the third level, he had to stop to catch his breath, wishing he hadn't jogged. He took the opportunity to look around, admiring the clean hallway and security lights. The apartment doors were red and the scent of fresh paint still lingered in the air. He glanced down at his phone to see there had been one missed call from Linda, and his stomach sank. He looked down the stairs and toward the street. *No. Don't get cold feet now. You've come this far.* And then another voice in his head said, *You are nervous and having second thoughts because you know this is shady as hell. Therapy would be cheaper and safer.* But instead of bailing, he started up the hallway, checking the numbers on each door as he went.

309.

311.

313.

He knocked, expecting his knuckles to come away red with tacky paint—they did not. For a handful of seconds, the wind gusted and carried on it a foul smell. In the next moment, the fresh paint scent returned, seemingly twice as potent. There was a noise from the floor below him. Something skittered along the hallway, making a dry, whispering sound like dead leaves—or the shed skin of a reptile. A loud, metallic *clang* caused Barry and stifle a scream. He looked over the railing and saw a shadow slinking away. Probably just a cat. Or a raccoon. He'd have to be careful on his way out. The quiet immediately returned, underscored by the birds chirping from the park and the rising chorus of night insects, eager for the daylight to go away.

313's door swung open, catching Barry off guard. Instinctively, he took a step backwards even though he saw right away there was nothing to fear on the other side of that red door.

A short woman with striking features, dressed in a white silk robe that fell a few inches shy of her knees smiled at him. He was unable to identify her as any individual ethnicity unless "exotic" was considered an ethnicity. She regarded him with almond-shaped blue eyes. Dark hair hung over her shoulder in a long braid, in contrast to her nearly porcelain skin. She smiled at him with full lips, revealing perfect teeth.

"Barry?" she asked.

"Yeah," Barry managed to get out. "I'm, Barry."

He stumbled over his own name. It almost came out as Blueberry.

She laughed, but the sound of it was warm and slowed his thundering heart.

"You sound nervous, sweetie," she said, her voice delicate. "Are you nervous?"

"I've ... I've just never done anything like this before," he replied.

"This is your first massage?" she asked.

"No. I mean yes," he stammered.

"Come in," she said. "Please. I will take good care of you."

He tensed at her choice of words. *What am I doing here?*

She moved aside and Barry stepped into her apartment. The lights were down low so he couldn't make out much other than it was sparsely but neatly furnished, along with some art on the walls—old and faded photos, by the looks of it. The aroma of incense permeated the cool air. To Barry, it smelled like the Fall. An unexpected surge of nostalgia hit Barry square in the breadbox. At first, he wasn't sure why, but then he remembered a younger, thinner Barry out on a Halloween date, sneaking a kiss with his now wife.

Guilt swooped in to replace the nostalgia.

You're doing this for your wife, he told himself. *You're making a sacrifice for her to break down this wall in your head.*

But that sure sounded like bullshit.

She closed the door, stepped behind him, and placed her hands on his shoulders, before giving him gentle nudge forward.

"Go through the door straight ahead," she pointed. "You take off your clothes, but keep your underpants on. Be with you in just a few minutes."

It's only a massage.

Once inside the small room, with the door shut behind him, Barry had to fight back a sob that was rising in his throat. Had it really come to this? Acid churned inside his stomach, and he pressed his mouth into the sweaty crook of his arm to muffle a wet belch that tasted like the spicy Chik-Fil-A sandwich that he'd had for lunch. He belched again and this time it burned. Barf o'clock was imminent. What in Christ's name was he doing there? *Call it off. Come up with an excuse and leave.*

There came a knock on the door.

"Are you ready?" a soft voice asked. "I don't want to rush you, but I have other customers today."

"Just a minute!" Barry said and nearly belched again. Before he knew what he was doing, his shirt was off, and his pants were down around his ankles.

He took a moment to gather his wits, folding his size 42 jeans and XXL shirt and placing them on a chair. He then got on the massage bed, pulling the sheet up to his chin and trying to ignore the swell of his belly.

"Are you ready now?" her voice came again, and her patient tone made him feel like weeping. He gazed up at the ceiling, focusing on a small water mark there, desperately trying to contain his emotions. For the barest instant, the water mark appeared to take up the whole ceiling.

"Yes. I'm ready," he said, a slight wobble in his voice.

A moment later, the woman was standing beside the massage table, looking down at him with her strange and beautiful eyes. He hadn't even heard her come into the room. Soft music was playing–had it been playing all along? The potent smell of incense made him sneeze, but in spite of that, the scent was calming. In fact, it made his head feel a little swimmy. Barry did not mind.

"Please roll onto your stomach," she requested, and he obliged, deciding that he would just stay on his stomach—that would certainly keep things PG. He heard her fussing with something and then she pulled the sheet down to just above his waist, cool air making giving him gooseflesh. Warm massage oil sprinkled onto his back and it felt as good as it smelled. Small but remarkably strong hands kneaded his shoulders, steadily working the oil into his muscles and right away Barry felt his tensions ease away, replaced by warmth. Barry almost felt drunk.

A siren wailed in the distance, rising above the music, creating a momentary distraction.

The foul odor he'd smelled earlier hit his nose again and he felt a cold draft on his back. His head cleared ever-so-slightly and his muscles started to tense up. The music became louder—Himalayan singing bowls—drowning out the siren, and her hands continued to work on his muscles. She massaged the back of his legs and the soles of his feet, working the oil in and the warmth along with it. Some of the tension faded—some, but not all.

"Please," she spoke. "On your back."

Her voice reminded him of wind chimes, melodic and mesmerizing. He obliged, the cold and stink all but forgotten as her slender fingers massaged his pectorals. Her hands trailed down to his midsection. And there they paused at the hem of the sheet. He opened his eyes and sat up.

"You are waking," she remarked.

And first he interpreted her words to simply mean he was awake. But then, horrified, he saw, the pointed rise in the sheet.

"You need relief," she said. "You poor thing."

Son of a bitch.

She placed her hands on him where he was hard, and he sat fully upright like he'd received a jolt of high voltage electricity.

"This was a bad idea," he said, clutching the sheet to his lap. Tears stung his eyes. "I'm sorry, I can't do this."

He clambered off the bed as he spoke those last words, entirely forgetting that the bottoms of his feet were slick with massage oil. Barry's feet maintained contact with the floor for roughly two seconds and then he was airborne. On his return to the Earth, his temple clipped the corner of the massage table, and it was lights out, Barry.

Barry awoke with the worst headache of his life. He could only breathe through one nostril and his sinuses and throat were on fire. He opened his eyes and blinked into the darkness surrounding him. For a long second, he had no idea where he was or how he got there. But then the nauseating details, the Rub Ladies Subreddit, the sweat-drenched drive, the incense and massage oil all scurried back into his skull like roaches fleeing the light. *How could I have taken things this far? How? Was I really planning to pay money for a handjob and cheat on my wife?*

And why was it so damn dark? Had he been ditched somewhere? And by whom? The masseuse's John? It didn't take his eyes long to adjust to the darkness, and Barry saw a familiar space. The massage table was there but tipped on its side. In the corner was the chair and his neatly folded clothes on top, but the recognizable similarities ended there. Dead leaves and trash covered the floor, and the stench of mold and dust was absolutely choking. Barry got to his feet, his head pounding, and fear making it hard for him to breathe. Desperate for more light and fresh air, Barry yanked back the curtains, and the resulting dust cloud sent him into a fit of sneezes. A dozen moths fled out through a broken window.

Cool moonlight spilled into the apartment, revealing paint that peeled from the walls decorated with faded graffiti. Bulging, black garbage bags leaned against one wall, draped with thick cobwebs. He was afraid to even contemplate what might be inside those bags. He took a step toward his clothes, and something shifted in the corner on the opposite side of the room, debris crunching under its weight. It was a dark shape hunkered in shadows, and Barry at first took it for only more garbage—what appeared to be broken broomsticks, wrapped in tattered trash bags and a mop with only black braids. But then the thing lifted its head, the oily black strands falling away to reveal smoldering amber eyes. It rose on those broken broom sticks, which were actually long, spindly limbs, to which hanging tatters of rotten flesh clung. Time ground to a halt and Barry found himself completely frozen in terror. He waited for the thing to pounce, and when it didn't, he forced himself into motion, backing toward the door and grabbing his clothes and his shoes on the way. Burning eyes followed him, and Barry could sense the creature coiling like a viper, preparing to strike at any moment.

I'm hallucinating, he thought. *She drugged me and I'm hallucinating. Or I have a concussion. Or both.*

He wrenched the door open, the screams of the hinges breaking the filthy silence, and dashed out into the corridor. Barry found himself in the same sparse apartment, but even in the weak light he could see it had been vacant for a long time. There was rubbish, fallen plaster, and little dead animals everywhere, and he was about to stop and put on his shoes when a crash from the massage room made his heart stop. He bolted up the hallway, no longer concerned about tetanus or MRSA as he imagined the creature lurching forward in pursuit. He dashed through the already open front door and down the stairway, descending two steps at a time. A commotion came from above him, and there was little question he was being pursued. A fresh sheen of sweat, along with dust and grime, coated Barry like a second skin by the time he got to bottom of the stairwell. He swung around and looked up the stairs to see what was following him, but all he saw were shadows. Beyond the landing, where he stood shaking, a neglected graveyard sprawled out where there had been the beautiful field of daisies earlier.

What the fuck is happening?

Without bothering to dress, or even put on his shoes, Barry ran all the way back to where he had parked the Subaru and was relieved to find the car still there, and more relieved still to find his keys in the pocket of his jeans, along with his wallet. His phone was gone, and he knew it had to be back up in that Godforsaken room, but he couldn't care less. He unlocked the car, tossed his clothes in, and climbed in after them. The moment the doors were locked, Barry had the engine running and the car in gear. Without so much as glancing in the rearview mirror, Barry sped away. Five minutes later, he found himself parked at a tired-looking McDonald's in an only slightly better neighborhood, sobbing as the adrenaline faded from his bloodstream.

What had he done? And what was he going to do? And what was that fucking thing? Had he lost his mind?

Once the tears had subsided, Barry slipped into his clothes and began the drive home. He had to tell his wife; he had to come clean. In the end, he hadn't gone through with it, so she'd forgive him, right?

He pulled into the driveway and noticed right away that Linda's car was not there. He checked the time. It was 3:00 a.m.–had she gone out looking for him? The thought put him on the verge of vomiting and he cursed himself for losing his phone. He rushed out of the car, not even bothering to lock it. Barry ran up the front walk, up the porch steps, and pulled on the front door. Locked. It took him nearly a minute to get his key into the lock, his hands trembled so badly. When he finally opened the door, he stepped inside to find the house dark and quiet.

"Linda?!" he shouted, but there came no response. The shout turned into a sob because he already knew what the silence meant. A light was on in the kitchen, and he rushed there. The kitchen was empty, and a note sat on the counter. Hands still shaking, he picked up the note and wiped away fresh tears so that he could read it:

Barry,

I am disgusted. DISGUSTED. How could you? When you didn't come home, I got worried, like an IDIOT, and I read your emails. And then your search history. And now you've been gone for two days. I KNOW WHAT YOU DID. And I HATE you for it. I am DISGUSTED. Do not try to contact me.

-L

The note fell from his hand and drifted to the tile floor like a dead leaf. White hot pain blossomed in his chest and robbed him of all breath. A flurry of disjointed, self-deprecating thoughts flooded into his skull, sending heat radiating out into his limbs and making him feel completely detached from his body. *Panic attack.* He was aware he was hyperventilating, but could do nothing to control his breathing. He stared at the condemning note where it lay on the kitchen floor. One note became two as his vision doubled and blackness began to bleed in from his periphery. He gripped the counter to keep from falling over, and fought the panic. Soon, his breathing was under control and then the tightness in his chest slowly released. He was both emotionally and physically exhausted, and a familiar numbness settled over him. He could do nothing about the mess he'd created, not at that hour and in his present condition. All he wanted to do was sleep.

Barry shambled into the bedroom and stripped out of his clothes. He climbed beneath the covers, not caring that he wore a suit of pure filth, and closed his eyes. Sleep came for him almost immediately. Later, Barry was awakened by the sound of the bedroom door opening. He didn't know how long he had been asleep, only that it was still dark outside.

"Linda?" he whispered.

"Shhhh," she said. "You're okay. It was all a bad dream."

"Thank God," he muttered, still mostly asleep. She pulled back the covers and slid into the bed. He was too tired to roll over and face her, but he would hug her the next morning as tight as he could without hurting her. The sickly-sweet smell of decay pushed into his nostrils and fingers like dry twigs slid up his bare arms to wrap around his neck. There wasn't even time to scream.

BROTHER

By Lauren Hellekson

Neglected grass crunched under his light footsteps in an attempt to reach the abandoned building's door unnoticed.

"Who builds houses around these things?" he whispered with an eye roll. His tone clearly meant to place blame on the audacity of the sleeping neighborhood surrounding this evening's destination.

Jordie Evans had been sneaking into abandoned buildings for what seemed like years. Ever since he met his best friend, Sam, two summers back, they'd been exploring local derelict spots together to bond with a little breaking and entering, discovering abandoned halls and provoking any spooky spirits that might be hidden inside in the process.

"Dude, stop shaking the door, you're making too much noise. Let me through." Sam was the lock picker in the duo and, though younger than Jordie, seemed to have an answer for everything, with the skills to match. Sam revealed when they met that he was a runaway, so he was on his own and always seemed to be in a state of nervousness, conducting himself with a sense of urgency. The assumption was made that his behavior was out of fear of someone coming to find him, which would result in their friendship being no more. Since Jordie firmly believed he was surrounded by idiots, to best protect Sam, he swore himself to secrecy about their friendship and Sam's existence in his life.

"Bro, I can't stand my mom anymore. We should hit the road together."

"You'll be 'hitting the road' in a different way if you don't be careful," Sam chortled, "you don't want what happened that first summer to happen again, do you?"

"Seriously, you know that wasn't my fault! And look, you're fine, plus we would have never met."

"Yeah, because you could have broken your neck if it weren't for me breaking your fall."

Sam set up his latest "ex-spirit-ment" as he playfully called them, another trade he seemed to know everything about, by lighting candles and pouring some oily liquid on the concrete floor. He handed Jordie a piece of string and told him to "tie a knot." With a chuckle and another eye roll, knot in hand, he knew he had to humor his friend before they could get busy with the real fun stuff.

"Don't start a fire with all those candles, Merlin"

"Nah, been there done that, I survived," Sam laughed

"OK, onto the fun stuff."

Sam went to his pack and pulled out a folded-up piece of what looked like cardboard. As he unfolded it, a tear-drop-shaped piece of plastic fell to the ground and Jordie picked it up, flipping it over in his hands.

"You can't be serious."

"I am, come on! It'll be spooky" he said with corresponding "spooky fingers," wiggling them in Jordie's direction.

On the dust-clad floor of the long-abandoned factory, the two friends took their seats opposite each other. In the flickering candlelight, the only sounds that could be heard were the unsettling scrapes of their seats. Lingering smells of fuel and smoke filled the hallways, lending a grimness to the atmosphere. Fingertips on the jagged planchette, unexpected movement began.

"S …"

"… is that you?"

"No, dude, shut up … A …"

"M," they said in unison, looking wide-eyed at each other.

"Come on, that's you fucking around."

"Shhhh." Sam adjusted in his seat, becoming more focused than before.

"N"

"O"

"T"

"M"

"E"

Sam tore the planchette from the bored with a smirk, "Got ya."

"You dick! I knew it was you!"

Nonchalantly, Sam knocked the nearest candle onto the board, allowing it to singe and burn while Jordie rummaged through his bag for the night's other planned source of entertainment. With a 4-pack of energy drinks and a few cans of spray paint, the boys set about their typical antics: TV show-style provocation, tawdry vandalism, and typical teenage debauchery lasting well into the early hours. At first light, tired, glazed over eyes guided them in their respective opposite directions until their next planned meet.

A pair of shaking hands, withered with age, light a crudely homemade candle on a tile floor. Palms rest on tight arthritic knees as an incantation is whispered. With a familiar retch, he leaves this vessel almost for the last time. The candle tips, but he cannot feel the sensations of the body, his consciousness only half-present. He doesn't smell the singeing of the polyester sleepwear. The blare of the alarm retreating into the recesses of his mind in this deep meditative state.

"You're late for work again?" Jordie woke up to his mother's voice in the hallway as his bedside alarm thundered into his temples. He hated how she was always nagging him.

"I called off last night, we were out late. It's fine."

"Honey, I'm trying to be patient with you. This is the third time this month you're not going to work. How can I help you?" Instead of answering the incessant criticism, he slammed the door in her face and buried his head under his pillow.

Within earshot, he heard his mother on the phone, "I just don't know what to do. He keeps staying out late and I just keep thinking about that missing boy … He still hasn't been found; Cheryl I just couldn't live with myself if–"

"Ok, this looks like a perfect spot for home base." Jordie unloaded the backpack, in which he had been collecting various pieces of suggested equipment in over the years.

"Can we try a new method this time?" The duo had found Silver Crest Asylum on a whim through the *GeoFind* app Sam said he had been playing on his phone. The game dropped you somewhere in the world, and through street view maps, you had to guess where you were. When he had found Silver Crest, he googled it and realized it was only a 2-hour drive away, settled deep in the woods. Perfect for some epic spirit stalking.

"This is the place," Sam explained, "It shut down a few years ago when one of the patients started a fire mysteriously–rumors said it was probably just a nurse smoking on the night shift and she blamed some spooky shit to not lose her job."

The looming structure seemed frozen in time. The smells of charred wood, melting plastic, and hot metal clung to the empty hallways. Signs of nature beginning to take its rightful place were prevalent in the cracked tiles swelling with yarrow and branches bursting through forgotten opened windows.

"You know I totally don't believe in all this magic whatever, right?" Jordie laughed as they walked through the halls together, lightly poking fun at Sam who was focusing intently on finding the perfect place to set up some kind of altar. Though Sam knew everything about the paranormal, Jordie, only cared to know everything about breaking stuff in old buildings.

"That's no biggie, you don't need to believe in *this* for it to work." The dramatics were certainly entertaining. Sam had a few instances over the last year where he would become extra focused on a new occult experiment, or weird crazy communication technique that never worked, and Jordie wondered when he would cut it out.

"Ok, just a little slice."

"Of my *finger*?"

"Just a tiny bit of—"

"OW! Damn dude!"

"Perfect."

But nothing happened.

"See dude, this stuff never works." Jordie pulled out *his* investigative device, a hammer, and started looking around for something to destroy. They stayed for what seemed like hours, screaming at the top of their lungs the provocations Jordie saw on the latest episode of *Spirit Exploits*, his current favorite show. It felt great. Jordie couldn't remember ever experiencing this kind of release during one of their usual adventures. He started to feel lighter, a tingle on his skin like something he'd never felt. This clarity had such a calming feeling; maybe things were going to be OK. He had been a little too hard on his mom lately. He thought about how he really wanted to just go home, talk to her, tell her about Sam and see if he could stay with them. Exhaustion hit Jordie before he even realized it; sitting down to catch his breath for a moment sent him tumbling into the deep darkness of sleep.

"It's time to wake up," a soothing voice lulled him back from the darkness of rest.

"Mom?"

"No, it's Dr Maeve. You have a visitor today." Sam blinked the sleep from his eyes, looking around his room in a haze. Everything seemed brighter. Cleaner. Where the Hell *was* he? He went to rub a headache from his temples, but his arm wouldn't lift past his waist. While trying to shift his muddled gaze to his wrist, he felt a heavy but subtle pain settle all over his body. "What is … happening … where–"

"Orderly! Let's get Sam ready for his visitor today," the doctor said with a calming smile as two men rolled a high-back chair into the room. Sam, realizing his wrists were restrained with buckled straps, tried to recall the last thing he could remember …

"Why am I here? Where's Sam? Where's my mom?"

The doctor snapped her fingers and pointed nonchalantly at Sam, "Sedation! Just his daytime dose; he has someone coming in in about an hour. Be mindful of those burns, they need re-wrapping."

His panic became liquid, and then all he saw was darkness.

Blinking away the dim, Sam awoke sitting in front of a mirror.

No, that's not right.

He wasn't smiling.

But it was him.

Right in front of–

"Hey Jordie," Sam whispered through Jordie's mouth, with a wink.

Jordie still couldn't speak as his sedative hung loosely around the muscles of his face and vocal cords.

"Thank you, Brother, for not believing in any of this." Sam stood as he slid an old box of matches across the table.

It had taken the being Jordie knew as Sam (but other humans throughout time and space only knew as "Ego") a little longer than usual to stabilize astral projection in that body. It took longer to stabilize it in a way where they could interact with the world outside the thick walls behind which they'd been confined. What would have been a full human lifespan, complete with the much-needed destruction, pain, fear, and death that was welcomed by these creatures, had been reduced to only a few precious years before being subdued and imprisoned. Why this behavior is both perpetuated and punished is what made these creatures so delicious to him. So satiating.

Though this cycle was brought to an end before they would have liked, securing the around-the-clock meds indeed proved so very helpful. After being transferred to the new Gold Crest, an institution that sounded a lot nicer than the dangerous but anesthetized criminals held in its walls and where Jordie now resided, they were able to sink deeper into a state of projection, extending their reach in order to find a body, at just the right time. Freshly uninhabited, and still warm. They never thought they would nab two in one night. A body to animate, and a body to befriend, who would eventually serve as the new permanent host? Kismet.

When Jordie fell on the young man a few summers back, he had severed his phrenic nerve: something that typically results in respiratory failure, but an injury that's clean enough for Ego to slip in and take the reins. They liked the youngness of this body, and would have been happy to keep it, but taking over completely required time, patience, and consent demonstrated by a series of ceremonial tasks to create anchor points—knots to complete the tether, and then transfer Consciousness.

Ego made their way towards the door. They would be more careful going forward, more creative. After all, they had a mother to go home to now. Jordie screamed in the direction of his old body, his life, and barely felt the prick in his arm from the syringe.

"There, there, Sam, let's get you back to bed—someone take these matches, we can't have another Silver Crest incident now, can we?"

THE RAIN

By Lorien Jones

The rain has been relentless for days. Grey skies, grey streets, grey rain—I don't mind it though. I enjoy being outdoors so much more in a good, heavy downpour. The smell, the lack of people, the calm. Today feels especially so, like the rest of the world is elsewhere.

As I continue the journey home, I don't pass a soul; the rain seems to have driven people into hibernation. A drenched black cat, its fur standing in spikes, runs along a low garden wall and skulks out of sight. It's late afternoon and the streetlamps are not yet lit, but being October, it's already dark and the heavy clouds are taking hours off what's left of the afternoon. Gloom seems to hang all around, oozing over walls, dripping from roof tiles and seeping across the pavements.

A small river runs in the gutter and over the cobblestones, eager to be elsewhere, as if sensing foreboding. Luckily, these boots were a good investment and have kept my feet dry over the past few days. I recall a famous Scottish comedian once saying, "there's no such thing as bad weather, just bad clothes," and I have to say I agree. My mind wanders to the contents of my fridge, wondering what to cook for dinner when I finally get home.

Glancing up from my feet, I'm surprised to see someone up ahead of me—an ancient-looking man, his skin hanging in folds against his cheekbones. He's wearing a long, light brown raincoat and a dark fedora style hat, from the brim of which the rain is cascading, just missing his hooked nose. Surprised to see anyone out at this point, I'm wondering why he is just standing there, oblivious to the deluge. His arms are hanging awkwardly down by his side, rain dripping from his fingers like candlewax.

I have a strong urge to cross the road to give this old man a wide berth, but manners get the better of me, and not wanting to appear rude, I holler an "Evening!" over the racket of the weather. He doesn't respond, nor move, nor acknowledge me in any way at all. As I begin to level with him, I worry that something might be wrong, and I reluctantly slow down. The last thing I want to be doing on such an evening is playing the good Samaritan.

The smell is the first thing to hit me. It starts damp and earthy, and quickly grows into an odour of rotting meat. You know—that awful metallic smell that instantly alerts you to the danger of foul meat, not to be consumed. The same mental warning triggers now, the inside of my nose starts to sting and my mouth fills with saliva in readiness to vomit. A weird, sweet undertone to the man's aroma comes next and is too much to bear. I lift my hand to my mouth as my shoulders heave with the effort of an empty retch. I'm thankful now that my stomach is still empty of an evening meal.

I want to walk away from this situation, but am also plagued with a nagging feeling of guilt at ignoring an elderly man, especially in this weather. Turning to face him, I begin to ask if he needs assistance, a move I instantly regret. Under the brim of his hat, one pale, watery blue eye looks blankly at me. The other eye is nothing but a cloudy grey ball, as if no iris or pupil were ever present. He slowly blinks, but as he does so, one eyelid seems to stick in its socket, and a milky yellow liquid oozes from the lower eyelid and runs slowly down his waxy, wrinkled cheek.

He opens his mouth to speak. His lips are dry and cracked as if he hasn't had a drink for weeks and his top lip curls into his mouth showing a distinct lack of teeth. His lower jaw seems to consist of blackened gum with jagged brown teeth protruding crudely here and there. His throat moves as if he's trying to say something, but the only noise to escape sounds like a raspy gargle. Something shiny and black begins to appear at the corner of his mouth, moving slowly outwards but I don't wait to find out what it is.

With a gasp, I turn fast on my heel and begin walking away from the man. With a shaking hand I rummage in my pocket for my phone to call the emergency services; they will be much better equipped to help than I am. And I'm scared, I'm not ashamed to admit it. I'm wearing my navy-blue raincoat and the lack of umbrella makes it impossible to keep my phone dry long enough to make a call. I lift the hem of my coat and try to wipe the screen on a dry part of my jeans, but it's no use. I decide to wait and ring them as soon as I get home.

I glance over my shoulder for one final check on the old man before I reach a turn in the road, maybe to make sure he is still OK, maybe hoping he has gone. To see him now following me is not something I'm prepared for, and I quickly look away, trying to calm myself from breaking out into a sprint. Again, my conscience gets the better of me and I wonder if he's trying to get help. Despite my pounding heart and clammy hands, I reluctantly look back again. The old man seems in no way to be trying to get my attention, but that one eye does seem to be focused directly on me.

He walks with a strange gait, almost like a shuffle, his legs in a permanently slightly bent, squat-like state. His shoes seem a few sizes too big for him, as if he's struggling to keep them on his feet. I now know I need to get away from this man. Whether he is in need or not is irrelevant right now; I'm beginning to feel like *I'm* the one who might soon require help. The houses I pass by are all in darkness. Where golden, glowing windows usually evoke a cosy, homey feeling on my evening journey, now they are cold, bleak, and lifeless, streaked with rain. I consider running up one of the small flights of stone steps and knocking on a front door. But the dark windows convince me that my efforts will be in vain, and I'm also reluctant to allow the old man to gain any ground between us.

I make the turn onto my street, the thought of being almost home is overwhelming and I speed up, my walk not far off a jog. The tree-lined street once offered shelter on sunnier days, but what's left of the brown leaves are being stripped from the branches by the endless rain. A soggy carpet of mulch now covers the paving stones, making a speedy walk home treacherous. A quick check shows the path behind me is empty, but the man's absence does little to abate my mild state of panic.

A small dog is trotting up the street towards me. I begin to wonder where its owner is, but I am beyond willing to offer any more help today.

As it nears me, I see it's a scruffy black and white thing, soggy and matted. As it comes closer still, I'm horrified by its appearance. The fur looks mangey and sparse, entirely missing in patches where the skin looks red and weeping with sores. The tongue lolling casually from its mouth has an unhealthy grey tinge and as the animal glances up at me, I see it shares the same cloudy, blind eyes as the man. How it can see where it's going, I have no idea. It passes me by, rounds the corner, and is gone.

    The rain always seems louder on my street, the fallen leaves working in unison with the rain in what sounds like a deafening round of applause. The streetlights finally flicker to life, but the effect is quite the opposite to that which I need. Everything now has an eerie glow, not the reassuring brightness I am craving. As I near home, I see something on the steps of my house. Not something, but someone. A small man wearing an old flat cap, and trousers far too short for him. He has only a thin white shirt which is wringing wet, the sleeves rolled up to his elbows, and over his shirt is some kind of thin waistcoat. His bare skin is filthy, the rain seemingly doing nothing to help wash it clean. He is looking away from me, up the street, but as I near him, I can tell he is in fact a young boy. I hesitate; I want to be home and away from this awful evening, but he remains sitting on my steps.

    A sudden clap of thunder makes me jump, and I can't help but gasp aloud. This catches the boy's attention, and he turns in my direction. His boyish features are long gone; a skeletal face looks back at me now. His eyes are so sunken, it seems for a second as though they're missing altogether. His thick, dirty blond hair is clinging to the sides of his face, small streams of water flow from it. His skin seems to be split at his temple and I think I just glimpsed some exposed skull. I feel my knees buckle beneath me and only just manage to stop myself falling onto the wet ground. I can't take my eyes off the boy, and he stands and smiles at me– the most sinister of smiles with decaying, black teeth, before turning and walking away.

    I steady myself against the tree trunk next to me, oblivious to the wetness against my skin. I feel bile rising in my throat and my vision starts to falter. Feeling as though I'm about to pass out, I consider sitting on those wet steps of home but I'm reluctant to put myself in the same space as that thing, that "child." Blinking hard to clear my vision, I blow out my cheeks with a few deep breaths and bolster myself for the last leg home. In a staggered lurch up the steps, I make it to the shelter of my front porch and search erratically for my keys, panic building as I do so. I thrust the cold key into the lock and let myself in, slamming the door behind me.

I rush to lock the door, but it does little in making me feel any calmer. Plunging my hand back into my pocket for my phone, I debate calling that ambulance, or whether now the police might be a better option. A bleeping sound lets me know the battery is about dead, so, cursing, I head to the kitchen where I left my charger this morning. That now seems like a lifetime ago. Walking into the kitchen, I reach to flick on the light and stop dead in my tracks. The back door is ajar, and pools of water have been tracked into the house.

Trying to allow my brain to catch up with what I'm seeing, I pause for a moment. I look up and see my phone charger, still plugged into the wall where I left it. Panicking that someone is now in the house, my priority is to call the police. Before I can move, I smell it: that rotten, rancid smell that I recognise all too quickly. My blood runs cold. I dare not move. Movement catches my eye and I see the mangey dog stick its head through the gap in the door, one soggy paw brazen enough to make it onto the kitchen floor in an almost threatening move. Those milky, blank eyes look up to meet mine, its teeth baring in a snarl, saliva hanging from its jowls. Then I hear that raspy gargle again, right behind me, and I feel damp breath on the back of my neck.

UNTIL THE NEXT TEN YEARS

By Allison Kurzynski

It had been a stroke of luck when LouAnne discovered the unassuming ad in the small local paper just as she was preparing to disappear into the night again.

It read:

> Family of Four seeks live-in Nanny
>
> Children: ages 3 and 6 months
>
> Applicant will be expected to act as caregiver and tutor
>
> Kitchen skills are a plus
>
> Sundays and Holidays off

LouAnne had set out on her own at an early age, chasing after a boy who had promised her his heart, only to be left stranded in an unfamiliar place. There was no going home once the relationship had fallen apart. Her parents had been devoutly religious; they believed that any woman who stepped out with a man with no chaperone was ruined. She had tried her best to make ends meet since then. She worked in the odd shop, and even a factory that allowed women to be employed. The long hours and low wages left her incredibly desperate.

With prohibition in full swing, it was easy to pick the pocket of a man that huddled a little too close to her at a bar. It didn't take long for pickpocketing to evolve into shoplifting, and shoplifting to evolve into embezzling. She took small amounts of money and supplies from the shops where she worked, thinking nothing of it.

However, this new life meant that she wasn't able to settle down in one place for too long. The concern of being caught encouraged her to leave before anyone noticed the discrepancies and theft.

The Carpolets were members of the Upper Crust. The father was the son of an Ironmaster, married to an industrial baron's daughter. It was odd that they were looking for a nanny on their own, without assistance from a professional company. Even after she purchased her bus ticket, LouAnne questioned the authenticity of the advertisement.

At the bottom of the ad had been the address with a date and time, indicating that all prospective applicants were to arrive on time to be considered for the job. What hesitation remained left her once she set her mind to chasing after the opportunity. The ticket for the bus was cheap enough. The town the Carpolets lived in was only a short half day's ride away. It was just far enough away to keep LouAnne from getting caught, should her transgressions be discovered, but close enough that she would make the date without hassle.

Leaving on such short notice left no lasting impression. The room LouAnne had occupied in the boarding house would be filled before the end of the week. The store that she had been working at would hire a new shop girl immediately. No one would remember she ever sulked around the corner before the month was out.

LouAnne couldn't believe her potential good fortune as she rode toward what could be her future. This could be the perfect job, and she could be perfect for it. There were no obligations to pull her from her duties to the family. Nor would anyone come looking for her if she didn't turn up elsewhere. LouAnne could simply disappear, just as quickly as she appeared.

The home was nothing like LouAnne had envisioned when she saw it for the first time. The bright cream color of the Carpolets home was like a beacon amongst a sea of green, a fortress atop a sloping hill, untouched by the neighborhood surrounding it.

Breathless from her walk up, LouAnne was struck with a wave of panic. No other applicants stood at the doorstep awaiting their turn. Concerned, she pulled out the small watch she kept in her carpet bag, and confirmed that she was, in fact, precisely five minutes early.

Something prickled in the back of her mind. Pushing forward, LouAnne climbed the stairs to the front entrance, each step feeling heavier than the last. Her heart fluttered. Her palms were sweating. There was no turning back.

Ornately carved oak, stained a rich brown, the door was just as magnificent as the house itself. It was not as inviting of the rest of the exterior though; the knocker was particularly off-putting to see: solid brass, heavy and harsh, in the shape of a ram's head. It glared in the sun, daring her to use its curved handle to disturb the house's residents. LouAnne gave a firm knock with her knuckles while returning the knocker's glare.

Minutes ticked by as LouAnne gazed out from the porch, taking in the view of the neighboring homes. The stillness ignited a joy she hadn't felt since she first set out into the world. However, the longer she looked out across the horizon, the more she became aware of the hair on the back of her neck beginning to stand on end. The unmistakable feeling of being watched prompted her to whip back around to face the entrance and see if she had somehow missed the door opening.

She was unsettled.

No one was behind her. The door was still firmly shut. For a fleeting moment, LouAnne was certain that she had seen someone out of the corner of her eye. Ever the rational individual, she quickly dismissed the thought, certain she was misjudging the unfamiliar shadows of the manor for something they weren't.

Impatience set in the longer she waited for the door to open. LouAnne finally heard the muffled sound of footsteps on the other side of the door, just as she was about to reach forward to knock once more. Correcting her posture, she stood ready to meet her potential employer and begin the next charade.

The air felt like it was being ripped from her lungs much like a tree ripped from the ground in a tornado. Her chest flattened with a sharp exhale. Her ears rang. Electrifying beats of her pulse coursed throughout her entire being. Hair stood on end. Eyes dried from refusing to blink.

One minute, the world slowed to a stop as excitement and anxiety over this new venture set in. The next, she found herself staring up at the clear blue sky, gagging on her own hot, sticky blood as it poured down into her throat from the gaping wound left by the shotgun, held within the delicate hands of an equally delicate woman.

Mabel Carpolet had the decency to look aghast and, one might even say, distraught. Her body shook from nerves, eyes widening in horror at the way the shotgun had eviscerated LouAnne's chest cavity. The force of the blast had flung the woman away from the door toward the top of the steps, and gravity pulled her body down that rest of the way so that it was splayed across the stoop.

The shock kept any pain from setting in during those last moments. LouAnne's eyes, wide with terror, rolled around in her skull like those of a panicked deer. She choked on the blood flooding her throat, a wet crackling coming from deep within her chest as her body fought to clear her lungs.

Linus Carpolet joined his wife on the porch seconds after LouAnne's body hit the steps. Unlike his spouse, Linus seemed unperturbed by the sight before him. Wrapping an arm around Mabel's quivering shoulders, he pulled her close. Once in her husband's arms, Mabel turned her face into his chest, dropping the gun to the floor with a clatter, shielding herself from the sight of the poor woman dying before her. Soft sobs escaped her throat as the adrenaline ebbed out of her body.

"Hush, my sweet, you did so well. The first is always the hardest," Linus whispered, recalling how he too had been a mess the first time he had assisted his father with the family ritual.

Her whimpering subsided as shock set in. He then turned his attention back to the body, which had finally stopped twitching. Extracting himself from Mabel's hold, he moved toward LouAnne to confirm that she was actually dead. Taking the first step down, he was startled when the eyes that had rolled to the back of the corpse's skull flared back to life and pinned him and Mabel with a horrified stare for one last second. Linus' jaw clenched as Mabel wailed.

Exasperated with her delicate constitution, Linus barked at her, "Enough of that, it's not alive, these kinds of automatic movements happen right after they die." He did not divulge that the body's eyes were not really looking at them. They were instead pinned on a point behind them.

Hidden deep within the dark corners of the home, dwelled a creature. Its smell of decay had been a constant companion to Linus for the last week, a reminder of what needed to be done. It was time to satiate its hunger and will, ensuring his family's safety.

LouAnne would not have been able to see much of it in her final moments. Linus knew that the last thing the woman saw was gray leather skin and rolling yellow eyes peering out from the darkness in glee. Her fleeting encounter with the beast was something Linus would envy. She would never know the stench of infection and rot that followed it.

To Linus and his forefathers, murdering unsuspecting individuals was a small price to pay to keep their home and wealth. A pact made three generations prior, each heir of the fortune would make the sacrifice of another life once every ten years. What was one life if it meant keeping the manor house standing, and the bank accounts full?

Did he feel guilt for what needed to be done? If he felt any, it would have been during his teenage years when he first learned of his family's secret. Shame lessened when the full weight of the family reputation sat upon his shoulders; with every kill, he grew more accustomed to the act. Now in his forties, as the head of the household, the once-per-decade sacrifice was as simple as changing out the ink in his fountain pen. It would take Mabel longer to grow accustomed to the rite. Younger than himself by twenty years, she was still bright-eyed and impressionable. Come the next decade, she would understand why it was so important to carry out the act. By then, his eldest son would also be old enough to learn why, how, and when it was to be completed. This body laid out on his front steps was like all the others before it: a means to an end.

Drawing a victim to the home had been a careful orchestration, one made easier by Linus' hobby. Owning a minor publishing company allowed Linus to acquire the contracts needed to print newspapers for the surrounding areas. When the time came, he just needed to switch out one of the thousands of papers printed, with one that had been run with the extra ad. After that, it was just a matter of the newspaper falling into the hands of the right sort of person. Someone unlucky enough to have the ambition to try and improve their social standing by working for *his* family.

Linus stooped over the body to confirm that it was dead, fingers pressed against its throat. He ignored the cold, congealed blood that transferred from its skin to his own hand. The dull eyes and cooling skin confirmed the lack of pulse, and that they could now begin disposing of the corpse. Nodding his head, Linus stood and turned back to Mabel.

"Bring out the sheet," he instructed.

Mabel nodded her head in meek acknowledgment of his demand, and hastened to retrieve the plaid sheet that Linus had placed on the foyer table the night before. Hands still quivering, she passed the fabric into her husband's outstretched hand, doing her best to avoid looking down to witness her handiwork. She did not wish to burn the image of the poor woman into her mind any more than it already was.

"Now, go to the cellar and get the buckets and rags. The hard part is over and I need you to clean up while I make short work of this here." Linus watched his wife retreat back into the house before shaking out the sheet, and throwing it over the remains. There was no need to be gentle, he mused, as he roughly wrapped the body up and threw it over his shoulder. It wasn't as if it was alive to protest the rough treatment. Groaning under the extra weight, Linus carried the corpse around the side of the house, to the exterior cellar doors.

There, he unceremoniously dumped it to the ground, allowing him to bend forward and toss open the heavy basement doors with a clatter. Grabbing the ankles of the body, he pulled it down the stone staircase. There in the dim lighting he discovered Mabel hurriedly wiping tears away from her face. Disgruntled, Linus released his hold on the body and stalked toward his wife. Gripping her arms tightly, he shook her.

"Listen here, you had the option to sit this out but you chose to do this." Mabel whimpered as he squeezed her upper arms harder. "I will not have you falling apart when there is work to be done. Now take the buckets and rags and get to work. Am I clear?"

"Ye … yes, Linus," Mabel whispered, before rushing to collect her items once he had let her go. Her husband's eyes bore into her back as she ascended the staircase he had just come down, grateful when she no longer felt their weight.

Once she was out of sight, he returned to work. Hoisting the body up once more, he flung it onto the laundry table that had been placed above the storm drain and removed the blanket. Confident that Mabel had been set straight and would begin cleaning the front entry as instructed, he retrieved the hand saw and garden knife from their resting place amongst the gardening equipment, and began the process of draining and dismembering the corpse.

Every slicing cut, every wet crunch, brought Linus closer to his objective. The smaller the pieces, the easier it would be to hide them all. It was a lesson his grandfather and father had ensured was ingrained in his very being. The lessons started with small game caught during weekend hunts, preparing him for the larger, more important game he would be dressing for the remainder of his life.

This was his fourth time completing the rite expected of his bloodline. By now, the task had become a delicate dance between himself and the body he tended. The fluid actions he executed reminded him of a well-practiced waltz like the one he and Mabel had danced at a wedding they recently attended. Steady and smooth, he worked in a sort of trance-like state, unaware of his hidden audience reveling in the shadows, soaking in the glory of the sins completed in its name.

Linus' work went well into the night. The disposal was only considered complete once no trace of the corpse could be found. Only then would he be able to climb the interior stairs, leaving the tainted work of Hell behind him and return to his carefully curated life above. Only then could he wash himself of the deeds done and join Mabel in their bed.

Even after a thorough cleaning, Mabel could still smell the sweet metallic tang of the woman's blood on her husband, while she herself smelled of the bleach used to clean away her very existence. Curled beneath the blankets, she could not stop the shivers that continued to invade her body, even hours after completing her part in the act.

Sliding into bed, Linus lent over his wife and pushed a strand of hair away from her forehead. "You did so well today," he crooned, stooping to leave a kiss on the crown of her head.

"I cannot do this again, Linus. It was so horrible. Her eyes, the way she tried to keep breathing." Mabel lifted herself into her husband's chest and clung to him for support, sobbing. She had thought she would be strong enough to be a participant in the rite but now she knew it would be a stain on her soul she could not live with.

Linus bit his tongue as Mabel cried on his shoulder. This would not do.

"Hush now," he whispered into her hair, "It's all said and done. So it didn't die quickly, the rite was still complete. We have ten years for you to settle into the family, darling. That's a long time to work through this pain."

She would have to, he thought darkly. If Mabel did not learn how to live with what they had done and would need to do in the future, well, there would be no need for an ad ten years from now.

"Rest now, my love. We have ten years ahead of us to enjoy. Do not let this darken our time."

He kissed her forehead. "Until the next ten years."

KANSAS FOREVER

By Amy Bennett

She wakes with a gasp that sends her coughing and sitting up in the blush of early morning light. Far off in the old farmhouse, she can make out the sound of soft snores that lets her know her husband Charles is downstairs, sound asleep. He could never spend the night upstairs in the bedroom in the summer heat. Evelyn pulls back the linen bedsheets twisted around her legs and steps softly to the washroom across the hall. With a match from the box on the sink, she strikes and lights an oil lamp and the porcelain is diffused in a soft yellow glow that flickers across the mirror's reflection before her.

Forty-five years stare back at Evelyn Prewett, "Evie" to anyone who knows her. The sweat has already begun to dry around her grey-and-deep-brown hairline, but the neck of her nightgown is damp and going cold. She's tired, but knows there's no use going back to sleep at this point. The rough lines around her eyes are a reminder of how much she's done to keep the farm running, and how much there's yet to get to in the coming day. Getting a jump on the long list of daily tasks would be helpful, she rationalizes as she washes up.

Waking up so suddenly and still resounding with a sense of disquiet after such a terrifying nightmare is new to Evie. She doesn't recall ever being plagued by nightmares or other sleep disturbances in her lifetime, and she remains on edge as the farm slowly wakes up around her. To Evie, it feels as though the sun and the birds and life itself is catching up to her after that odd, rough start. The last fragments she can recall are the rage she felt looming from the person coming for her in the dream, in the blue work shirt. The shirt was straining at the creases as an arm came down from over their head, right toward her face.

'What could that even mean?' She ponders idly.

Evie blinks and turns the cold tap on hard and shakes the leftover dread out of her mind with icy water. The heat outside never seems to relent, but the well water is reliably cold. Puzzling over the nightmare's origin, she can't recall having a bad day in recent memory. No bickering with Charles, no problems with the grandkids, and it unnerves her how this nightmare needled its way into her sleep. Something's changed, but she can't quite determine what it is. As the minutes go by, the feelings and images of the nightmare fade as she moves through the motions of her routine.

After dressing quickly in a cotton dress, Evie begins to boil water for the coffee and slip on her workbooks by the back door. A feeling like déjà vu comes over her as she peers at the leather and frayed laces of the other pairs of boots sitting beside the door. They remind her of the dream and the sound of hard steps across a wood floor, speeding up and getting louder as they come up fast behind her. But her recollection of the dream fades, and that gives her a small sense of relief.

With a furtive look over her shoulder into the still-dark kitchen and parlor beyond, Evie sighs, swings the creaking wood door shut behind her and sets off across the yard to take care of their meager but necessary livestock. The goats and chickens provide more through the Kansas winters than the town's general store can, if the roads are even in a condition to be taken in the first place. If she times it right, she can get back to the house as the water is getting hot and the sun is just peeking over the low hills of corn on the horizon. The sun will help ease the day to normalcy, to the peace she craves.

The bleating of the goats startles her back to the present and the morning continues as she knows it would, caring for the animals as she listens to the grandchildren play in the side yard. She prepares food and leaves it warming on the stovetop for when they're finally tired enough to come inside. Evelyn's husband eats when he wants but takes to staying in the parlor, listening to CBS incessantly.

Charles keeps the Philco radio turned on all the time these days, now that he's retired. At 58 he was let go from the factory as a 20-year foreman when a larger company bought out the failing paper mill. Since then, his forced retirement has made him bitter, as though he deserved something more, or missed a vital mark on his life's trajectory. Evie knows he loves her; he was just never taught how to show it just right. When they're good they're good, though, and right now, they're good. She thinks now and then she should just talk to Charles and sets out to look for him, but every time she tries, he's out in the barns or fields, busying himself in the distance. He doesn't look up. Evie goes back to taking care of the farmhouse.

He'd raised their children with her the best they can, to the tune of three grandchildren, all under the age of nine, who stay with them often, much to Evie's delight. They help keep Charles young; Evie's convinced herself of that. When she stops to listen, she can hear the kids playing on the porch, their little feet running back and forth. Even when they're not visiting, she swears she can hear their patter on the old planks and undulating voices just beyond the windows. It's one of the many delightful sounds of her family farmhouse. She just likes it better when she can hear it.

Several nights pass, and again, the nightmare worms its way into Evelyn's sleep. The blue work shirt she can see moving toward her is stained down the right side, Evie is staring at it as she peers at this person from behind a shuttered door. She's in a tight space, pressed into other clothing hanging on either side of her shoulders. It's a worthless hiding place and Evie realizes it in her dream, but she has no control over what's happening, all she can do is buy time before this person, *this man*, she thinks, finds her. In the dream she seems to blink and then the man is closer, just outside the thin wood doors of the closet space she's standing in. She wishes she could run but her body is restricted like its underwater, under mud, under the weight of a mix of terror and desperation. Her panting increases and her heartbeat matches it as she stares in silence at the blue shirt creep closer through the slats. She wishes she could flatten herself into nothing against the back wall but she's seemingly backed herself into a corner and has no choice but to make a break for it.

The faded denim blue shirt sleeve gropes forward in the oil-lit darkness toward the narrow space Evie is in. She hesitates and then lunges forward with both hands out, shoving wildly and hoping to knock her assailant backward, if only for a moment to startle them. All she can buy is time, but there's a sliver of her mind that knows this is a nightmare, and there's an awful ending coming. The final swing comes seconds later to the sound of her breath ragged in her throat, and the dreamscape snaps away into darkness.

Sweating and heaving, Evie sits up and fumbles for the edge of the blankets. She's twisted up and reaches her arm out for Charles, forgetting for a moment that he's likely asleep downstairs. She glances toward the armoire against the far wall and sees both of their clothing hanging limp in the damp summer air like ghostly people standing in a line. The wood doors hanging open give Evie an unsettling feeling and she looks away, pulling herself free from the tangle of bedsheets to make her way to the bathroom and out of the grip of the nightmare. The after-effects wash down the drain with the icy water while the first songbirds awaken and chirp in the near-darkness. Their calls ease Evie slightly, and let her know morning isn't far off. She may as well stay up and start the day.

Time passes, but the nightmare interrupts Evie's sleep every so often, and she can't help but feel jittery after she wakes. The images she remembers are few: two slatted wood doors, a final swing before her heart seems to jump from her chest before her own bedroom's darkness envelops her again. She hears the children playing, she prepares the food and tends to the animals, but an unpleasant dread follows her in her waking reality like a dull headache on those mornings. It confuses her because nothing *seems* amiss. The farm is doing well, the summer days are pleasant, and the kids are healthy. She can't quit the feeling of uneasiness that follows her through the house on the mornings she wakes from the nightmare, but at least by the end of the day, she can't quite remember what she was so afraid of anymore.

There's a distance with Charles that has always been there, just under the surface. He wouldn't understand what this feeling was, and she doesn't want to change their peaceful home with any distress for the family, especially not on her account. She'd never want to trouble the grandkids either. The chores at home can't be put off and no one is going make Evelyn Prewett out to be a weak woman, prone to hysteria or overexcitement. She carries on with her days and after some time, forgets about it altogether.

Evelyn awakens to the sound of heavy footsteps. She's standing in a cold, dark room, confused but alert. It was like she had drifted off one second and only a moment later awoken in the darkened room of a nightmare, a room familiar but implacable. Simple wooden floors. More heavy steps, closer this time and thudding onto wood that cracks on each footfall. Were they coming up stairs? She moves unconsciously, at the will of the dream. She's heading for an opening, two wooden doors with slats. The attacker is getting closer, but the dream sequence resonates as terrifying as reality.

A blue shirt and heavy breaths of a man creep through the room toward the doors. The slats are just far enough apart to see his torso and legs. If only she could look up, if only she could see this person after her. The adrenaline of fleeing for her life has left her almost manic with exhaustion and agony, but she remains locked in the nightmare. In a moment of lucidity, Evie looks down beside her. There's clothing pressed up against her side, limp in the heat.

Is this the armoire?

There's no time left to wonder what she's seeing, and she can't hold onto the control over the nightmare. The events move forward, she pushes through the doors with both hands out and scrambles toward the open doorway of the room.

Her room.

The hallway is dark, like it's closing in around her, but for the floorboards in front of her, and the anguish of muddled, uncoordinated dream movement brings a new flush of terror as she tries harder to pump her legs, to run faster. Evie is convinced she can beat the nightmare before it plays out.

Whoosh.

Her body turns and her eyes lock on the arm in the blue shirt. Evie squeezes her eyes shut and screams. In an instant, she's awake again and in the bed she recognizes. She can't hold the fleeting dream images in her mind, and sighs deeply, turning over slowly on her side. The armoire stands solemnly against the far wall, the doors open. Something about it now feels sinister to Evie, and she pulls herself out of the room in a few hurried movements. The oil lamp, the sink, the cold water. This is the routine she knows before morning breaks.

She dresses, and turns to leave the bedroom without pulling open the curtains. There's something about the room that doesn't feel quite right but she knows the family will be downstairs, waiting for her. That will be peaceful, and at this age and this long in the life she's lived, all she wants is her peace. Finding that through the farm, the family and the farmhouse that's been in her family for generations is what she knows she has to focus on. In not too many minutes of busying herself around the property, the nightmare slips away.

The summer buzzes along, warm and teeming with life. Inside and out of the farmhouse Evie takes on her tasks. Now and again, she's reminded of her family members, especially going through the cleaning and finding cherished belongings hidden in the closets or tucked away in drawers. As she carefully resets a lace runner she's reminded of something her grandmother spoke to her of when she was a little girl. *Soothsayers.* Apparently, there'd been someone in the town who knew the weather and upcoming births and deaths well before any of the three arrived. Evie wonders if the odd sense of unease that follows her some mornings might be attributable to some extra sense of knowing, seeing something bad or good a little early. In her case, quite bad. The idea unsettles her, but she keeps it to herself. Charles would consider her to be having female peculiarities, a conversation with him would be useless, and she doesn't want to rile him up. She tells herself there's probably a normal reason for the lack of peace to her days and the growing dread as night folds in over her, but that only satiates the surface of her anxiety.

Tonight, Evie switches off the Philco after Charles begins to snore and heads up to the bedroom. Halfway upstairs, the sound of static abruptly blares out around her as though someone's turned the radio knob between stations and cranked the volume up. Startled, she turns and runs back to the parlor, expecting to see Charles at the machine. As she turns the corner into the room, the static stops. Charles is nowhere to be seen.

Shaking with adrenaline, Evie stands dumbfounded looking at the radio. It is off, it's usual electrical hum cut to silence. There's no sound of static, no sound at all, Evie realizes. No crickets chirping or sounds of the summer evening. Dead silence meets her as she turns slowly in the room. Where she was certain there were still lamps lit, there's only darkness throughout the rest of the downstairs now. One flicker of light bounces off the rafters at the top of the stairs. Taking a tentative step forward, Evie calls for Charles. Her voice comes out weak like it's difficult to speak.

Making her way slowly up the stairs, she follows the glow of the bedroom lamp light to the end of the hall. The room is cast in a warm glow, but it's hotter than it should be. Sweat beads across her forehead and upper lip as she begins to cross the room. There's not a sound but her own breath and the scuff of her bare feet on the wood floors. The silence is as confusing as the sound of the radio, and in her desperation, Evie trips forward toward the bed and calls out for Charles again, but the sound of her voice is hollowed out. She looks frantically around to find something to defend herself with, but the room is sparse and there's no time as heavy footsteps sound behind her, downstairs. Evie's breath catches in her throat. It sounds like more than one person. Something might have happened to Charles and now they're coming for her.

Standing in the middle of the room, Evie glances around quickly for a place to hide. The sparsely decorated house at the edge of the woods has never been full of rich furniture, and the bed is too low to squeeze under. More footsteps, closer this time and coming up the stairs. Evie weighs the best of her options and tiptoes to the armoire, climbing inside the tall wooden piece of furniture older than her, as quietly as she can. Standing between the wire hangars she eases the double doors closed with an inch in front of her and a thin line of sight into the room.

The heavy steps approach at the door as Evie keeps her body still, breathing shallow and quietly. The footsteps are louder as they enter the room and cross the floor. The cedar wood planks trigger her memory and for a moment and she feels a disturbed familiarity to the situation.

Summoning whatever strength she can, she shoves forward as a shadow crosses the floor. As the shirt sleeve appears, Evie pushes out against the armoire doors with both hands and the man stumbles backward several steps. Evie knows she shrieks the words *"Get out!"* as she flings herself forward, but she can only hear it echo in her mind.

Leaping barefoot toward the door, Evie catches the shadow of a second person standing in the room. They're hard to see in the dark, and only their outline is visible. *This isn't part of the dream,* Evie thinks as she swings around the doorframe and propels herself down the hall. A terror that's been fermenting for months rises inside her as the hallway stretches out before her. She can't seem to run as fast as she knows she should be, and a sob rips from her throat. Evie turns around against her will, powerless to stop her body from doing it as the nightmare takes its course in disjointed, agonizingly slow seconds. The blue work shirt meets her vision as she stands at the top of the stairs. She's tried to fight the nightmare every brutalizing second, but she can't wake up and she can't change the events playing out before her. With a swish of air coming down toward her face, a woman's excited voice accompanies it:

"Can you give us another sign of your presence?"

Evie screams, and everything goes black.

The first light of morning sliding between the curtains, painting everything a soft blue, is the first thing Evie sees as she wakes up. Disoriented but calm, the nightmare fades as she blinks and sits up. Pulling back the bedsheets, Evie crosses the room and shuts the doors of the armoire before lighting the gas lamp in the washroom and splashing cold water on her face from the tap. As she stops to listen, the sound of Charles' snoring downstairs is as reassuring as always, and Evie sighs, resolved to get to the tasks of the day that keep the farmhouse running. She knows she had a bad dream last night, a vivid one, but she can't recall quite what made it so bad.

From the kitchen, she looks out to the parlor and sees the Philco radio in the next room, accompanying the soft sounds of sleep from her husband. The kids will be up soon, and the animals are probably stirring already. The whine of summer greets her at the back door and the sunrise begins in full. Tying the laces of her boots, she stands up to face the row of wooden pegs and clothing hanging next to the door. A green coat, a straw hat and two of Charles' denim work shirts. Taking in the faded and stained blue weave of the shirts, Evie blinks. For a split second a sense of confusion washes over her, but she shakes it off and sets off across the yard to begin another summer day at her family's farmhouse. If there were ever a more beautiful, peaceful place to exist, Evelyn Prewett couldn't think of it. The long summer days on the farm were always her favorite.

    This is where she'd like to stay forever.

THE WRITER

By Bizzy Blank

Rose sat hunched over her keyboard, as she'd spent almost every hour for the past three days. She needed to get it all out before she burst out of her own skin. She typed and the clacking of the keyboard jostled her coffee. Coffee was required when you'd been up for three days straight. The crawling feeling up the skin on her legs and heavy breathing on the back of her neck had almost subsided; that was how she knew she was almost done. When she was working, she felt almost inhuman, like something else took over. Finishing an entire book in three days was nearly impossible, but Rose managed to do it again and again. This would be the tenth book she turned into her editor; her publisher loved her, of course.

As she typed the last sentence, she shut her eyes, just for a moment. A wave of relief flooded her entire body. She sighed, knowing it was only temporary. The time between when she finished her book and when she recovered from lack of sleep was an unsettling period. Rose always felt like she was being watched. She did not handle lack of sleep well. She closed her computer and worked on cleaning up the wreckage around her; coffee mugs and water glasses crowded the space, almost to the point of toppling over the edge of the table. As she slid the last mug into the sink, she noticed a long scratch down her arm. She really needed to be more careful when she was in her creative zone. She always ended up hurting herself without realizing it.

She made her way to the bathroom to take a bath before crashing into bed. Rose needed some time to come down from the writing high before she was able to sleep. She undressed and stretched. All that time hunched over made her back ache. The warm water would help her to ease her pain, still her heart, and clear the ringing in her ears. She noticed some bruising around her ankle. While she was writing, she must have had it pressed against her chair. She'd always been less than aware of her body; Rose either had zero awareness of pain and sensations or been totally consumed by it. This had made life difficult for her.

As a child, she would have spells where she felt her skin crawling. She was convinced something was wrong and there must be bugs or a ring worm inside her. Her mother was so alarmed at her erratic behavior to try to tame the bugs that she took her straight to the emergency room. After many negative tests and consultations, she was diagnosed with OCD. Rose's mother was pleased to finally have something to point to when she acted in a manner that drew attention. She'd always drawn attention. The attention was never wanted.

She was one of those people who had an inviting spirit; strangers naturally gravitated towards her. Rose, herself, felt very introverted and rarely started conversations with anyone. Yet somehow, every time she went out, there was a stranger drawn to her, spilling their deepest secrets. Rose didn't mind. She was a good listener. She nodded in all the right places and showed genuine concern for the stranger. *This must be why they are drawn to me*, Rose thought to herself. The trauma dumping left Rose feeling drained. Her sister, Sarah, told her it was because she was an empath. She absorbed other peoples' energy. It felt a little far-fetched to her, but she didn't have any other explanation. In high school, she learned to channel the energy into writing. Rose created fantastically horrible worlds where she wrote the stranger's secret and turned them into demons. She wrote for herself; to focus and get rid of the skin crawling energy she felt.

Now, as she sank into her bath, she could breathe a sigh of relief. Her body melted into the warm water. Rose's eyes were almost closed when she saw something go past her door. She blinked and rubbed her eyes. She lived alone, there couldn't actually be anyone or anything out there. She talked herself through relaxing each group of muscles. Rose often saw things after writing because she was so sleep deprived. She blamed all the hours immersed in the wretched worlds she created; her brain had a hard time transitioning back into reality.

Finishing her bath, she made her way down the hall to her bedroom and curled up. She felt her body sink into her mattress, finally relaxing. Her body settled enough to drift off. With her eyes closed, she heard light footsteps in the distance–three soft steps. She pulled her covers over her head. The steps grew louder. She clamped her eyes shut and stilled her breathing. If she didn't move, it couldn't get her. She stayed still for so long, she fell asleep.

This was the same cycle that occurred every time she wrote, and Rose grew more and more reclusive as she aged. She continued to produce books, her fan base growing with each release. She did not do public appearances for her books, and the mystery surrounding her led to almost a cult-like following. Everyday her mailbox was flooded with letters from fans. She did not read them unless the envelope caught her eye. Some of these fans felt so drawn to her that they scrawled letters, manically spilling their secrets in pages upon pages. Rose nailed her mail flap closed and directed her sister to have her mail sent to a holding facility.

She had the same routine every day. Her sister would drop her groceries off and Rose would set about her routines. She would check the door and rooms in her house to ensure she was alone and the things she heard were only in her head. She made herself a healthy meal and chased it with a glass of whiskey. She checked the doors again and sat in her cozy recliner with an enemies-to-lovers romance novel and finished the night in silence. Rose became a hermit.

In a few weeks, her symptoms faded and she felt more alive. She was able to take walks around her yard, and people pretty much left her alone. One night, after dinner, she heard a new voice

"There is one more" it whispered.

One more what?

She'd stopped writing when she stopped leaving her house. But tonight, she felt the old familiar feeling. It was a hand wrapped around her ankle. It was squeezing to the point of pain. She froze.

Why was it back?

Nails down her arm. Hot breath at her back.

"Go. Find them and write," it growled. The voice grew louder. The hand gripped harder. She did not know what she was supposed to be looking for, but she had to get out of her house, if only to get away from it.

Rose went to the grocery store near her house. She stopped at the baskets of flowers near the entrance, and she picked one up to smell it. A man slid in next to her and picked up a different flower to smell. He smiled at her and began talking. This was how it always started. Small talk was not needed; she was just a vessel for their secret demons. They were the fuel for her books, though the strangers never knew. After he had emptied his heart of his demons for her to care for, he left feeling lighter. She slumped a bit as if the wind had been knocked out of her; it was a familiar feeling. She didn't mind it as much as the breathing on her back that had urged her there in the first place. Rose made the trek home, hoping she could get some rest.

The cycle had begun again, but this time was different. No matter how much she wrote, the skin-crawling feeling would not subside. She tried everything. She wrote and wrote and wrote. Trying to walk away, she felt a pull right back. Rose finally broke down and pulled out a bottle of liquor. She wrote and she drank. She typed to the point that her fingers were blistered. When she finally finished, she didn't bother clearing her space. She lay her head down on the desk to sleep there.

Three days later, Rose's sister, dressed in all black, walked into the parlor where Rose's body was being held. Hush whispers spread throughout the service. They could not believe that *the* Rose Sherwood was dead. People lined the walls, hoping to get a glimpse of the reclusive author. A little girl and her mother walked in behind Sarah. The little girl pulled on her mother's sleeve.

"Is that her, Mommy? Your favorite writer? I will be like her when I am older. I will be your new favorite writer," she told her.

The man standing at the casket turned to face them. His eyes were dark and sunken, as if Rose's death had greatly affected him. He walked past the row of people in the back of the room. They were familiar to him; he'd helped her create their existence. Each one crawled from the depths of each stranger pouring out their long-held secrets, following her home. They whisper, urging Rose to write them into existence so that they could live on. He made his way past the little girl. She walked over to him.

"It's OK to be sad," she said, patting him on the arm. "Everyone is so sad she is gone. Did she write any more books?" She asked him.

"She wrote her last, but I see her talent in your eyes," he said, touching her cheek as he walked away.

The little girl watched him go. Soon she began scratching and slapping at her arms. She walked over to her mother in a panic.

"Mommy, I think I have bugs under my skin."

To Be With Her

By Karly R. Latham

I wake in a cold sweat.

I saw her again—the woman who haunts my dreams. Ever since she first appeared, images of her have been swimming in and out of my mind all through my waking hours. My once-organized desk is now overflowing with notebooks, each filled with sketched drawings of her. Hours of my day have been eaten away trying to capture her dark hair falling delicately to her waist and even more, trying to capture the longing in her eyes.

Does she long for me as I long for her?

Sharp knocking comes at my door as my mother's voice echoes through the heavy wooden door, "Thomas! You must come out. It's been days! You have duties to attend to. Your brother would never have acted so irresponsibly."

I make no reply. I hear her sigh and lean her head against the door. Mother knocks again and says in a softer tone, "Have you at least eaten today?"

The heavy silver lid of my dinner platter is lifted and placed down once again. "Please, Thomas, you have to come out," she says, before pounding on the door again, threatening to have the butler unlock the door. She finally gives up and leaves with an exasperated sigh.

As her heels tapping against the hardwood floors recede, my thoughts return to her—my dream woman. I care little about my duties or the endless social gatherings and charity balls. They are trivial at best. Women fawned over me, begging me to fill their dance cards and hoping to win my fancy, as if any other woman could compare to her beauty.

My friends assumed I locked myself away like a love-sick puppy, not understanding her hold over me. My passion for billiards and hunts has long disappeared; she has replaced everything I once loved. Now my days are spent counting down the hours till nightfall. Nothing matters anymore except for her.

The first time I awoke and saw her pale figure shrouded in shadows, it terrified me. I sat bolt upright, yelling, "Who are you?!"

She stepped forward then, allowing me the briefest glimpse of her. Now, night after night, she appears, standing tantalizingly out of reach in the corner of my chambers as she stares at me.

Her visits come more and more frequently until I am driven mad with a mixture of curiosity and desire. Why does she haunt me? The anticipation of her visits weighs heavily upon my mind. Day in and day out, I think of her. I lay down at night, awaiting her arrival and hoping to know more. I can feel her beckoning me, silently calling my name from whatever realm she resides in.

When she is here, the world around me feels so vivid, as if my waking life is the dream and this is reality. I can feel the air swirl around in my room when she appears, as a cool caress pushes my night clothes. Her eyes penetrate my very soul. She's the picture of perfection, filling me with a thirst I know I'll never be able to quench.

She moves a little closer each night, and my breath catches in my throat each time, entirely overcome by her beauty. The delicate features of her face, combined with the deep color of her eyes captivate me, both familiar and yet unknown all at once. The need to unravel the mystery of who she is overcomes me.

Finally, I open my eyes to see her standing within my reach. Passion floods my system as her long raven hair tumbles past her shoulders. Reaching my fingers out slowly, just to feel those silky raven strands, my fingers pass through her. Disappointment tastes bitter in my mouth. She remains still, smiling pleasantly at me. I need her like I've never needed another woman. My gaze travels down her pale flesh to see her dressed in a simple white gown before coming up to study her face.

My eyes focus on her soft lips. I would do anything to hear her speak. Desperately, I ask, "Please, I must know what to call you. Won't you tell me your name?"

Her eyes stare into mine. My heartbeat quickens as she opens her mouth. I hardly dare hope that she will finally grant my deepest wish and let her voice fill my still, silent bed chamber. Her breath catches slightly, making my ears strain for the slightest sound. Instead, she slowly reaches a hand to me, and anticipation fills me as I study her long, slender fingers.

Her eyes plead with me, begging for me to understand, before she lifts her fingers with a frustrated expression. She flickers and disappears. Frantically searching the room for her, I cry out, "Please, come back!"

The air shimmers in front of me once more. She reappears, wearing a delicate gown embroidered with little blue flowers—something about the pattern of the fabric scratches at my memory. I've forgotten something important, but what?

I move to reach for her once again, but pause as fear etches itself across every inch of her face, and her mouth opens wider in a silent, endless scream. Shock has me whirling my head around, searching for the cause of her distress, "What is it? Why are you screaming?"

I brace myself, thinking her wailing cries will wash over me any second. Part of me wishes they *would* wash over me. I would gladly drown in a never-ending stream of her sound just to hear her voice, but no sound escapes her lips.

I don't know what she is seeing or reacting to, but I want to understand. Was she hurt? What is she trying to get me to understand? Why doesn't she speak? I have an endless list of questions, and I fear I'll never receive an answer to them.

Daylight warms my skin as I wonder if perhaps she will come again tonight. Hours pass as I watch the sun travel across the sky. I lay down and close my eyes. I hear my name whispered: "Thomas."

My eyes fly open, and my heart beats frantically in my chest. After quickly lighting a candle, I peer around in the dark. My room is as empty as it was when I laid my head down.

I lay down again, and finally, there she is, once more standing before me. Only this time, something is different. Instead of staying still, watching me from the shadows, I reach for her, sighing as I finally hold her in my arms. She feels solid as she nestles into my grasp. After all this time, my deepest desire has come true.

Smoothing her hair back, I see her smile as she says, "Thomas, I've been waiting."

Confusion sweeps over me. What does she mean? She has been coming to *me*, not the other way around. "Yes, of course, my love, I would never stop looking for you."

A smile spreads across her face as she climbs onto my bed and sits beside me. "Will you lay with me, Thomas?" I feel the bed indent with her weight upon it. I put my hand out and felt the warmth radiating from her skin.

How is this possible?

Perhaps this is yet another dream. I can't tell if I'm awake or asleep. Reaching down, I pinch my thigh hard enough to make me wince. This is real. I eagerly pull her to my side, letting my hands roam across her gown. "You're here. I can't believe it."

The longing I have felt for ages overcomes me as I bring my lips toward hers. Her mouth eagerly meets mine, and it isn't long before I lift her skirts to bury myself in her warmth. "Oh God, Bethany, you feel so good."

Her eyes flash.

"What did you say?"

Suddenly she's straddling me, with her hand wrapped around my throat. The air between us feels different. Barely controlled rage comes off of her in waves. I open my mouth to speak, but now my voice cannot escape. My limbs are frozen in place as she whispers, "Say my name, Thomas. I want you to remember me."

My eyes fly to her face, searching the expressions dancing across it. Her mouth hangs open as she stares at her stomach before reaching down. Lifting them slowly, with tears running down her face, she showed me her fingers dripping with red. "How could you?"

I roll away from her in horror, only to see *my* hands stained red. "What is this?"

I took her into the gardens, pressing her against a bench, loving the small sounds of desire she made for me. *Bethany.* I remember the way she felt moving beneath me.

"Thomas, please, I don't think we should … "

The gardens faded away, replaced with her shoving past the butler into my bed chambers breathlessly saying, "Why haven't you responded to my correspondence? I have news."

Her hand flies to her stomach. "I'm with child."

I wake gasping, looking around my bed chambers. They finally find her again standing in the corner of my room. Bethany stood before me, her beautiful white gown stained red.

"Bethany, please, I don't understand. Come lay with me again."

She doesn't make a move towards me. She only stands there, staring at me with accusation in her eyes. I feel a cold weight in my hands. Looking down with dread, I see it. Clutched within my hands is a blood-stained dagger.

"Thomas, look at what you did."

Memories of that night flood back to me, and I gasp in horror, "What have I done? Oh God, what have I done?"

Bile rises to my throat as the stale air suddenly suffocates me. Getting to my feet, I stagger towards the balcony doors. Pushing them open and lean over the edge, heaving until the contents of my stomach empty onto the ground below me.

Behind me, the air stirs. Turning as I wipe my mouth, I see her striding towards me, looking just as she did that night. With blue flowers dancing along her gown and hair perfectly curled, she walks towards me and places her hands on my chest.

"Please, forgive me." Even as the words left my mouth, I feel her push me. My scream echoes through the morning light, only to be cut off by my body hitting the ground. Blood fills my mouth as I feel her land gently beside me. She curls herself by my side, wrapping her arm around my waist.

"You remember me now, don't you, Thomas?"

About the Authors

MALLORY CYWINSKI

Mallory Cywinski is an author, publishing editor, graphic designer, and paranormal investigator. She has her B.S. in Human Development and Family Studies from Penn State University, and she lives with her husband, son, daughter, and rescue dog near Philadelphia, PA.

Her debut book, *Making Friends with Ghosts*, and her children's book, *The Roasty Toasty Ghostie* are both available now on Amazon. Her writing has also been featured in Volumes 1 & 2 of *The Feminine Macabre: A Women's Journal of All Things Strange and Unusual* and on *Atlas Obscura*. Her latest novel, *Desperate Creatures*, a steamy paranormal thriller, will be out in Winter 2023.

She'd happily go miles out of her way for a peppermint oatmilk latte, preferably from a café with claims of a haunting. Follow her adventures in ghost hunting and writing projects on Instagram and Facebook @coffeebooksandghosts.

KARLY R. LATHAM

"Hi, hello ..."

Stories have shaped Karly's life from an early age. She spent her school years devouring stories and diving into different worlds to escape her own.

Karly finds an odd sense of comfort in the macabre; she is particularly drawn to the books and films with the final girl—who has been to hell and back and survives. She's survived her personal trials by fire and came out a little singed, but stronger. Developing PTSD was a catalyst to change her life; she is forever grateful because it helped her find her voice as a writer.

Karly is a native Texan, hiding in the AC year-round with her three spawns and polar bear masquerading as a dog. Honorable mention goes to her cat, who insists on being a terror. Outside of her life as a writer of terrible and occasionally spicy things, she is a tarot reader and medium, specializing in helping the living and the dead better understand their dark side. Her work all weaves together, creating a tapestry of the human experience and what it means to survive it.

A Collection of Eyes, the first book of Karly's 3-part series, *The Collectors*, is available now on Amazon.

To keep up with Karly, find her social media @karly.latham.

AMY BENNETT

Amy L. Bennett is an artist and paranormal investigator based in Upstate New York and survives on heavy metal and Diet Coke. She's been weird her whole life and wholly encourages others to engage in the strange and unusual too.

Her writing has been featured in both *Haunted Magazine* and *The Feminine Macabre: A Women's Journal of All Things Strange and Unusual*.

Together with her fiancé and partner-in-weird, Ryan Bradway, they're 'Amy & Ryan's Weird Adventures' on all socials.

Also find her on Instagram @onestrangeamy and at supernaturalspot.com.

Stay Weird!

BIZZY BLANK

Bizzy Blank is a spooky-loving tarot reader with an affinity for all things strange. A dark sense of humor and sense of adventure leads her down all sorts of paths! She has turned her passion for the macabre into a collection of ideas expressed through her art and stories.

Find her on social media @bizzybcoven.

TORRENCE BRYAN

Torrence Bryan loves control. She loves to control lives, to control stories, and most importantly of all, to control your emotions. Her stories will make you think, and leave you wondering exactly what goes on inside her twisted little head. When she isn't writing dark tales, she writes romance about rainbows and butterflies.

Find her on social media @torrencebryan.

E.E.W. CHRISTMAN

E.E.W. Christman has been a freelance writer and editor for more than a decade. Their work has appeared in a number of magazines, anthologies, and podcasts, including The NoSleep Podcast, *Riot Diet: A Fatterpunk Anthology*, and *Tales to Terrify*.

When not working, E.E.W. enjoys all things horror, practicing martial arts, and sinking their teeth into a fantasy series. You can read more about them and their work on their website: www.eewchristmanwrites.com.

AMELIA COTTER

Amelia Cotter is an author, poet, and storyteller with a special interest in the supernatural, history, and folklore. Her books include *Where the Party Never Ended: Ghosts of the Old Baraboo Inn*, *This House: The True Story of a Girl and a Ghost*, *Maryland Ghosts: Paranormal Encounters in the Free State*, the children's book *Breakfast with Bigfoot*, and the poetry collection *apparitions*. Amelia's award-winning poetry and short fiction explore the themes of anxiety, isolation, and trauma, often incorporating supernatural elements. Her work has appeared in journals like *Barren Magazine*, and Amelia is a frequent contributor to *Haunted Magazine*, *The Feminine Macabre*, and Troy Taylor's *The Morbid Curious*.

Visit her official website at www.ameliacotter.com or write to her any time at ameliamcotter@gmail.com.

HARLOW DAYNE

Harlow Dayne is an old school dark fantasy writer and artist. She got her start in horror zines in the 80's and 90's, and a couple of her drawings appeared in Leilah Wendell's 2003 hardbound coffee table book *Necromance—Intimate Portrayals of Death*. Her favorite short fiction appearances were in *Frightmare: Women Write Horror*, and an anthology called *In Creeps the Night*. All of her horror work has been published under the pen name Morgan Griffith.

Last year, Harlow published a memoir of her lifelong paranormal experiences called *Plugged-In to the Paranormal*, which is available on Amazon.

Find her on social media at Harlow Dayne.

MAE DEXTER

Courtney Powers, writing in this anthology as Mae Dexter, lives in Upstate NY with her husband, two children, and their cats. This one goes out to her long-suffering editor, J. Mahoney: thank you!

When she isn't attempting to write spooky stories, she writes about magic, witches, and enemies who eventually become lovers. She's currently writing her first novel, *Bound by Water*.

Find her on Instagram @maedexterauthor.

LOKI DEWITT

Loki DeWitt has lived in several different places, but currently lives in Arkansas. He has loved horror since a very young age when he was introduced to the genre by watching a number of 80s horror movies with his dad (despite his mom's protests). Years later, he began writing in the dreaded land of fan fiction. While his stories were not original, they let him sharpen his skills for the days ahead when he would tell his own stories. Now an adult, Loki retains his overactive imagination and takes great pleasure in unleashing it on readers.

Find him on the following platforms:

Instagram: @lokidewitt

Twitter: @comixpunk

Facebook: Desk of Loki

BETHANY DRILLSER

Bethany, aka Betty, is based in Salem, MA and is often inspired to write short stories by odd things her kids say, which is where *Daisy, Daisy* originated. Her first paranormal thriller novel is in progress. She's a Halloween and dog fanatic, and mostly keeps to herself and her family, drinking tea and spending too much money on Autumn candles.

KARINA HALLE

Karina Halle is a screenwriter, a former music & travel journalist, and the New York Times, Wall Street Journal, & USA Today bestselling author of River of Shadows, The Royals Next Door, and Black Sunshine, as well as 70 other wild and romantic reads, ranging from light & sexy rom coms to horror/paranormal romance and dark fantasy. Needless to say, whatever genre you're into, she's probably written a romance for it.

When she's not traveling, she and her husband split their time between a possibly haunted 120-year-old house in Victoria, BC, and their condo in Los Angeles.

She seems a bit boring in her bio but I assure you she's a big ol' goof in real life. For more information, visit www.authorkarinahalle.com.

KATHARINE HANIFEN

Kay Hanifen was born on a Friday the 13th and once lived for three months in a haunted castle. So, obviously, she had to become a horror writer. Her work has appeared in over forty anthologies and magazines.

When she's not consuming pop culture with the voraciousness of a vampire at a 24-hour blood bank, you can usually find her with her two black cats or at kayhanifenauthor.wordpress.com.

Find her on the following platforms:

Twitter: TheUnicornComi1

Instagram: @katharinehanifen

JORDAN HEATH

Jordan Heath is a writer, artist, and podcaster living in rural Indiana with his wife in a bustling house filled to the brim with their children and animal companions. Known for his tales of the strange and unsettling, the bulk of his work is inspired by true accounts of Forteana throughout history.

Driven by an unending desire to explore the blurry edges of our reality, you can find him more nights than not sitting on his porch, buried in one dusty tome or another, with his trusted Wolfhound, Violetta, at his side.

Find him on Instagram @jordan.heath and at linktr.ee/Campfirepodcast.

LAUREN HELLEKSON

Lauren has been investigating the paranormal for over 15 years in a technical/equipment-focused way. She has explored various methods of spiritual practice all over the world and has held educational workshops on witchcraft, meditation, and metaphysical exploration over the past 6 years. She holds a variety of spiritual practice certifications and has trained and worked with a multitude of practitioners in fields ranging from Shamanic to the paranormal applications of mechanical engineering.

Her debut title, *Dark Moon Light: Discovering Your World with Magic, Mysticism, and the Paranormal*, was published March of 2023 and held a #1 spot on Amazon's New Release list in *Ghost & Hauntings* and *Supernatural* genres during its pre-sale and ranked in the top 20 New Releases in *Ghosts & Hauntings* genre after its release.

She currently is an investigator and educator with Lauren Haunts, an interactive, educational, and fun way for paranormal investigator hopefuls to learn more about objective investigating through LIVE hunts, equipment builds, and chats hosted on TikTok and YouTube.

Find her on TikTok, Instagram, and YouTube @laurenhaunts.

NOELLE W. IHLI

Noelle Ihli is a thriller-suspense author with a reputation for fast-paced, terrifying novels that readers have a hard time putting down. She was born and raised in Boise, Idaho, where she still lives with her husband and two sons.

When Noelle isn't writing, she's scaring herself with true-crime documentaries, and staying up late reading the latest releases in the thriller genre.

Find her on the following platforms:

Instagram: @noelleihliauthor

Facebook: Noelle Ihli Author

JOY JOHNS

Joy Johns grew up in the wild backwoods of Florida, dodging alligators, swimming with baby lemon sharks, and on one occasion, living her bucket list dream of out-driving a twister.

She was published first at the ripe old age of five in the local newspaper and was bitten by the writing bug then and there. She holds a bachelor's degree in English and Film which she acquired on an ongoing adventure in the UK where she explores foggy haunted castles, the rugged wilds of Scotland, and the chained libraries of Hereford.

She lives on the Welsh border with her husband, a small jungle of houseplants who she has named, and a worrying number of ghosts.

Find her on Instagram @the_wild_herstorian.

JASON A. JONES

Jason A Jones is an industrial painter by trade. He enjoys writing in his spare time and hopes that others will enjoy it too. He collects vintage horror novels and loves to spend time with family and friends. He currently lives with his wife in central Indiana.

Find him on Instagram @thehorrornovelnut76.

LORIEN JONES

Lorien lives in the heart of England, UK, with her partner and two daughters. She has a life-long fascination with all things ghostly, and would often rent books from the library as a child, only to sleep with the light on.

Lorien turned her passion into work when she created "The Ghost Book" in 2013, which advertised ghost hunting events for companies, as well as documenting British haunted locations. She now spends her time between her family and haunted pubs in her endeavour to explore and document historic buildings with her new venture, "Alehouse Haunts."

After watching Michael Jackson's *Thriller* as a girl, followed by *Night of the Living Dead*, a fear of zombies was instilled. Lorien used this fear as a base for her short story, "The Rain."

She is a writer for *Haunted Magazine*, and her work has also been featured in *The Feminine Macabre*.

Follow her on social media @alehousehaunts.

ALLISON KURZYNSKI

Raised in Chicago, there was never a short supply of spooky stories growing up. A fan of the macabre, Allison has always enjoyed reading stories that make you need to turn on a light. An avid fan and participant of the early 2000s online Role Playing Groups, she has been honing her writing style for 15+ years. It is now that she has begun to turn her attention to writing her own stories, looking to invoke that same sense of unease she's enjoyed in books her whole life.

Find her on the following platforms:

Instagram: @spookyallicat/allicat1813

Threads: spookyallicat

TikTok: allicat1813

Twitter: beatha_dubhach

CASSIE MAROZSAN

Cassie Marozsan is a creative soul who lives in a spooky world of vibrant color. She has six children and resides in a conservative, prominently Amish town in Ohio. While hiking and walking trails, her imagination goes crazy with art projects and stories she later gives life to. With a not-so-good background of her past, she enjoys her quiet lifestyle but loves bringing chaos to paper seeing what craziness comes out of her clear, sober head. She loves monsters and cryptids, but thinks the scariest monsters are people and what lives inside of them battling to get out.

Find her on Instagram @cassiesland.

MORGAN MCKAY

Morgan McKay (it/they/she) is a genderqueer, Autistic, disabled writer from south Mississippi. They have been writing since they were seven and had their first poem published when she was 13. She's polyamorous and has 3 amazing partners who have helped them rediscover their love for reading and writing. In its spare time, she enjoys playing video games such as Animal Crossing & Skyrim, watching Doctor Who, and playing with her pit bull, Pugsley.

Follow her on Instagram @morganmckay_writes, as well as on Facebook & YouTube @cozywanderings.

HEATHER MOSER

Heather Moser grew up in the foothills of Appalachia, and her heart is squarely in collecting tales and diving into historical records. Her latest project includes recording stories from all areas of Appalachia from the spooky to the mundane.

She is a classics professor, author, and researcher. She is most proud, however, of her roles as a researcher and producer for the film production company Small Town Monsters and helping launch Small Town Monsters Publishing! You can find her work in other anthologies as well such as *The Feminine Macabre* Volumes 1, 3, and 5.

Follow along with her projects on Instagram @paganhistorian.

SHAWN PROCTOR

Shawn Proctor's writing has been published in several literary journals and anthologies, including *Crab Orchard Review, Flash Fiction Online, Podcastle, Galaxy's Edge* and *Daily Science Fiction*. He was nominated for Best New American Voices and is a WYRM's Gauntlet Champion. His middle-grade fantasy novel, *The Ex-Calibers*, was selected for the Write Mentor Summer Programme in 2020.

He earned an MFA in Creative Writing from Rosemont College and BA in English with a Concentration in Professional Writing from Kutztown Universty. He is a member of The MGNarwhals, a writing group for aspiring middle grade authors, and the Codex Writing Group for professional SFF writers.

Find him on the following platforms:

Twitter: shawnproctor

Instagram: @shawnproctorfiction

PHIL ROSSI

Phil Rossi–author, musician, podcaster, and paranormal investigator–has a passion for story-telling, matched only by the pleasure he derives from keeping his fans awake at night. *Crescent*, Rossi's debut novel, was originally released as a podcast in 2007 and *Crescent*, along with *Eden*, *Harvey*, and other Phil Rossi stories, has seen download counts nearing the millions, taking listeners around the globe on a dark and twisted carnival ride into world of nightmares and things that go bump in the night. *Crescent* went on to be an Amazon bestseller and was soon followed by *Eden* and then *Harvey*.

Rossi's writing has been paralleled to Stephen King, Philip K. Dick, and HP Lovecraft. He has a flair for vivid and often chilling imagery that lends itself to engrossing narratives and an undertone of inescapable, creeping dread.

Phil Rossi is a professional musician in the Washington, D.C. metropolitan area, creating and performing music spanning from solo acoustic to industrial to techno. In 2019, Phil launched his paranormal podcast, *Don't Turn Around*, an exploration of the paranormal as it relates to the human experience. *Don't Turn Around* quickly led Phil into paranormal investigation himself, and the founding of Old Spirits Investigations along-side his long-time pal and fellow author, Tee Morris.

Follow him on social media @dontturnaroundpodcast.

STACEY RYALL

Stacey Ryall is a writer and artist from Melbourne, Australia. She is the creator of the independent zine 'Unknowing' which examines the strange locations, mythology, mysteries, and dark history tales of Australia (www.unknowingau.com). Her work has also been featured in *Haunted Magazine*, *Strange Days Zine*, *The Feminine Macabre*, *Myth & Lore*, and *Short & Twisted*. She has degrees in Creative Arts and Professional Writing & Editing.

Find her on Instagram @unknowingau.

AMANDA WOOMER

Writer, lecturer, and dark historian, Amanda R. Woomer (she/her) was born and raised in Buffalo, NY. She is a featured writer for the award-winning *Haunted Magazine* and *The Morbid Curious*, as well as the author and co-author of 15 paranormal books for kids and adults, including *Harlots & Hauntings*, *A Very Frightful Victorian Christmas*, and *The Art of Grieving*. She is also the creator of *The Feminine Macabre* and the curator of The Traveling Museum of Memento Mori. Her fictional work has been featured in numerous anthologies from Zombie Pirate Publishing, Blunder Woman Productions, and others.

Follow her spooky adventures at spookeats.com and on Facebook, Instagram, and Twitter @spookeats. You can also follow *The Feminine Macabre's* journey on Facebook and Instagram @the.feminine.macabre and The Traveling Museum of Memento Mori on Facebook and Instagram @museum.of.memento.mori.

Made in the USA
Middletown, DE
20 September 2023